Copyright © Elaine Johns 2014.

The right of Elaine Johns to be identified as the author of this work has been asserted by her in accordance with the Copyright, Designs and Patents Act 1988.

All rights reserved. No part of this publication may be reproduced, stored in a retrieval system, or transmitted, in any form or by any means, electronic, mechanical, photocopying, recording or otherwise, without the prior permission of the copyright owner.

This book is a work of fiction. All characters and events are from the author's imagination and any similarity to people living or dead is purely coincidental. Some names and places, although real and in the public domain, have been fictionalised.

Acknowledgements:

Thanks to the many friends and family who have been helpful throughout the writing of this and other books:

Alli Francis-King (who always believed in me). Jennifer Hoare, Anne Kemp, Patricia Dupuy and Jo Rayner (Alpha and Beta Readers). Michele Ashworth who generously gave her time. Lesley Baxter and Helen Watson for their friendship and support.

Special thanks to my lovely man, Larry – for his unselfish and unstinting support and expertise, even when he was busy writing his own books. And for Matt and Sam who sometimes had to put up with a scruffy house and takeaways.

Elaine Johns was born in Belfast and came to London to attend the Italia Conti Performing Arts Academy. She made records with her twin brother, Derek, which 'scraped' their way into the charts in her teens. She has travelled the world as a musician, playing the flute and singing in big bands where she met her partner, Larry Johns, a jazz saxophonist and novelist. (See his website: www.kornwall.co.uk). They played in night clubs, hotels and cruise ships, returning home to a residency in the rooftop club at the London Park Lane Hilton.

Her twin brother, Derek, may be better known to those who follow the BBC Series 'Casualty' as Charlie Fairhead. Derek, who is known to many of his friends on the series as 'the apothecary' has gleaned quite a lot of medical facts over his many years of appearing in the series, but as he himself will freely admit, he only knows enough 'real medicine' to actually kill you.

Elaine was a print and television journalist in Bahrain for 4 years and is now a freelance, writing mostly short stories and articles for women's magazines. She has written several books in different genres including Crime/thriller, Contemporary Women's Fiction and Children's. She lives in Cornwall and writes every day. She and Larry have two grown up sons: Matt, a jazz pianist and Sam, an engineer. Elaine loves reading and music and getting the most out of life whatever it throws at you. Elaine also teaches a part-time creative writing class at Truro College.

Ice cream for Breakfast

Elaine Johns

Chapter 1

Americans say ass instead of arse. They're different from us. Less up-tight. The tiny American pensioner in front of my reception desk looked like a delicate miniature. She barely came up to counter level.

"Thanks, Hun," she said. "You've been real helpful."

Hun? I'd only just met the woman.

I looked down to check my name badge. It was still there. But maybe she needed glasses. Her small, tanned face was like a wrinkled peach and the wispy, white hair no more than a thin halo. I suppose she'd shrunk with age. Is that what I had to look forward to? A ripple of depression overtook me.

Ignore me. I'm not usually this bitter, or *mean to senior citizens. But it's been a bad day, and my normal cheerfulness has vanished thanks to the family from hell complaining about the size of their en-suite and because their T.V. wasn't a massive flat-screen, like the one they had at home. Why hadn't they stayed home then?*

"All part of the service," I said.

The old girl was sweet, and at least she'd said thanks. Not everyone did. But even so, I'm happy to be the capable and smiley type that guests expect to find behind their hotel reception desk. For I enjoy my job. But like I said, you've caught me on a bad day.

"Stevie? Strange name for a girl, that." The woman had figured out the name badge bit and smiled. So I smiled back, despite the fact that I'm not a girl but a fully grown woman, and even on a rough day don't look anything like a guy.

Blame my mother for the Stevie thing. I always have. And I suppose I could have had Stephanie Anderson printed on my name tag, but anyone who knows me says I'm definitely *not* a Stephanie. Still, after thirty-four odd years of being called Stevie, and all the smartarse comments, I've grown into it.

Anderson, I've always been happy with. I share it with an American novelist, a Nobel physicist, a foxy lady in Ireland, and that actress who played Scully in the X-Files. Google has its uses.

"How the hell am I s'posed to park on that pocket-bloody-handkerchief you've got out front!" The man's face was screwed up and scarlet. Hard to tell if it was anger or blood pressure, for he could have done with a few pounds off, most of it from around his middle.

And if life was fairer, it would be *me* getting angry. He'd been rude. Had pushed up to the counter out of turn, elbowing in past the old lady I'd been dealing with. Some people leave their manners at home when they come on holiday. And lots of people came on holiday to Newquay, the Cornish Riviera. It wasn't Saint Tropez, but when the sun shone and the surf was up, it came in a decent second.

Saturday. Changeover-Day. It was often a challenge. When one set of guests left and the next arrived expecting to stay at The Ritz when they'd only paid for the economy version. The guy leant heavily on my chipboard counter and pushed his face in closer to mine.

"Can I help you, *Sir*?" Sometimes the word stuck in your throat, but I was a professional. Plus I needed the job.

"Car park!" he said (a little harshly, I thought) and pointed to the Peugeot abandoned haphazardly across our front drive. It was a family car. With a family still in it.

"Sir, the sign out front directs you to the large parking area at the rear of the hotel."

"Sign? What bloody sign? I never seen no bloody sign."

I looked him in the eye, not something I'd recommend to the novice, and passed across one of our courtesy slips with *Hotel Royal* written on its header. There wasn't much 'royal' about the place, unless you count thirty mediocre bedrooms, some with dodgy plumbing and floors that slope, and a restaurant badly in need of refurbishment.

"Write your name and licence number on there, if you would, Sir. First right onto the road, then right and right again will take you to the parking lot. If you'd like to bring your luggage in now, I'll have someone help your family up to their rooms."

The man grunted, wrote something on the slip, flung it across the counter at me and headed back out to his car.

"Unpleasant man," said the old lady.

The in-house phone rang. Which was just as well, for it saved having to think up a reply. It was a definite no-go-area, discussing guests with other guests. We may not be The Ritz, but we were still a long way from Fawlty Towers.

"Shit, Stevie. How long does it take to answer a bloody phone?" My boss didn't wait for an estimate. "Just get your butt down here, Alfie's about to walk out." *Alfie's our cook.* "He's had a fight with the K.P. again."

"Which one?" I asked. It might make a difference.

My boss, Harry Evans, didn't bother to learn Kitchen Porters' names. He didn't see the point, for they never stayed long. Harry wasn't known for his people-skills.

7

"The spotty kid with the jeans half-way down his ass," he said.

Harry came from the British side of the pond, but he always said ass anyway. He'd watched loads of American movies and often slipped into a confusing Brooklyn accent. He was a Yankees fan, pronounced New York *Noo Yawk* and I believe he even thought he was cool. Harry definitely wasn't cool; still he wasn't a bad bloke. He had a few rough edges, but I'd had worse bosses.

"Frigg's sake, Stevie. What is it with the kitchen staff? And why does this Prima Donna of a Chef only want to talk to you? He's trying to throw me out of my own God damn kitchen, the one I paid for."

Why does he want to talk to me, Harry? Well, maybe because I don't start every conversation with a swear word, like you. Or it might even be the faint waft of body odour that Harry carried around with him. Although most of us were used to that by now.

I thought about going back to bed. Sticking my head under the duvet and coming back on duty when Changeover-Day was over. But instead, I stuck a 'back in five minutes' sign on my reception desk, smiled sweetly at the old American woman who still seemed to be waiting for something and let out a small, hard-done-by sigh. It wasn't as satisfying as swearing, but life is often a compromise.

Chapter 2

It's sometimes said that we humans are a race of problem solvers. You'd be wise to add problem makers to that. My boss Harry makes more than his fair share and expects me to solve them.

Like Changeover-Day, when he took his snotty attitude into the kitchen and we almost lost another good K.P. These poor kids get paid a pittance to do the most menial, skanky job on the planet, and then they're expected to salaam to a mediocre cook who calls himself a *Chef*. Harry (an innocent abroad when it comes to kitchen etiquette) jumps in with both feet when he doesn't know a crème brûlée from a custard tart.

There's an uneasy truce in the kitchen now. But I don't kid myself that it will last, for Alfie, our cook, is not an easy man to get along with. He comes with tattoos across his knuckles that say 'game over' and questionable cooking skills. When he's having a bad day, he takes out his anger on the nearest body to hand, usually an unfortunate Kitchen Porter.

Our present full time K.P. - the one with spots and 'trouser issues' - is a willing lad and there was no way I was going to lose him. So, I've wangled an hourly raise of fifty pence for him. Not much compensation for the grief Alfie gave him, but the guy seemed made-up. And I've massaged Alfie's ego (calling him *Chef*, and dropping him a pack of Marlborough). I've also moved one step closer to a stomach ulcer. But it's all part of the cut-and-thrust of the hotel business and when things are going well I really *do* love my job.

But maybe that won't be enough, for there are doomsday rumours coming out of the staffroom. Mostly Doris, our *head* chambermaid – we only have two – and Doris has a nose for the latest gossip. I try to steer clear of the rumour mill, but fear that the Royal was going bust and might not even make it through to this year's summer season wasn't something I could ignore. The place was my home. Not a metaphor, for I actually lived in the tiny, attic flat.

"Hey! You Stephanie Anderson?"

"Eh?"

"I'm looking for a Stephanie Anderson," the guy shouted in my face, like I was in the first stage of Alzheimer's. "Got a packet to be signed for."

It was the postman's choice of name that had thrown me. For I'm clearly not a Stephanie - as you know.

"Oiy! Stevie. I was here first. What about this invoice?"

Another man waved a paper dramatically in the air. It could have been anything. "Boss says I'm not to come back without the readies in me hand."

I looked at the hand. It was large, like the rest of him.

His name was Skelly, and he was one of those muscle-bound guys you see in gyms, bulking up their biceps. He brought us cheap house wine and booze with labels I'd never heard of. The kind that fell off the back of a lorry somewhere. I didn't like the idea, but Harry told me to stop worrying. None of the guests had ever complained and it saved him a few bob.

"Sorry, Skelly. You'll need to see Harry about that," I said. "Not my department."

"Will somebody *please* sign for this? I've got the rest of my round to do." The postman slid an assortment of envelopes across the counter followed by the large brown packet he'd been trying to off-load.

It was addressed to: Stephanie Anderson, Hotel Royal, Newquay, Cornwall, U.K. It was mine, so I signed. At least it got the postman out of my hair, and I sent Skelly off to Harry's fancy office outback. The place suddenly went from the madness of a three ring circus to the quiet of Dead Man's Gulch.

I took advantage of the lull to get myself a coffee. Then I settled at my desk in the small, airless cubicle behind Reception that some architect with a sense of humour had called an office. If anyone wanted me they knew how to ring a bell.

The coffee was great. That was one of the reasons I'd gone out on a limb for the young K.P. His coffee was legendary. Weapon's grade.

I peered at the stamps on my package. It seemed to come from Canada, but I knew no one in Canada. I gave up guessing and opened the thing.

There were two letters inside, one from somebody who called herself my grandmother. I didn't know I had a grandmother. Well of course I *had* a grandmother; technically everyone needs one of those. But my mother had never talked about her and there were no photographs anywhere, like there had been no evidence in our family home of any kind of family. No sisters, brothers, father, grandfather, no aunts, uncles.

It was a state of affairs that I took for granted as an adult. Something I'd grown into, though not easily, as a child. But even now, there were times when I had this weird feeling there was somebody out there tugging at me, someone with my DNA. My mother always insisted this was wishful thinking and I suppose she was right, for surely she must know. No grandmother then. So I'd figured she was dead.

She was dead. I grabbed for the coffee to steady my nerves. Imagine how you would feel. One minute you have no grandmother. The next you do. And then suddenly she's yanked dramatically from your grasp; slips through your fingers before you can say hello Granny.

How did I know the woman was gone? The letter, for one. It began by saying that if I was finally reading her letter, she was now dead and it had been forwarded to me by her solicitors in Ottawa. She'd sent a photograph too, and the effect of having this artefact in my hand was surprising. I forgot to breathe and whatever jelly you have in your bones – I'd never listened properly in human-bio lessons - seemed to solidify.

"Hey. That looks just like you. Got that blazing red hair of yours, though hers is more like wire wool. And the eyes. Yours are green too. And look ..." Doris stabbed a fat, stubby finger irreverently at the photograph "... she's got the same little pug nose. Like somebody's stuck on a bit of putty."

"Yeah, okay. Thanks for that, Doris." Doris had made one of her silent entries; something she was famed for. It helped with her eavesdropping. "This mean you've finished the first floor?"

"Coffee break."

She looked pointedly at the mug on my desk. A shop steward sort of look that said she knew her rights and was a reader of Karl Marx.

"Fair enough," I said. It wasn't wise to upset Doris. She had power beyond her job description and she was a good worker. Like me, her wage didn't match the galley slave role she played in the Royal. Harry was a cheapskate, but jobs weren't that easy to come by, not ones where you could walk across the road to the beach and had your own built-in accommodation.

"Who is it then?" She poked another dangerous looking finger at the picture.

I thought about telling her to mind her own business, but like I said, Doris was a useful person to have on your side.

"It's my grandmother," I said, and the words felt like they'd landed from some alien planet. "She's dead."

"Sorry for your loss. Maybe she's left you something in her will." Doris looked at the other envelope, the one I hadn't opened yet. "You hear that ruckus coming from Harry's office?"

"No," I said and wished she'd go, so I could read the rest of the letter. I hadn't thought about a will, and the idea seemed mercenary, especially when I hadn't even met the poor woman.

"Not looking good, babe." *Doris insisted on calling me babe in her more relaxed moments.* "Skelly's in there threatening to break Harry's arm if he don't get paid. Place is on its uppers, Stevie." She took up a feisty stance, and folded her arms across her ample bust. She was all bosom and batwing arms, the sort of figure that might have intimidated some.

But I'd got the hang of Doris some time ago. Beneath her rock hard exterior beat a generous heart and once she'd taken to you, you were allowed odd glimpses of it.

"Right," she said. "I'll be getting on then."

Good, I thought. Call me uncharitable, *and I don't think I am*, but my grandmother had just died.

Doris was right about the photograph, though. The resemblance was spooky, except for the wire-wool hair. Though I should come clean that my own thick mane of mahogany red hair could also resemble a pot scrubber before I'd attacked it with the straighteners.

I thought about the nose. I wouldn't say mine was pug, or like a lump of putty some unfeeling sculptor had just stuck on as an afterthought. I've always considered my nose jaunty and pert, if anything.

"Stevie! Thought you said I could have tomorrow off."

It was Joe Hines, part time receptionist in this house of fun. I like Joe and I've come to think of him as a friend. He's thirty-two, closer to my age than anyone else here and I suppose that's why, when Joe first came to the Royal last year, some of the other staff tried to pair us up. They worry about my love life. Bless.

And it's true that Joe and I see eye to eye on many things, music for one. We both like Jazz. He's an intelligent guy and somebody you can have a grown up conversation with. A glorious looking man and impressively tall. I have to look up at him, but then I have to look up at most people. He has fine chiselled features and fabulous blond hair – which I suspect he dyes. But he'll have trouble with his hairline when he's older, for he's already chasing after it.

Still, there was no way Joe and I could ever make it in any romantic way, for he sails under a different flag. I don't think anyone else realises that Joe's gay. And frankly it's none of their bloody business. I guess somebody who looks like that; you assume his bedroom history includes a tonne of classy women. But Joe had confided in me, although he wants to stay in the closet as far as everyone else in our little family is concerned. I suppose he's seen prejudice at first hand.

"Well?" he asked.

"Well what?" I countered.

"The staff rota." He waved a flimsy paper in front of my eyes, like some kind of proof were needed that we actually operated a staff rota. "It's been changed. And you promised me *faithfully* I'd have Tuesday off this week." The sad look in his eyes and the way he emphasised the word faithfully made it sound like I'd broken some kind of blood-oath and could never be trusted again.

"And I *gave* you tomorrow off," I said. "I'm covering your shift myself. Let me see that thing. Where'd you get this? It's not the one I printed off for you." It looked like the dog had eaten breakfast off it. (Harry has a dog but we try to keep it away from the restaurant and kitchen areas in case of food hygiene inspections.)

"Misplaced mine," he mumbled, looking uncomfortable, for in most things Joe was a perfectionist. "That's the one from the notice board in the staff room."

The staff room was a small space that Harry hadn't been able to think up another use for. It had once been a storeroom, so there were no windows in there and it was hardly luxurious. He'd thrown in a couple of dog eared sofas for staff morale and an antiquated coffee maker, and the navy blue carpet was now threadbare in places. But despite its shortcomings, the place was a cosy retreat. Somewhere you could meet friends and gripe about what life threw your way.

I looked at the staff rota. The print out had been altered, the names scratched out and rewritten in red ink. "That mess isn't my writing," I said, "and I'd hardly have put the two of us down for a full shift together on a Tuesday night. They're not exactly queuing in the aisles this week."

"That's what I thought."

"Looks like Harry's scribble," I said.

"It's our anniversary tomorrow." His voice took on a whining tone. "Wilbur's got something special planned. I can't let him down."

Wilbur was Joe's life-partner; a decent man. I liked him.

"Leave it with me. Some kind of foul up. I'll sort it."

"Bless you, Stevie. You're a brick. I'll be in town shopping before my afternoon shift."

I shuffled the two letters and the photograph in front of me back into their brown envelope, shoved them in my desk drawer. I could take a hint; the Gods were against me this morning. But if they changed their minds, maybe I'd get a chance later to read the rest of my grandmother's letter and study the face in the photo. The one that looked so much like me that it must be my grandmother when she was young.

She'd lived in Canada, which sounded far more exciting than the council estate in Enfield where I'd grown up. A place where I'd watched my mother give up her unequal struggle with the damp mould, and sink into a sad complacency.

But watching my mother settle for second best in life and going off to her mind numbing job, day after day, had one positive effect on me. It had made me determined not to follow her down the same road. To go to college. To aim for something in life. I'd learned early on to stand on my own two feet. So, I suppose if I had anything to thank my mother for, it was that.

I took in a long, calming breath and tried to find the serenity that one of my friends who did yoga insisted was out there somewhere. I'd just reached some sort of peaceful plateau, ready to take on whatever challenges the rest of the day had to offer, when a noise like a siren erupted throughout the hotel.

Shit! Failed again. It was the day in the month when we tested the fire alarm. And I'd forgotten to put out the warning notice for guests. Any minute now I'd have them flooding to the front desk twittering on about shock, and the more astute of them trying to get money knocked off the bill for psychological trauma. Then Harry would join in and look at me like I'd personally started World War Three. Some days you'd be better off working as a traffic warden.

Chapter 3

"You change the staff rota?"

"Meant to tell you," said Harry. "But stuff's been hectic lately."

I thought back to Doris's latest keyhole report. And how Skelly had threatened to break Harry's arm if he didn't come across with the money he owed. *Hectic* wouldn't have been the word I'd use, but then maybe I'm picky.

He shuffled uncomfortably in his seat like his haemorrhoids were playing up again, said "Got some people coming in tomorrow night. *Special people*. I want us to make an impression. That guy Joseph's got a lot of class; looks good in the uniform, posh accent."

"And what am I, Harry? Something the cat sicked up?"

I can be rash at times. The mouth rushes in while the brain's still figuring stuff out.

"Stevie, you look great and you're one hell of a worker, but you can be a smartarse when somebody tees you off."

"A what?" That was rich, coming from Harry who peppered most conversations with swear words.

"Look girl, you do a great job."

"Yeah, right." I've been patronised before, so I recognise the signs.

"But for reasons best known to me, I want you *both* out there on the desk when these guys come in on Tuesday night. Big beaming *meet and greet*. Courteous, professional, charming."

"And you don't want to tell me why."

"No."

"Oh."

"Last time I checked it was me who paid the mortgage, owed the bills and didn't sleep nights." Harry's face hardened. "I want you both on Reception tomorrow night even if there's a nuclear attack, got it?"

"Got it."

He waved a dismissive hand towards the door and looked down at the papers on his desk.

I needed an Aspirin. Doris was right, we were in trouble and Harry wasn't sleeping nights. Usually, Harry slept like a baby. Not that I had personal knowledge of his sleeping habits. Yuck! He was a tub of lard and fifty-five if he was a day. But trouble-free sleep was something he bragged about.

*

"What you want me to do next, mein Führer?"

Joe was only baiting me, but his insults were wearing thin now, so I shot him a sarcastic look. It was hardly my fault he'd lost his night off tomorrow. *Life can be a bitch. Join the club.*

"Try growing up," I said. "And go whinge at Harry instead of me."

So far, today hadn't been one for the record books, unless you measure it in crap value. And I suppose if you were an optimist, the upside was that things could only get better. I try to be an optimist. And that's why, when I wrap up here and hand over to Joe, I'm going into town to look for a new smart-casual top to wear on my date with Nigel tonight. Someone would need to be an optimist to go out with Nigel. But maybe the guy's got hidden talents that haven't been discovered yet and a night out at Butcher's Bistro will do the trick.

I know I shouldn't go. It can only end badly. For me. For Nigel. He's a decent enough man, but he's made *boring* into an art form. He delivers our fresh fish, so there's usually a faint smell of Mackerel wafting from him, which I'm hoping tonight he will have overcome with a good aftershave.

So why go? Why touch the man with an extra long bargepole and a pair of reinforced rubber gloves? Nigel has worn me down after countless fumbling attempts to get me on a date, and I suppose I figured that if we finally went out it would bring a dose of reality into his life. That he'd stop thinking of me as some sort of prize to be won, but see me as I really am. Human, feet of clay, sometimes cynical, sometimes confused by life, loyal to friends, looking for companionship and love - like so many other people on the planet - and so far been disappointed.

I'd started the New Year with a new slogan – *All Men are Bastards*. But I had a fair enough excuse, for a slimy, smooth talker I'd dated for two whole months had borrowed a 100 quid and hadn't been heard of since. So I guess you can add naive to my list of virtues and vices.

Two months was a record for me. At least since my partner and I broke up two years ago. I hadn't realised we'd broken up till I came home from work one day to find that my flat had no furniture in it. A moving van had shifted the lot, and he'd set up in the Midlands with a 24-year-old nurse from Halesowen he'd met on the beach. You had to admire the guy's planning skills and grasp of logistics.

That's when Harry had offered me my own place in the hotel, for a small rent that he takes from my salary. He calls it The Penthouse - *a sense of humour, it's a gift*. My place is certainly the highest point in the building, the attic. It's tiny. The floor slopes and in places the roof slopes to meet it. So, it's just as well I'm not tall. But it's all mine. No kitchen, no living room, just a miniscule bathroom and a bedroom so small that only a bed and a wardrobe fit.

The phone rang in my office.

"Hey, Stevie. You put up the Karaoke poster out there, yet?"

It was Harry and I'd been hoping he'd forgotten about the Karaoke poster. But Harry was a frustrated performer and the highlights of his week were the two Karaoke nights he ran in the bar.

Monday and Wednesday, come flood or famine, Harry would entertain guests with the lame Karaoke backtracks he'd got Joe to download. These nights attracted a smattering of people, ones who hadn't yet discovered the delights of the British Legion Club down the road where you could buy a pint for a fraction of the price that we charged in our 'newly refurbished cabaret lounge' – the bar. Once the night progressed, Harry often managed to drive away the few remaining customers with his tired jokes that staggered their way to punch lines.

"Oh, and Stevie?" *What now*? "Phone up that guy with the keyboard. Young bloke. The one who played that background shit for us at Christmas."

Harry had a way with words. "Matthew?" I said.

"Could be. You know me and names."

"You want *Jazz* in the bar?"

"Sure, why not. Bit of culture for Tuesday night. Show these guys from London we're not running a cheap sideshow down here. And tell the bloke to wear that white tux he wore at Christmas."

"You want him tomorrow night?"

"Problem?"

"Only that it's short notice. He's a muso. These guys usually get booked up months ahead."

"Do your best. And if you can't get him, try and book somebody with a bit of class. No bloody stand-ups with mother-in-law jokes. And try to keep the price down. You know the form."

I knew the form. Cheap. But with a touch of class. Yeah, right.

I riffled through the rolodex. Maybe Matthew Barry would have a cancellation. If he had any sense he'd be fully booked, but that wasn't the attitude, of course. I'd do my best to get somebody decent to play, for there had been a hint of desperation in Harry's voice.

We needed to pull something out of the fire or the Royal might go down in flames. We may not be the most sophisticated, or elegant, or most sought-after hotel in a town where you fell over the things every step you took, but we did the best job we knew how with the tools to hand. And we were a family. A strange family with all its quirks, but a family just the same. None of us felt like leaving to start over again.

I managed to book the pianist, but had to agree to an extra twenty pounds. New year, new price, he'd said. I guess he'd made some New Year resolutions as well.

So, things were looking good. Positive vibes were out there somewhere, and I hoped that would include my date with Nigel. I was finally off duty and could head into town; get myself that new top and a turkey and ham sub. No way I'd chance eating anything that came out of Alfie's kitchen, not for a while yet. He might still have a grudge because I'd been kind to the K.P.

I remembered it was Monday, so made one more pass by Reception. Joe was standing behind the desk looking bored.

"Put the Karaoke poster up," I said. It would give him something to do.

"Jesus! He's not still doing that. Not after that bloke threatened him last week."

"You know Harry. He's an optimist," I said.

"He'd need to be."

"Just put the bloody poster up, Joe." Maybe Harry was right. Maybe that was all we needed for the Royal to survive. A proper dose of optimism.

*

February's a mean, hard month to get through. It's often cold. The joys of Christmas forgotten and the next one almost a year away; it can also be a depressing time. But let's hear it for optimism, for this year February's a leap year. And any woman mad enough to propose – my advice would be to go for it anyway. Give the men what they deserve. *Notice my irony and bitterness kicking in there?* I try to hold it back, but I'm still remembering the 100 quid and my stolen furniture. So you'll hardly blame me.

February's noted for something else, as well. Valentine's Day. As if there wasn't already enough pressure out there for us singletons, this is the time it really piles on. People in work sending you lame cards with doves or hearts on, or those pathetic little love-bears kissing each other, and sniggers from the staff as they wait for you to open them.

People mean well, I guess. But I refuse to fall in with this stuff anymore. I've sat in a restaurant with lots of other romantic hopefuls, a mass produced red rose on every table - guaranteed to be scent-free; red candle shimmering in its glass bowl, and eating my way through a three course meal that included oysters. (I'm not that keen on oysters.)

What's the point? Anyway, romantic love isn't something you can buy. Is it? Maybe I'm wrong. I'm not an oracle. But surely if you love someone like that, you wouldn't have to wait until February the 14th to shower them with flowers and chocolates.

I shuddered as an unsettling thought floated in from the dark side. *Nigel*. Please, dear Lord, I'm begging you now – don't let Nigel send me a Valentine card.

I was going to meet the man in an hour. That's probably what it was. My subconscious, like some patrolling, suspicious nanny, was preparing me for the worst. Or, maybe the best. Who knew? But I had serious doubts about Nigel, about actually sitting at the same table with him for any length of time. What would be a reasonable time to eat and run without taking a scouring pad to the guy's self-esteem? I may be a smartarse and a cynic at times, at least according to Harry, but I'm not unkind.

*

In one way it was easy. For a start there were no expectations (on my part, at least) of anything romantic or serious leading from an encounter with Nigel. No pressure about whether my underwear was sexy enough. The man wasn't going to get near it.

I considered myself a bit like a social worker. Meet the guy. Try to have a passable evening without too many embarrassing lulls in the conversation. Get the date over with in as civilised and humane a way as possible, while making it clear there would be no future contact between myself and Nigel Jameson.

I got there first, which surprised me. I'd imagined him camped out on the doorstep of Butcher's waiting for it to open, for he'd always struck me as someone who took being on time seriously. So I had a drink at the bar. And then I had another. And looked at my watch. Cheek. He was already fifteen minutes late and I was two drinks ahead - but the glasses were small.

Well, if he thought I was going to sit here looking like some loser who'd been stood up, he was living in a fantasy world. *And me doing him a favour*. Bastard. I was right, all men were bastards. I got ready to leave.

The phone rang. The barman picked it up. "Nope, she's still here" he said and looked at me pityingly. "Want to talk to her?"

It's not a comforting feeling, being discussed while you're only a few feet away. It's like you're an object. I'm not a raging feminist or anything, but right then I was one step away from burning my bra.

"He's late." The barman nodded at the phone.

"You don't say."

"Says he'll be another ten minutes. Wants to talk to you." He held out the phone.

I pulled back from it at first, like it was a snake ready to strike. It had been a long time since I'd been stood up. Then I changed my mind, decided to give Nigel the full blast he had coming. "If you think I'm going to sit here all night..."

The phone went dead. I handed it back to the barman. Was that a smirk on his face?

"Lost the signal."

"Sure," he said. "Another drink? This one's on the house."

"Did I want his pity? *Or* another drink? I'm not much of a drinker, but I had one anyway. I figured it would dampen down the anger that was threatening to take hold. I could feel my face redden, my lips tighten into a thin, pinched line, and I expect the tiny red veins had already appeared in my eyes. Joe insists they're a warning sign that the volcano named *Stevie* is about to erupt. Not that I lose it often, at least not often enough to warrant anger management therapy.

I waited another twenty minutes, to see what pathetic excuse he could come up with. Some breadsticks (I was hungry) and another wine helped pass the time. He'd said ten minutes, but then Nigel-the-fishman-Jameson seemed to live in Neverland.

I was laid-back and mellow by the time he arrived. Chardonnay can do that to you. And maybe that was why his entrance made such an impact on me. Who the hell was this? Surely not the man who delivered our wet fish. He'd cleaned up really nice. Don't you hate that expression? But then I was three-parts hammered, so finding sensible thoughts that weren't clichés wasn't easy.

"Hell, Stevie. I am really, *really* sorry." He took my arm and steered me towards the table that had been waiting for us. "Can you forgive me?" he asked; a forlorn look on his face.

"Uh?"

"Got stuck behind an accident at Mount Misery roundabout."

"What?"

"Penzance. There was an accident. You okay?"

"Sure." But I wasn't.

Assumptions can be dangerous things. I'd assumed that the Nigel who delivered our fish and always looked slightly crumpled, the Nigel who discussed the weather or the current state of fish stocks when forced into conversation, was the *real* one.

I don't know how he did it, but there wasn't even a faint whiff of Mackerel about him, and he was the most un-crumpled I've ever seen him. He wore the expensive, well cut suit with an ease that said he hadn't borrowed it from a mate. I sucked in a breath and looked at the man sitting opposite me as if I'd seen him for the first time.

Maybe tonight wouldn't be a washout after all. I did a quick mental check of the underwear I'd decided on. Definitely not the sexy stuff, but not too bad considering. I'd worn the small NVL pants. I had the no-visible-line underwear in three different colours: white, beige and black. They only did them in three colours where I could afford to shop. I'd randomly picked up the black pair. Sometimes things just happen for the best, even when you haven't planned them.

Chapter 4

Looking back on it now, on the other side of last night's meal at Butcher's, I realise I can be every bit as patronising and condescending as Harry when he's on a roll. My lack of expectations. The presumption that I was doing Nigel a favour by going out with him. I blush to the roots of my very red hair.

"All under control?" Harry was on patrol and had made several surprise inspections, checking on me, checking on the professional look of Reception. He was giving me a headache. Then again I'd already started off with one, for I'd come on duty with the hangover from hell.

"All good here," I reported, with a jauntiness I didn't feel. But I was a member of the local Am Dram Club and the skills I'd learnt there came in useful at times.

"Excellent." Harry did some more pacing. "What about our boy wonder? What time's he coming on duty? He's not taken the hump, has he?"

"He'll be here," I said, not wholly convinced that Joe would turn up in time to parade for these fancy visitors of Harry's. Maybe he *had* taken the hump. It was his anniversary, after all. But Joe knew the bottom line. We all did. Harry Evans might be a skinflint, but he was a boss who mostly left you to get on with it. He was happy as long as the place ran smoothly (most of the time) and he got to do his 'I'm a jolly-host' bit with the guests. Except recently he hadn't been sleeping nights, but I guess he had that in common with a lot of people.

"You hear about last night?" Harry asked.

"Last night what?" I said, thinking that my own version of last night had given me enough to chew on.

"Never mind. If you need me, I'll be in the bar taking inventory."

"George sick?" I asked. George was our barman. A tight-lipped little guy with the face and manner of a weasel. Weasels are like ferrets, but George could have passed for either. I didn't like the man. Guests often complained about him, about his bar skills - which were basic - about his sour face and surly take-it-or-leave-it attitude, like he was doing customers a favour instead of the other way around. George was not a natural for the customer service industry. I'd tried to talk Harry into getting rid of him, but the rumour went that George knew where the bodies were buried and had something on Harry that made him impossible to sack.

"Depends on your point of view," said Harry.

"What?"

"Whether George's sick or not."

"Ah." It was the closest he'd ever come to admitting there was something odd about our barman.

"When Joseph gets in I want you to go and double check that Chef's happy with tonight's menu. Any problems, I need to know about them *now*. I'm having dinner with my two guests and I don't want to be embarrassed by any crap that comes out of that kitchen."

Get yourself a new cook, then, Harry. But I didn't say that. It looked like the man already had enough on his plate. *Ta-da! Take it away, pun.*

Harry left. Doris arrived. The two were practically interchangable. Same weight, both had similar facial hair, except that most of the staff were more scared of Doris than they were of the boss.

29

"Hey, babe. What about George and his glass jaw," said Doris.

"Eh?"

"'Course. Your night off, wasn't it? Seems you and me missed a real doozy," Doris said, a smug look on her face. "Cook saw the whole thing kick off."

"What, with George?"

"George and a guest."

"Dear God! No wonder Harry's worried."

"Seems one of the punters put our snotty little barman's nose out of joint. George threatened to smack the guy, but even our George ain't daft enough to throw a punch at a guest *inside* the hotel. Looks like the guy from room twenty-five got in there first, was waiting in the alley for George when he did the empties. Put him out with one punch. Broke his jaw."

"Twenty-five?" I said. "You sure?"

"'Course I'm sure." Doris stuck her chin out defiantly. "Poor old Joseph was right upset by all accounts. When he sent for the ambulance, the guest threatened to go for *him*. You know what our Joseph's like, quiet sort of lad. Shouldn't think he's used to that kind of violence."

"And it was definitely Mr Whitely? He's no sweetheart," I said, "but breaking George's jaw. Wow!"

A part of me said, "Go Mr Whitely!" But then you can't just go round breaking barmen's jaws willy-nilly, not even if they are arrogant little toads like George.

"Bloke had some beef on him, mind," said Doris. "Bloody great fists." She shuddered. "Skinny little runt like George wouldn't stand a chance."

"What happened to him?"

"Told you. They took him to hospital."

"Not *George*. Mr Whitely." God, it was a pantomime. Who said communication was easy? "The guy from room twenty-five," I said. It was the man who'd been so rude on Changeover-Day.

"Gone."

"What you mean, *gone*?"

"Him and the family up and vanished. Not a trace left in their rooms. Left them like pig sties."

"God, their bill," I said. "Wonder if Joe made out their bill."

Doris sent me an old fashioned look. "Wake up, Stevie. Would you pay *your* bill if you were thinking of doing a midnight flit?"

Poor old Harry. He might as well put up a sign. Free board and lodgings, help yourself. And as for Joe – would we even see him today?

Thinking about him brought him through the front door.

"You hear about last night?" he said, a glint of excitement in his eyes. They were all at it, bringing me up to date. Like rubber-neckers at an accident; getting a kick out of someone else's bad luck.

"Get round here quick," I said. "I've got to check on the kitchen."

Joe still had his mouth open when I left.

I felt sour. But that could just as easily be because I had a headache that would show up on any orbiting satellite and wasn't sure if I'd made a spectacle of myself with Nigel last night. I'd drunk industrial quantities of wine, and I don't remember him drinking anything. I don't even know how I got home. My attitude to him had gone through a dramatic change. I wanted him to think well of me. And how could he - if I'd staggered up the back stairs to my room like somebody whose next stop was rehab. He'd said I had class. But that was *before*, when he'd asked me out. And I'd spent the night proving him wrong, behaving like some mindless ladette.

I'd hardly be seeing *him* again, other than delivering fish. The thought made me feel flat and disappointed, until I remembered that Valentine's Day was on the horizon. Maybe there was hope for all of us.

Chapter 5

Our noble leader is at his happiest when he's doing the genial, mine-host bit, walking amongst the guests, asking about their day on the beach, or how they were enjoying the Royal's fine dining. He was on a rollercoaster to nowhere with that one, for they might as well go to the Fried Chicken restaurant down the road. (Obviously, I use the word restaurant advisedly here.) Except, it's cheaper there. So you get the same amount of fat grams for less money, and they've got cooks in there who aren't likely to deck you if you argue with them. Maybe even somebody with an NVQ level 1 in Catering.

Harry was at it again. Regaling his captive audience in the restaurant with his comic anecdotes. But I sensed an edge to his voice, a tension that wasn't usually there. He maintains that talking to guests while they're eating is the best policy, for they're trapped and can't go anywhere. I say it brings him the closest to Basil Fawlty that any hotelier would ever want to get.

I grabbed his arm and steered him away from the family at table seven. They seemed relieved.

"Chef's happy," I said. *Alfie had been whistling which was unnerving.*

"Great," said Harry. "Food looks okay, too."

I couldn't decide if he was trying to convince me or himself. Okay's a relative term. This was somewhere between a burger bar and haute cuisine. A little closer to the burger end, but it looked fairly edible, so maybe the extra twenty quid Harry had promised 'Chef' for the night had brought on some long overdue miracle in the kitchen. I wouldn't fancy eating the stuff myself, but then my stomach was still queasy after a night of firing alcohol and hot chilli sauce into it at Butcher's. It could be some time before it was ready for anything cooked by Alfie.

"Where'd you like me to set up?"

"Eh?" Harry's voice echoed the puzzled look on his face.

"My gear. Am I playing in the restaurant or the bar?"

"It's Matthew," I reminded him. "The guy with the tux," I whispered. It was a description that would cut to the chase with Harry. No point in using the word musician around my boss, for he'd only upset the guy by telling him not to play too much of that classical or jazz crap.

"Right." Harry eyed the young man suspiciously. "Can you play show tunes?"

Dear God, Harry wasn't going to try his Rogers and Hammerstein again, was he? He saw himself as a singer. But he was the only one who did.

"Sure," said Matthew, a resigned look on his face.

"Where's the tux?" asked Harry.

"What?"

"Just leave your stuff here," I told the guy and pointed to a space in front of Reception. "I'll keep an eye on it while you park out back. Right on the road and . . ."

"I know," he said and smiled a charming, innocent grin. "Right and right again. You told me at Christmas."

"So?" I looked at Harry when the musician had manhandled his final speaker in and gone off to park.

"What?"

Sometimes communication doesn't seem worth the trouble. "Where *do* you want him? I asked. "The guy's got his meter running and these blokes of yours haven't arrived yet."

"They'll *be* here," he said, kind of defensive.

"Just thinking of you. This guy runs over his contract hours, it's time-and-a-half."

"Shit, Stevie. Everyone's a friggin' comedian. When's the last time I paid anybody overtime?"

"So, I'll put him in the bar, shall I?"

"Shove him in a corner of the restaurant. Take out the table near the door. Guy's thin, he should fit in there. Might even block off the draught they're always whingeing on about."

"Not the bar, then."

"You'd be sod-all use in the army, girl."

"Yeah?"

"Useless at taking orders." Harry smiled. He was back to his old self again.

I gave him one of my best sighs. *He* wasn't the one who'd have to ask the waiters to shift the restaurant furniture, but he looked as if he didn't care.

*

"Miss. We'd like to register." The two men had the look of used car salesmen about them, except they were hauling golf bags as well as their flashy luggage.

"Have you booked?" I asked.

"Leave this one to me, Stevie," said Harry and hustled up to shake hands with the new arrivals. "These gentlemen are my guests."

My heart sank for him. *Gentlemen*? If these were Harry's fancy out-of-towners, I could write the script. *Freeloaders*. Promising him new money to put into his struggling hotel, while just out for a freebie golf holiday. I couldn't believe Harry didn't get it. Like all of us, he had his shortcomings. He was only human, but of the many things Harry was or wasn't, you could never call him naive. He was street-wise, maybe a bit too much sometimes for his own good. And yet here he was wearing blinkers that blinded him.

I'd have to start looking for a new job. We all would. And the sort of rent I could afford would only get me a crummy winter let, or a caravan. I was in my mid thirties, had gone down the crappy student-let route in my youth and wanted a bit of security now, a few home comforts. Not some skanky, damp flat in a run-down building where the hallways smelled of sweaty socks and greasy spag-bol, and the grass never got cut, and the boiler wouldn't work.

"Is *that* what all the fuss was about?" said Joe, looking at the retreating backs of our new guests and Harry struggling to shoulder an over-size golf bag. "What I gave up my anniversary dinner for?"

"Looks like it," I said.

"Disappointing."

"Yeah."

"Think the rumours are right, Stevie?"

Maybe Joe was already drawing up figures on a balance sheet. Wondering if between them, Wilbur and he could still make their mortgage. They lived in an upmarket place, near the boating lake.

"Who knows? Best not discuss it till we know for sure, eh. You know what this place is like for gossip."

"Sure, but it's . . ."

"*Disappointing.*" I smiled. "Yeah, I know."

Joe should get out more. There were a whole lot more interesting words I could have introduced him to. None of them ladylike. And maybe it was good that he was here. Otherwise I might have gone through a repertoire of swear words that would have impressed an army drill sergeant.

*

From an unpromising start, the evening went well. There were no kitchen tragedies. The stand-in barman Harry had hired was a professional. No one broke anyone else's jaw. And Matthew, the piano player, even seemed to enjoy himself. He'd had the tuxedo in a wardrobe bag and looked handsome and sophisticated and played something from South Pacific when Harry asked him, but thankfully Harry didn't sing. He was too busy buttering up his guests and pouring red wine down their necks – the good stuff that he usually saved for himself – and handing out the brandy and cigars like there'd just been a birth in the family.

And both 'Joseph' and I acted like real professionals. Cheery *meet and greets* plastered to our faces. Harry was right, Joe looked great in the grey uniform blazer with the logo H.R. embroidered on the pocket - and the slim fitting grey slacks suited him. But then, I don't think I looked too bad either. Not for someone who'd drunk a vat of wine the night before, and whose red hair could resemble wire-wool when it wasn't tamed.

The thought reminded me of the woman in the photograph, obviously my grandmother in her younger days, although she hadn't dated it. I went into my office to go through the letters. It was quiet and things were running smoothly, so I figured I'd earned a few minutes to myself.

The handwriting was spidery, like you'd expect from someone very old. Not easy to read. I squinted at the faint lettering and considered the option of laser eye surgery.

"My dearest Stephanie,

"If you are finally reading this letter, it means we have met at last – although one of us is in the hereafter. I have instructed my solicitors to get in touch with you, but being the drama queen that I am, this will only happen once I am *demised*.

"I don't know how much your mother has already told you. Knowing Isobel, probably none of it. It was a mammoth task to even drag your address out of her. But I've kept my oath to her that I would not upset your life or hers by getting in touch with you. You know how she hates face-to-face confrontations. But dying can be very liberating and has, I believe, released me from any previous promises I made to her. My daughter was always a strange one, but don't be too harsh on her, for you don't know all the facts. I still love her as only a mother can. And one day, Stephanie, I hope you'll get to know the unconditional love that a mother lavishes on her children."

Unconditional love? Obviously my grandmother had it for my mother, but could I really say my mother had it for me? I still sent her birthday cards every year and a catch-up letter at Christmas. But she never replied. She was the reason I'd moved down to the West Country, to be closer to her in Plymouth. To keep some kind of link going, but it had been one-sided. Two years ago we'd had a fight and she'd made it plain she wanted nothing to do with me.

"My reason for writing is two-fold. Gosh, but that sounds cold and clinical and really I'm not like that. One part – and this is the selfish bit – is that I need to get something off my chest before I peg out. That process has already begun, but don't get all sentimental and fuzzy on me. Especially as the reason you're reading this letter at all is that I will finally have rammed the pearly gates with my Fiat Punto and my solicitor will by now have forwarded it to you. The letter, obviously, not the Fiat Punto."

A small tear escaped from the corner of my eye. I had tried not to cry, but the woman and I had the same sense of humour. And now, thanks to my mother, I would never get to meet her. I tried to pull it together and went back to my grandmother's letter.

"The other part and in my mind the *most* important (for I'm an ancient old bird whose passing will hardly rate a mention and life will still go on without me) is that I worry about you being lonely and never having the chance to meet your sister."

"Stevie, room number seven's complaining about their heating again." Joe's head came round the corner of the door. He let his jaw unhinge and I noted absent-mindedly that he looked as if somebody had smacked him in the mouth.

"What the hell's wrong?" he said.

"Uh?"

"You – you're white as death. You're not pregnant, are you?"

"Jesus, Joe!"

"What?"

I felt the letter slip from my grasp and flutter to the desk. "I've got a sister," I said.

"Is *that* all? I thought you were going to faint."
And that must have been when I fainted.

Chapter 6

Maybe it was better that I didn't have a man; things were less complicated when you only had yourself to think about. Independence has a lot going for it. And I could still wear my furry red socks in bed without worrying about looking sexy or glamorous. Or go out when I fancied it, without some man asking where I was off to. Or, even worse, giving me permission. Hey! Maybe I really *am* a Feminist.

Nigel's absence had been noted by several, but they hadn't laboured the point which I was grateful for. Some other guy dropped off our fish from Newlyn today - and nobody asked him about Nigel. Maybe he was sick, but I didn't think so. The man was avoiding me.

There was another thing noteworthy about today's fresh fish delivery – the arrival of two large, expensive lobsters in the order along with the usual white fish. Normally, we only had Coley, the cheapest fish Harry could buy and still claim that he sourced 'fresh local produce' for the kitchen. The sudden appearance of the lobsters was somehow *significant*, for it meant that Harry was still trying to impress his two special guests. But they didn't strike me as special, or entrepreneurs, just a couple of flashy freeloaders stringing poor old Harry along. But what did I know? I'd just lost another man. But at least I'd gained a sister.

The idea was still new and exciting to me. It was also puzzling, because my grandmother had said that my sister, Sophie, left Canada just before Christmas to look for me. Either my sister was a slow worker or she'd changed her mind.

Sophie and Stevie. I ran the names across my tongue. It felt like some kind of hackneyed double-act. Clichéd - corn straight from the cob. You'd think mother would have been more original, given us different sounding names. Had she been working her way through the alphabet? Or maybe the woman was just plain tired. Far as I know she'd never had any luck with men, at least not ones who wanted to stick around and bring up a family. This is just something she hinted at, for we'd never had a proper discussion about my father, and I couldn't remember any male ever bouncing me on his knee. And surely you'd remember important stuff like that. And Sophie. Why couldn't I remember Sophie?

Sophie had gone to live with our grandmother, had been brought up by her in Canada according to the letter. Had the job seemed too daunting for my mother? She would have been young then and alone, but how could you give one of your children away. And was Sophie older than me, or younger? The letter didn't say, but I assumed she was my baby sister.

I tried to imagine her. Why didn't I remember her being born? If I was her big sister, then shouldn't I remember? Unless stuff had been so awful back then, that I'd wiped it from my memory.

"You okay now, babe?"

"Sure." I smiled at Doris.

"Gave them all a scare last night, from what I hear, you keeling over like that. Not pregnant, are you?" Doris let her eyes stray to my stomach, which - I'm the first to admit - wasn't as flat as it once had been, but was definitely *not* hosting another generation of the Anderson clan in there. For that, you need some kind of biological event to take place – like sex.

"No," I said emphatically. "What the hell's wrong with everybody? Of course I'm not pregnant and any rumour that says *that* had better be killed off at birth! Got it?"

Birth? Why had I said that? One of those Freudian slip things, because the old biological clock was definitely ticking away. But I'd never even thought about babies, not until now – and I didn't need any complications in my life. I mean my mother had hardly been a shining example of nurturing motherhood. But my grandmother, now she seemed different...

"Well?"

"What?" I said.

"I asked if you thought I spread rumours. But you weren't listening - floated off somewhere. Where were you?" asked Doris, her tone accusing.

Not here obviously. "Sorry, Auntie D," I said, hoping my pet name for her would bring us back to some sort of status quo. I reached over and put my arm round her shoulder. "Didn't mean to hurt your feelings. Stuff's been weird, lately, is all."

"Oh? What kind of stuff?"

"When you two have quite finished with your mother's meeting, I think you'll find that number seven's complaining about a lack of fresh towels in their en-suite." Harry looked pointedly at Doris. One of those 'if the shoe fits, wear it' looks.

But he was dealing with the best here. She gave him her stony glare and tapped the watch on her arm. "Even slaves are allowed coffee breaks," she said.

Harry's thoughts glitched, but only for a second. I think Doris frightened him at times, for when called for, she could pack the punch of a small nuclear warhead.

But Harry soon came back on track. "Well, Doris. Maybe *you* would like to go up to the Hendersons and explain the finer points of your work schedule, and why they don't have any dry towels for their shower." He stared her out. "In your own time!"

*

"What the feck am I supposed to do with this crap?"

"And good afternoon to you too, Alfie." It wasn't often cook phoned me, for relations between the two of us had been strained lately. So, obviously he needed a favour.

"I been trying to get Harry for ages. He's not answering his phone."

"So, I'm the oily rag?" I said.

"You're his 2I/C, right?"

"Am I?" I'd no idea what that meant.

"When he's not here, like. You're Second-in-Command."

Ah. Got it. Alfie must have spent some time in the army. He wouldn't have learnt his culinary skills there, for they actually *taught* you how to cook. I always assumed he'd learnt any little he knew from a stint in a prison kitchen somewhere.

"Harry's on the golf course," I said.

"What the feck's he doing there?"

"Call me a traditionalist, Chef, but I presume he's chasing a little white ball around with some sort of club or other."

"You're a fair tit when you set your mind to it, Stevie."

"One aims to please. Now, what can I do for you?"

"Tell me what he wants doing with these two feckin' lobsters, for a start."

"Ah." I had a feeling that would be coming. As soon as I'd seen the delivery note. For Alfie didn't strike me as somebody who'd had a lot of dealings with lobsters, dead or alive. God, then it hit me. "Shit, they're not alive are they?"

"Well, they ain't dancing no tango nor nuthin'," he said. "But they ain't passed on yet."

"You sure?"

"Sure, I'm sure. I ain't stupid. I did what it said on the instructions."

"And?"

"You're supposed to poke them in the eye," he said. "Check they ain't snuffed it."

The thought of some poor lobster quivering in its boots as Alfie stuck his thick, podgy finger in its eye made me feel queasy.

"Right."

"So - what does Harry want me to do with this bloody lot?"

"He didn't say?"

"Like I'd be phoning you if he did."

"Okay. I'll try and find him."

"Make it quick."

"Why?"

"I don't like the look of this pair. And it says if they look sleepy you should get them cooked straight off."

"And do they look sleepy?" I said.

"How would I know? I ain't their mother. But I don't want *nobody* accusing me of poisoning no customers."

Should have thought about that before you stepped into a kitchen, then Alfie. But I wasn't stupid enough to say that. We already had enough problems with a hotel that was slowly going broke, two wise guy investors who were squeezing Harry for a week's free board, and two confused lobsters ready for a kip.

I made a decision. If Harry wanted the lobsters for that night's dinner and if they were likely to go off (did lobsters go off?) then they needed to be cooked. What Alfie was supposed to do with them after that was anybody's guess.

"Cook them," I said.

"Duh!"

Got it now. I'm not usually that thick - or maybe I am. He wasn't sure how.

"I'll Google it."

"Yeah – well do it quick. These guys don't look too happy. Think I should put them back in the salad drawer?" he asked.

"How the hell would I know? I'm a receptionist."

"It said on the paper. Keep them cool and moist," he said. "Put them in a salad drawer."

"What, even if they're still alive?"

"Sure, 'swhat it says for the live ones. And boil them straight off if they look sleepy – or if they've passed on, like."

Dear God. It felt surreal. "Well, do it then. Put them back in the salad drawer. Meanwhile I'll look up Utube or something. You want to take a look?"

"Nah. You do it, Stevie. I trust you."

Course he did. I may have been slow on the uptake, but I'm not bloody stupid. Somebody ends up in hospital with food poisoning from a dodgy lobster and it would be me he'd blame. I started pressing keys on the computer. There must be something out there to tell the uninitiated how to cook a lobster.

*

"These came while you were out." It was the new permanent barman. He was called Christopher Newly. He'd arrived early that morning and so far I hadn't seen much of him, other than a swift introduction when I'd made a weak joke about his name, it being appropriate and all, him being the new man at the Royal. But some people have no sense of humour.

I looked blankly at the massive bunch of flowers, the cellophane still intact around them and their stems stuck into the ice bucket of water. I assumed they must be for one of the guests.

"*You* put them in water?" I asked, thinking it was quite enterprising. Not particularly a man-thing to do. "Our last barman would never have thought about it. Ten out of ten for initiative," I said and smiled. *Building bridges*. The man looked at me like I'd grown an extra limb.

"Yeah, well. I've heard your last barman wasn't much of a brain surgeon. Hardly set the bar high, did he?"

Great! This guy was going to be a hoot. I'd only been trying to be friendly, make him feel at ease in the new job. Pearls before swine and all that.

He thrust the ice bucket and the flowers at me. "Well, you want them or not?"

"Sure," I mumbled, and then thought about his rudeness. We were all colleagues together, after all. For better or worse. Maybe going down with a sinking ship.

Maybe not. "By the way I've got a name," I said and pointed at the badge, clinging to my lapel for all to see. "Stevie. Call me that or Miss Anderson. Up to you."

"Not *Ms*, then?" It was meant as an insult, for he pronounced it miz and held onto the 'z' like it was an angry bee. I knew then I wouldn't like the guy.

I grabbed the flowers from him and walked around to the back of Reception.

"Hi Stevie."

"What you doing here?" I asked Joe.

"Got in while you were on the golf course."

"I wasn't *on* the golf course. Just in the clubhouse, looking for Harry. Alfie's had a crisis of confidence in the kitchen and wanted me to go look for the boss."

"Yeah? Anything I should know about it?"

I looked at Joe, all bright eyed and anxious to please. "Nothing you should worry about." What he didn't know couldn't hurt him and he couldn't do anything anyway, not unless he knew how to make Lobster Thermidor. I'd looked it up. It was an old fashioned recipe that had fallen out of favour with foodies. So I guess it would fit right in here. Apparently one of Harry's extra special guests had mentioned his liking for it.

"Fair enough."

"So. Why *are* you here?" I asked.

"Overkill, I know. Both of us. Reckon Harry's still keeping up appearances, like we've got loads of staff floating around, all with great grins on their faces. Two extra waiters in the restaurant as well."

"God's teeth. He'll smile himself right into bankruptcy."

"Money brings money, Stevie. Gotta look successful," said Joe. "I mean would *you* invest in a business that looks like it's going down the tubes?"

I guess Joe was right. You had to speculate to accumulate, so they said. I wouldn't know. I've neither speculated, nor accumulated. But then the two guys that Harry was wining and dining didn't look as if they had either.

"They're fancy," said Joe. "Who they for?"

I was still holding onto the ice bucket. And the flowers. "No idea; that new barmen said they'd been delivered earlier."

"What's he like?"

"Pass. Right - if you're here now, I'm going for a coffee. Need to see Alfie anyway." *The two birds with one stone theory – always useful.* "Here, get these to whichever guest they're meant for."

Joe took the flowers and read the envelope. "These are yours, Stevie. Wow! The man's no cheapskate, is he? Maybe he's got money we don't know about."

"What? Let me see that."

Life can throw you the odd surprise, but this was a real belter. Not only had Nigel *not* written me off, but he had the heart of a poet. The card read: Every moment spent with you is like a beautiful dream come true. Okay, maybe not a *real* poet, but as close as I'd been to one.

Joe read the rest of the card over my shoulder.

Sorry haven't been in touch. Been busy here. Hope lobsters arrived okay.

"Dull," he said - a slight sneer in his voice. "For a poet, I mean."

I gave him a withering look, for Joe could be pompous at times. I felt the need to come to Nigel's defence. "And you're Shakespeare, I suppose."

"Ah," he said, like he'd arrived at some great truth. "Smitten, eh? Who'd have guessed – you and the fishman."

I couldn't think of a reply, but made a dignified exit, heading in the direction of the kitchen.

"And what's he mean about the lobsters?" he shouted at my retreating back.

"Mind your own bloody business," I said.

Chapter 7

"Get that mutt out of my kitchen."

Benjy was Harry's black Labrador, a dog with a sense of adventure. He figured he was a *hotel dog* and should have the run of the place - and the kitchen was an area he felt naturally drawn to.

There were two philosophical and opposing schools of thought on this. One was Harry's who preferred to keep Benjy in the office with him. The other was Benjy's whose natural instinct was to break free from the confined space of Harry's office and retreat to the more promising setting of the kitchen. Like some World War Two prisoner, he saw it his duty to escape. The office was small. The dog was large. The kitchen had leftovers. No-brainer.

The young K.P. skidded to a messy halt, fell to his knees and flung his arms around Benjy. The dog's successful capture brought a look of triumph to the lad's face. The K.P.'s name was William, though everyone called him Smithy – except Harry of course, who had no idea what his name was and mostly called him 'mush'.

Funny thing about dogs. They often *do* look like their owners. And Benjy had the heavy jowls of his master and a similar breadth around his middle. Neither he nor Harry were lightweights, but I guess that's natural if you spend your time in a hotel and have a fondness for the kitchen - Benjy, not Harry. Harry's fondness was for the locally made pale ale called Betty Stogs, brewed by Skinners. He thought of himself as a connoisseur and he drank enough of the stuff to qualify.

Harry spoilt his dog rotten. He'd been heard to say that he felt more affection for Benjy than he had done for his wife, now ex. But, by all accounts - mainly Doris - the woman had been a loudmouthed, in-your-face, brassy blonde who made it her mission in life to strip as much cash as possible from Harry's bank account over the shortest possible time scale. No wonder the man claimed he'd rather have animals than people. I guess that was why he'd become a cheapskate.

The dog was led away in disgrace by the grinning K.P.

"And wash your bloody hands before you come back in my kitchen!" shouted Alfie after the young lad. This, I felt, was more for my benefit than any deep-seated love of hygiene on the part of our cook. "Right, let's get on with these feckin' lobsters, then," he said.

I hadn't been looking forward to it. Not that I was going to cook them, but I'd learned enough from my limited research to figure out that the process could be a barbaric one - at least for the lobsters. So, I'd agreed to come down and translate my small knowledge into a hopefully less painful experience for the doomed Crustaceans. Alfie wouldn't give a monkey's either way. He'd be perfectly happy to plunge the poor bloody things straight into boiling water and watch them writhe in agony. "I've heard they don't feel nuthin'," he'd told me. *Sure!*

"Did you put them in the freezer, like I said?"

"Still in there. Ten minutes, you said. But I don't see the point."

"Numbs the lobster before cooking," I said and pretended not to notice his astonished look.

A timer went off and Alfie took the lobsters out of the deepfreeze. There was a huge pot of water on the cooker.

It had been at a fierce boil for several minutes now, so there was no turning back.

"Right," he said. "Let's do it."

I refused to look at the things. "Okay, two tablespoons of sea-salt for every four pints of water," I said, reading from my list.

"Check."

"Fierce boil," I said.

"Check."

"Hold the lobster behind its claws and drop it head-first into the boiling water."

Alfie did this with what can only be described as gusto. I forced myself to watch the tails writhe up and down before he put the lid on the pot.

I thrust the instructions for massacring poor innocent lobsters into his hand, shoved my hands over my mouth and ran towards the exit. I threw up in the staff toilet. It wasn't only what I'd seen that made me sick, but I remembered the last two bullet points on my print-out.

- Do not remove the lobster from the pot before the shell has turned bright red.
- You'll know the lobster is properly cooked when an antennae comes away easily in your hand when gently pulled.

The process was brutal, but I didn't think Alfie would have too many problems with it, certainly not the ethical kind. I knew I would take some time to recover. It's not easy being an accessory to murder, if only on the lobster front.

*

It was Wednesday night. Karaoke night in the cabaret lounge of the Royal. The wall of replica Victorian mirrors gleamed, their ornate brass frames glinting in the recessed mood lighting. The mirrors were a testament to the housekeeping skills of Doris who took a special pride in polishing them, like they were her own personal property. They also pulled off the optical illusion of making the room look bigger. Candles already flickered on the tables around the dance floor. I'd talked Harry into those. He hadn't been keen at first. All that extra cost! But their rosy glow added to the atmosphere and their faint aroma, cherries with an overtone of almond, had been popular with the guests.

I'd tried my best to be subtle with Harry, to suggest he skip the Karaoke bit for tonight and just sit up at the bar with his guests. Didn't want to see him make a fool of himself in front of the two morons who'd been taking advantage of him for the last couple of days.

But my boss was nothing if not consistent. He carried on setting up the equipment on the small stage and sent me off to his office for a bottle of champagne for the two guys; I hadn't even bothered to learn their names - they were creeps.

"Hi, Gorgeous." The older man gave me a flashy smile, a full-frontal of his dentures, as I set his free champagne on the bar in front of him. He patted the barstool next to him, lingering slowly over the action, as if to infuse it with extra meaning. It was pure sleaze and I felt a queasiness plant itself in the pit of my stomach. "Come and join us."

Harry's ears pricked up and he gave me a warning look. But I'd no idea what he was warning me against. I can do many things. It says so – right there in my C.V. But mind-reading isn't one of them. So, I excused myself, *politely*. Not a smartarse comment in sight, for I didn't want Harry having a coronary.

"Thanks, that's kind," I said. "But I have to get back to work." *Kind*? The word almost stuck in my throat. The man looked like a bloody perv and there was definitely a leer on his face. I left the bar like I was in some sort of race.

Harry came rushing out after me and ran me to earth in my office. There was barely room for both of us in there; he must have weighed in at around two of me. I pulled the desk back so that he could get in *and* close the door. I had a feeling we'd need the door closed. It was a cosy space, but useless if you were in the business of cat-swinging.

"What the hell was all that about, he asked?" His voice was angry.

"He asked me to join him." I said, calmly. I wanted to be angry too, but there was no point in both of us ending up in therapy.

"And you flounced out like some stuck-up-fucking-brat."

"Don't you fucking swear at me, Harry Evans! You may be my boss, but you don't fucking own me and neither does that fucking creep."

"Oh, very mature, I'm sure."

I pushed the desk back, jamming him against the wall and Harry relented, showed me the palms of both hands like I'd won a special prize.

"Look, it's obvious Gerry likes you. Though God knows why. You're a pain in the ass." He smiled to show this was a joke. "Couldn't you just humour the bloke for a while? He's very important to me, and surely just having a drink with the guy wouldn't hurt you. It's not like I'm asking you to go to bed with him or anything. Where's the harm in that, Stevie?"

"It's called whoring, Harry. And I signed on here to be your Head Receptionist not a bloody prostitute. You'll have my resignation in the morning. Meanwhile, I'll finish out my shift tonight, for I'm a *professional*. And if you find yourself near a dictionary, I suggest you look up both meanings of that word. If I'd wanted to be pawed by some creepy perv, I'd hang out on a street corner and wait for the kerb crawlers. I don't need your loser hangers-on to do the job. Got it?"

I stormed past him and headed for the kitchen. I needed a coffee. I could do with a cigarette as well, for my hands were shaking badly. But I'd given up smoking for a year now. It seemed like a good time to start up. Cook would have one. He always nipped out to the back alley for fag breaks. *And Alfie and I were on good terms now*. He owed me.

Chapter 8

"Bastard!" said Joe.

"Yeah, bastard," I agreed.

Wilbur had been the first to say it. But I don't know if he was talking about that creepy bastard, Gerry (I can't believe I'd even remembered his name) or Harry.

It was one o'clock in the morning and we were in Joe and Wilbur's lounge. It was one of those rooms that you dream about. Perfect. Navy blue and green scatter cushions – satin and velvet – piled up on two enormous white leather sofas, luxury wooden flooring and long, midnight blue velvet drapes. I called mine curtains, but these were definitely drapes. White fur rugs were scattered around, so I'd taken my shoes off as soon as I came in the front door. I felt like I'd walked into the centre fold of a glossy magazine. Joe had taken a course in interior design.

It had been Joe's idea that I go home with him. My own planning had stopped short at walking out of the hotel and booking into some cheap surf lodge for the night. But he convinced me that walking the streets at midnight looking for a bed wasn't a good way to start my new life. *A new life*? It wasn't until then that the whole thing truly hit me. What I'd done. How many bridges I'd burned behind me. But sometimes you had no choice.

I'd felt like an intruder in their home. But that was before I'd drunk a bottle and a half of Cabernet Sauvignon - 13.5%. Now things seemed about as perfect as they could ever get. Joe and Wilbur were social drinkers and only had a glass each. Probably because

Wilbur had to be up at seven in the morning to go to work, and Joe was turning in for the eight o'clock shift in Reception. I reminded myself that they both had jobs, whereas I was now unemployed. I still had to write out my resignation, but that was a formality. Nothing in the world could make me set foot in the hotel again. Yes, I'd definitely made the right decision. It might have been one of those spur of the moment and heat of battle ones, but it was clearly the only sensible thing to do.

At half past five in the morning, throwing up red wine and the cheese and ham paninis that Joe had made the night before, I began to regret the way I'd stormed out of the Royal, my job, my home and something that had been the focus of my life for the past five years.

My head throbbed with the kind of pain only a hangover can give you. It was a vicious, vindictive pain that reminded you hangover headaches were self inflicted wounds, and you were getting what you deserved.

I stumbled through an unfamiliar landscape towards the kitchen, looking for some form of pain relief. There'd been no Asprin in the bathroom cabinet and I could hardly walk into Joe and Wilbur's bedroom to ask where they kept their drugs. So I put the kettle on and settled for a cup of tea instead. I remembered that I'd started smoking again, and thought about the half empty packet still in my bag, but this house had no ashtrays in it. So, the boys must operate a smoke free zone.

The boys! It was hard to think of them in there together, snuggling up like a couple of lovebirds. But I guess that was my problem and not theirs. They were good people and when I needed it, they'd given me succour. *Succour? Well, I'm not on top form right now.* But I couldn't stay indefinitely. I'd need to make plans. Place to live. Job. My clothes and stuff.

That would be the worst bit, getting my things out of the hotel without running into Harry or even worse, Doris. Having to explain to the others why I'd gone.

"You okay, Stevie?"

It was Joe and he managed to look just as fabulous first thing in the morning in a dressing gown as he did in his uniform. What is it with other people? My hair did an imitation of a haystack every morning, and all the wine I'd drunk last night had collected in the deep, sagging bags under my eyes. Note to self: teetotal from now on.

"I'm fine, thanks." My nose should have grown at least a foot. But I figured that Joe had his own problems and didn't need to be worrying about drunken women who'd just lost their jobs. "I'll be out of your hair soon. I'll find somewhere temporary today and take it from there."

"You'll do no such thing. Wilbur and I talked it over and you're welcome to stay here. Get yourself sorted."

"You're princes, both of you. But I couldn't do that. I've seen it before, been on the other end of it. You try and help someone out and they start to get comfortable. Don't try very hard to find their own place."

"You wouldn't do that. I know you. You've got principles, Stevie." Joe dropped his head, embarrassed.

"Like some tea?" I asked.

"Sure, that'd be good. There's some of my Lapsang souchong in there. He pointed with his chin towards an old fashioned caddy.

I'd been thinking more along the lines of a teabag. But when in Rome . . .

*

"Right, that's the last of it." The van door closed on all my worldly goods. It didn't seem much, not for almost thirty-five years on the planet. But then we are more than our possessions, right?

"Sure I can't take you back to Joe's place? Be a bit more humane than that fleepit you've rented."

"Thanks but no thanks," I said. "Firm believer in standing on my own two feet." *Yeah – straight into bankruptcy, like Harry.*

"Commendable."

I thought so too. But maybe I wouldn't have used that exact word. But then Nigel was like that. A bit quaint and conservative, especially for somebody his age.

Funny how things turn out. Who'd have guessed I'd end up in a refrigerated fish van with Nigel, all my belongings packed in the back and heading for my new flat? New to me, but obviously not NEW, not for the sort of money I could hand over. It was more in the shape of a bedsit, but I suppose that's all my last one had been. I stifled an unhappy sigh, for it wasn't easy leaving my old life behind. No matter how much I'd moaned about it, I'd felt part of a family and now here I was being transplanted into some alien, unknown soil.

Nigel had been like an old fashioned knight in armour. And let's face it – he *was* old fashioned; some ancient throw-back to a gentler age, when men tipped their hats, held doors open for women, and friendly neighbourhood coppers cycled by whistling *The Sun has got his Hat on*.

He'd been brought up to speed by Joe and immediately offered the fish van to move my stuff for me. I'd worried that he might get in trouble with the boss, but he'd just laughed that off. Said he and the boss were very close. Good for him! Wish I could say the same thing for me and my boss. Ex-boss, I reminded myself.

I hadn't seen him, or any of the others. Had just packed my things as fast as I could and taken them down the back stairs of the hotel to the van waiting in the car park.

"Ready?" Nigel eyed me with sad, doleful eyes. He had the ability to look like a Cocker Spaniel having a bad day. Not that there was anything wrong with Spaniels. They were lovely dogs.

I nodded. I didn't have the energy for speeches. It had been a hard three days, but I figured I'd worked miracles in the time. Pulled myself together - I'm never quite sure how that works, but I'd had a go. Found somewhere to live. Had my hair cut into a short, *edgy* style, the salon's words, not mine. It had been liberating, seeing all that red hair fall to the floor. I got the feeling Nigel wasn't too keen, though he didn't criticise it, just said he liked women to look feminine. But everyone else says the new, spiky cut suits my personality better. I don't know if I should be pleased or insulted by that. But I'm glad I was brave enough to do it.

I'd also got myself onto the books of an agency and would take any kind of work that came along, although Admin or Customer Service is my thing, and I feel more at home in a hotel than anywhere else. But right now, beggars couldn't be choosers. I had a bit of money, but not enough to be out of work for more than a month.

I hadn't heard from Harry. I hadn't expected to, but at some point he'd have to give me my wages. He knew the score. He'd had my resignation, just a three-line-straight-to-the-point letter. No frills. No recriminations. I'd tried to be professional.

I wondered how things were going for him, and if the losers had agreed to invest any money. I doubted they had any, but then I wasn't always right. Maybe the hotel would survive. Maybe Harry would survive. I wasn't vindictive and they were my family – all of them, including Alfie and I missed them already. I sighed again. Nigel heard me and looked sideways. He was trying to find something to say. He seemed a sensitive sort of man, but he was still a man. They weren't that good at the touchy-feely stuff.

"Well, here we are. You sure about this?" He eyed the place dubiously.

It was the only way you could eye the place. But at least it had a roof and a front door and I had my own key once again. So, a result.

"It'll be fine," I said, radiating confidence. "The toilet works and there's a shower."

"Yeah, but no kitchen."

"I'm not much of a cook," I said. "There's a Subway down the road."

He left me once we'd piled everything into my living area. I didn't want anyone around, didn't know how long I could hold back the waterworks. I promised to call him as soon as I was settled in and we'd go out for a meal, or the cinema, or something. It would be good, I'd said. And it would, for Nigel seemed like a kind man. Not bad looking, and not too tall, a point in his favour, for it made me feel better about my own height, or lack of it. He was three years older than me and looked striking - when he took the trouble to dress up. And he had an air of confidence about him when he was with me, something that was never there when he delivered our fish. Hark at me – *our* fish. Maybe we'd be good for each other.

I unpacked my kettle and made a cup of tea. With a teabag. It was more *me* than some fancy leaves that had been smoked over pinewood fires. A few salty tears trickled down the side of my face. I'd tried to hold them back, but sometimes your body just won't listen to your head.

My face never took well to crying. It had the light complexion that went with red hair and easily gave in to messy blotches left behind by tears. The guy who cut my hair had said my few freckles were 'cute' but then he would say that, he was taking my money. He also said he found redheads mysterious and sexy. But he was gay. So maybe we weren't.

I thought about my sister Sophie. Wondered if she had the family red hair. If she could go into the sun without breaking out in a mass of freckles. Angle dust, I used to call them. It made me feel better about them, but that was when I was ten. Was Sophie tall? I wasn't and neither was my mother, and it was hard to tell about my grandmother, she'd been sitting down in the photograph. Was my sister a beauty? What was she doing now? Where *was* she? And why hadn't she tried to find me? It couldn't be that hard.

I should stop feeling sorry for myself. All things change. Change was *good*. I sipped the tea and smiled and thought about Doris and how she'd be quizzing Joe about my sudden disappearance. Joe had promised he wouldn't talk; neither waterboarding nor having his finger nails pulled out could make him, he'd said. But Doris had a way of dragging stuff out of you.

I closed my eyes and relaxed. Maybe I'd start yoga; a new beginning to go with the hair. I inhaled a long, slow breath and a faint waft of fish filled my nostrils. And I wondered how long my belongings would have the smell of Nigel's fish van clinging to them.

Chapter 9

"Miss Anderson, Ma'am - this is an unexpected pleasure. I wasn't sure if our letter had found you."

"Yes, I'm sorry. I didn't realise I was supposed to get in touch. Not until I read the letter properly this morning. Things have been manic."

"I know that feeling, but an email would have been just fine. Didn't want to put you to any trouble."

The accent made everything sound exotic and I suddenly felt dull compared to this man, Clarence Adams, sitting at a desk somewhere thousands of miles away. He was an American and I wondered if I'd got it wrong.

"You *are* the Harding and Willis who wrote to me from Ottawa?"

"That's us Ma'am."

"Only, you don't sound Canadian."

"I'm an import. From Virginia in the good old U.S. of A."

"Ah."

"As your grandmother's solicitors and executors, we will be sending a copy of her will to all beneficiaries."

"So I don't need to be there for the reading?"

I could hear the man chuckle. "Not necessary, Ma'am. The *family gathering* in an oak-panelled room – that's the stuff of T.V. shows. Rarely happens."

"Oh."

"You sound disappointed."

"Just that I assumed my sister would be there as well – and I've never met her." Not that there was any way on God's Good Earth I could afford a ticket to Canada.

"I see. Well, of course, I'm not in a position to comment on other beneficiaries. At least not until you've received your copy of the will."

"Hypothetically – if my sister *was* named in my grandmother's will – and you couldn't find her, would that make a difference?" It sounded bad. Like I was just thinking about any money coming my way. Not that there would be much; this was *my* family we were talking about, not the Rothchilds. But I wasn't. I'd rather have had a chance to meet my grandmother than take her money, but I couldn't lie; the money would be useful. *Any* money.

He gave a discreet cough as if he was deciding exactly what would be ethical to divulge on the phone, or maybe the man was just arse-covering. Everybody did that, and I guess lawyers took it to the extreme.

"Hypothetically?" He seemed to be mulling the word over. Perhaps he liked it. "Well, we are instructed to liquidate and distribute your grandmother's estate between the main beneficiaries. It's sometimes a challenge to locate all the beneficiaries – speaking hypothetically you understand . . ."

"Yes, I understand." I was madly trying to read between the lines. "And will that make a difference?"

"Not to yourself, Ma'am. If one is missing, it just makes our job as executors harder, that's all. Now that we have confirmation of your address, a copy of the will should be with you in a few days, along with the letter of special instructions your grandmother wanted you to have. After that, it's just about the process and how long it takes to liquidate and divide Mrs Warburton's assets."

"Mrs Warburton?"

"Your maternal grandmother."

I remembered to give him my *new* address which still felt alien to me, but I guess I'd grow into it. I hadn't lingered on the phone after that and I hoped that Clarence Adams understood. I pictured him behind his mahogany desk, in his silk suit and tie, with his client lunches, and me with my 6 inch meatball sub, wondering where my next job would come from. He wasn't likely to understand, was he? I'd put thirty pounds on my phone and calling him was costing me £1.49 a minute. But I could be wrong. Maybe he was a sympathetic guy who knew that we didn't all operate on expense accounts, or wear designer labels. Some of us had to make do with faded black joggers that had seen better days.

*

"Sorry about this." Nigel nodded at the line of traffic crawling its way along the Hayle bypass through the miserly, single lane.

"Not your fault," I said.

But the words didn't seem to relax the man beside me, gripping the steering wheel so fiercely that the skin on his hands was pulled tight and his knuckles shone white. I wondered if there was something wrong, for Nigel wasn't usually this wired up. But I didn't know him well enough yet to poke around in his private life. So I left it. Perhaps he didn't like sitting in traffic.

We were on our way to St Ives. So far, the journey had taken well over an hour. It was a record. Even in summer, when the roads were crammed to bursting with holidaymakers, you could get there in forty-five minutes from Newquay. But the exodus of holiday visitors back to their homes kicks off a strange phenomenon in Cornwall. Somewhere, in an office run by the Highways Department, a man with a power complex and a three-piece-suit starts shoving pins in a map. That's the signal for gangs of construction workers to pour onto the selected bits of road, making them traffic black-spots. The man in the suit has a special name for this exercise. He calls it a road improvement scheme. The drivers who have to navigate it use other, more colourful names. This is also the time when share prices of companies making bright orange traffic cones go through the roof.

Ours wasn't a journey for the fainthearted. But we got through it and once we'd arrived in St Ives, Nigel relaxed slightly.

"This is nice."

"Yes, it's nice," I agreed. And it was. Doing things with Nigel was 'nice'. But the blandness of the word said a lot about our relationship. He was kind, which was good, of course. No one wants a proper bastard who's going to whack them around, but there were times when I wished that Nigel had a little more fizz in him.

It was Tuesday night, the time when jazz lovers flocked from all over the county to the St. Ives Jazz Club. It prided itself on being *The Last Jazz Club before New York* and you could hardly argue with that, for the next stop was the Atlantic Ocean.

We had a couple of hours before the gig started and were walking down towards the seafront, to a restaurant that I liked. It served mostly fish - we were in St Ives, after all.

"All except your choice of restaurant." He smiled to take any sting out of the criticism.

"And what's wrong with it?"

"Fish," he said. "When you see fish all day, it's good to have a change."

This was the first time I'd asked him to do something particular on one of our dates. Usually I just went with the flow – *his* flow. We'd been seeing each other every Monday and Friday since I'd left my job three weeks ago. Those were the nights Nigel had said were better for him. He hadn't invited me out on Saint Valentine's Day. Yes, I *know* I said it didn't matter, but it turns out that it did. The fourteenth had been a Sunday, but of course any couple with a shred of romance in their souls had booked tables at intimate restaurants on Saturday night.

I'd waited, but nothing happened. It was neither Monday nor Friday, but I thought he'd have made an exception. Still, Nigel was no Don Juan. But maybe that was good, right? A steady, dependable bloke. A bit stuck with routine. I hadn't asked him what he did every other night of the week; he'd tell me if he wanted to. He was a private sort of person, and there were times when I could feel him clam up and I had to back off.

He'd been to my place - as you know, it's hardly a mansion, but I didn't mind him seeing it. But he hadn't once invited me to his, and when I'd asked where exactly he lived in Newlyn, he'd become edgy.

Tonight was a Tuesday. So it was a sort of test, if I were really honest. Would he be happy to break out of his mould? Happy to go along with something *I'd* suggested. But there was a special concert on at the club, a trio from New York that I wanted to see and I hoped to test the waters with Nigel, see if listening to jazz upset him as much as it seemed to some other people. It was sometimes an acquired taste. He hadn't refused, but there had been a kind of undercurrent. Could be that I was reading too much into stuff, though. I've been known to do that.

"Old world charm, eh?" There was a touch of sarcasm in his tone.

"Authentic Kitsch". I agreed. *Ignoring it.* So, okay. Maybe the restaurant décor *wasn't* the most subtle, but we were here to eat. I eyed the pieces of net strung haphazardly from the ceiling and the old fashioned glass fishing weights. Even now, beachcombers still managed to pick them up, but more likely these were the kitsch replicas used by decorators for the interior design of fish restaurants.

I wondered about the tension in the air. Didn't know if it came from me, or him. I don't like atmospheres; try not to add to them. But Joe accused me of being moody sometimes. So maybe I am.

"And you'll be having fish, I suppose?"

"Maybe," I said.

"What about the lobster?" He pointed to the entry on the menu. "You could always give them a few pointers on how to cook it." He laughed.

I'd told him about Alfie and the lobsters. I remembered how the tails had writhed. And suddenly I didn't feel hungry.

Chapter 10

"How's the job search going?"
"Not a business in the county hasn't had my C.V."
"Any bites?"
"Only from the fleas in my place."
"Stevie! I told you to stay with us."
"Joke." I put my hands up in mock surrender. "Not a flea in sight."
"It's horrible. *Horrible*! You having to stay there. Your talents wasted." Joe put his hand over his mouth. Sucked in a dramatic breath.

He was a loyal mate and had come out to meet me at a coffee shop in town.

"I'll live," I said. "But you're right, It's depressing. I've applied for ten jobs so far. Not so much as a reply back or an interview."

"Bastards!"

"Yeah. But most of them were for care assistants. Or cleaners. Not a lot out there in our line of business right now."

"What about me talking to Harry?"

"I won't go crawling back to Harry. I wasn't in the wrong."

"I know that. But he's suffering. We really need you and if I suggest it . . ."

"No!"

We sank into silence and I sipped my latte. It tasted bitter. Everything tasted bitter lately.

"Harry give you your wages, yet?"
"What do you think?"

"I think he should've done, by now."

"That's what I think too," I said. "But then maybe he's waiting for the end of the month. Anyway, I might end up buying and selling Harry soon."

"Yeah?"

"I've been named in my grandmother's will."

"Wow!"

"I'm not buying the penthouse yet. But it was a sweet thought."

"Sure. But every little helps, right?"

"I need something *now*, Joe. Need to get a job."

"Then, let me talk to Harry . . ."

"Never! Know the funny thing?"

"What?" he said. And like me, Joe looked as if he could do with hearing something funny.

"Well, about two weeks ago I applied for a job looking after an old lady in Falmouth."

"What, a companion, like?"

I laughed. "Not even, that. A support worker. Care assistant. Whatever. Know what that means?"

"No idea."

"You help them to live at home. Do anything they can't. This old girl needed 'personal care', washing and stuff. Couldn't get to the loo by herself or wipe her own bottom," I said, remembering how I'd talked myself into the idea that I'd be fine with that. I could do it. You could do anything you put your mind to. You needed money, you went out and earned it. All work had value. I believed that.

"Shit!"

"Exactly. Know the *real* hoot, though? They didn't get back to me. I can't even get a job wiping people's arses."

"Bummer!"

"Yeah, bummer. You're priceless, Joe."

We both laughed. I laughed till the tears rolled down my cheeks. I laughed long after Joe had stopped laughing at his own joke. But then my laughter was more like hysteria. It wasn't that funny.

"How'd it go at the club last night?"

"Okay."

"That good, eh? Thought you were looking forward to it."

"I was. The music was great."

"And Nigel?"

"Rough. We had a row afterwards. He hasn't phoned me since."

"Maybe he doesn't like jazz."

"Yeah, maybe," I said. But I had a feeling it was more than that.

*

Two days later, Joe arrived at my bedsit with a letter. *Delivered by hand*, it said on the envelope. I opened it. It was some kind of vindication that I was right and Harry was wrong. He'd acted out of turn, he wrote, asking me to go and sit with that plonker - *plonker*, eh? Maybe Harry was getting more refined in his old age. Normally he'd have used a different sort of word. He asked me to forgive him and come back 'home'. He missed me. Everybody missed me. From Harry, that was as close to an apology as you could get.

"Well?"

Joe was fidgeting from one foot to the other like he was standing on hot coals.

"Well, what?" I asked.

"Did he give you your wages?"

I looked at the cheque. "Sure, and a bit more. Says he knows I'll have to give a month's notice on this place and he's giving me a month's rent to pay in lieu." I eyed the figure on the cheque suspiciously.

"That's great. Well, he wants you back, right?"

"Sure he wants me back. Can't live without me." I grinned.

"So? You're coming?"

"Maybe."

"Stevie, you are the most infuriating, bloody woman on the planet. You waiting for a better offer? Or maybe you still fancy wiping some old biddy's bum."

"Could be. Anyway, how'd he know how much I was paying for this place? Insider information?"

Joe blushed to the roots of his dyed blond hair. "In a good cause," he said.

"You might have had the decency to let him pull out the odd fingernail first."

Joe Hines laughed like a drain that had just been unblocked. "You're back, yeah?"

"I'm back!"

*

"You're back." Doris was a master of the short one-liner.

"Couldn't get a better offer, eh?" The barman had a smart mouth on him. But, although I didn't want to admit it, he had hit some type of nail fair and square on its head. I still didn't like him.

"Haven't you got something to do?" I asked him, my tone neutral.

"Yeah, and I've been doing it for the month you've been gone."

"You'll know how to get on with it then," I said and walked back to my office. Joe was busy taking care of the front desk and all was right with the world. Well, *almost*. If things were perfect in my life, that's when I started to get paranoid. I know - it's hard to get it right for some people!

"Good for you, girl." Doris invited herself in and sat down in the one proper chair in my office.

"What?"

"That little bugger Christopher's far too cocky for his own good. I don't trust him. His eyes are too far apart." *Too far apart; too close together. Sometimes it was hard to get things perfect for Doris as well.* "Least with George you knew where you were. He was the same every day. TBC."

"To be confirmed?" I said, puzzled.

"Total bloody crap."

"Anybody you *do* like here, Doris?"

"Sure - you, Joseph, Alfie . . ."

"How *is* Alfie?"

"Well his cooking ain't got no better, but least he's bloody honest. No side to him. Not like that squirt of a barman."

"Oh?"

"Something about him, Stevie - he ain't all he seems. Course Harry thinks the sun shines out of the bloke's arse cause he can make cocktails. Forever sucking up them pair. But I don't like him. Cook don't like him neither, says he's bad news, tried to talk his nibs into firing him."

"Woman on the phone for you, Stevie." Joe stuck his head round the door, a quizzical look on his face. "Says it's personal. Want me to put her through?"

"Old? Young?" I could feel my heart pound. Maybe it was my sister.

"Oldish."

"Oh."

"Yeah? You want to talk to her?" he asked.

Doris cocked her head to one side. "You ain't psychic, are you? You'll not know who it is till you talk to the woman."

"Yeah, thanks Doris." I pointed to the door. "I'll catch up with you later. Okay, Joe. Put it through."

"What kinda place you running down there? Some ponce just put me on hold."

"Good morning to you too. And Joe is *not* a ponce, but a perfectly nice man. He was only making sure you weren't some loony-tune that I didn't want to speak to."

"He sounded like a pouf to me. And what d'you mean, some looney-tune? What way is that to talk to your mother?"

"Look - can we start again, Mum?"

"Bit late for that, wouldn't you say, Stevie?"

I didn't bite back. But if that's how she wanted it. Stilted. Uncomfortable. Laced with blame. I could do that too. "Okay. What did you want?"

"Why should I *want* something? Maybe I just decided to have a chat with my daughter."

"You could have done that anytime in the last two years." I had a flash of inspiration and immediately felt ashamed of myself. Of my cynical thoughts. *But the timing was right.* My grandmother had just died. She'd left a will. It was as if my mother had read my thoughts.

"I phoned to tell you that your grandmother died."

"What, the one you never wanted to talk about, you mean?"

"I had my reasons," she said. "Families are complicated things, Stevie."

"Not *everybody's* family."

"Have you heard anything from your grandmother?"

"How could I? She's dead, you said."

"Before that, obviously. I see you haven't changed. Still awkward and headstrong."

"You should know. The fruit doesn't fall far from the tree." What the hell was I doing this for? Getting into yet another battle with her. Why couldn't we just have a conversation, like normal people?

"She asked for your address. Didn't she write to you?"

"She wrote to me," I said.

"And? God, it's like draining blood from a stone. What did she say, girl?"

"I am *not* a girl. And she told me about your other daughter, for a start. That I had a sister you've been hiding from me all these years." There was only silence from the other end. "Well?" I prompted. "Where is she? Where is Sophie? I have a right to know."

"The woman was old. Probably going doolally," she said. "Why would you believe her?"

I thought about the solicitor. When I'd spoken to Clarence Adams and mentioned my sister, he hadn't denied it. Hadn't said that she didn't exist. But then again he hadn't confirmed it either. He'd been tight-lipped about the other beneficiaries. Maybe that was it. Was my mother digging away, trying to find out if I'd been left something by my grandmother?

"Stevie, why would you believe some demented old woman over me, your mother?"

What could I say to that? I was confused. I wanted to believe I had a baby sister; somebody called Sophie, waiting out there to be found. Someone else in my life. But maybe my grandmother really was one brick short of a small building, and she'd made it up. If Sophie was real, why hadn't she found me? Who was I supposed to believe?

"So ..." I couldn't answer that. And she knew it. It would only mean dragging up the past and she knew me. Knew I couldn't go through it all again. And yes, even if the woman was demented, I was still tempted to believe her. To believe her instead of my mother. For my mother had lied to me before.

"So . . . You take care, Stevie."

"That's *it*? After two years, that's it? Listen, Mum - you want to come visit? I could sort out a room for you. Free holiday. Stay a few days. Be a break for you."

"Nice idea. But we'd only fight."

"So, why'd you phone – *really*?"

"Tell you about your grandmother, like I said. Thought you might like to know."

"Oh."

I put the phone down. My mother already had. Just like that. *Disconnect* - it was a word that covered our relationship over the years.

"You okay?" asked Joe, hovering in the doorway. He did a pretty fair hover.

"Grand," I said and started to cry. Noisy, heaving sobs that surprised me. Years of bottled-up regret that finally found their way to the surface. "My grandmother's dead," I said.

"I know," said Joe, gently. "Here," he pulled a tissue from his pocket. "Wipe your eyes and go have a ciggy."

That's when I realized just how good a friend Joe Hines truly was – pure gold, twenty-two carat. There was nothing he hated more than smoking.

Chapter 11

Harry winked at me. I don't think I'd ever seen him wink before. It was unnerving. He was glad to have me back. *Honeymoon period.* Once he got used to seeing me behind Reception again, fielding the awkward customers that he didn't want to deal with, the honeymoon would end. And he'd be back swearing at me. But I think I preferred that to this strange new management style of his. Maybe he'd taken a course in motivating staff.

"Our room slopes."

The elderly couple in front of me hadn't long arrived on the Pearson's Travel coach. The Pensioner's Express, we called it, and Harry was always glad to see it. It meant he could pay off some of his overheads again. It kept business ticking over, but the downside was that he would have complaints about the heating and would have to turn it up. Pensioners got cold. One hand gives, the other takes. Nothing is perfect; maybe in the next life. I'd come back 'home' on Changeover-Day. What did I expect?

"What's your room number Mr and Mrs. . .?"

"Askew," said the man, helpfully. "Room thirty."

I heard a strangled splutter from Joe behind me. He was sat at the small desk in the back of Reception and had been drinking coffee and eating a weird looking cup cake that Doris had produced as a celebration of my return.

I tried to ignore Joe. As puns went it was on the weak side. Moderately funny. But not for this sweet pair - well, they looked sweet at the moment. Time would tell. We had several rooms where the floors weren't level, like walking across the Himalayas, but nothing to worry about, the building was old, but safe. It was inspected every so often (by the Pearson Travel Company as well) and had always passed muster. But I could see where Joe was coming from. If your room had a sloping floor, then I suppose you couldn't have a better name than Askew.

"My wife tried to look out the window, but the floor dips."

I dragged up an image of room thirty in my head and Mrs Askew trying to look at the view. She was small, only came up to her husband's shoulder. We'd need to put her on a box. Not that she'd have much of a view from there, anyway; the back of the hotel, the alleyway, the fire escape.

I searched the listings for other rooms. The only ones we had left were the real dogs that no one would want to go into. Ones where the plumbing was noisy and guests had complained they couldn't sleep.

"I'm really sorry, Mr Askew," I said, "I don't have an alternative that I can offer you at the moment. But in two days I can shift you into one of our larger rooms at the front of the hotel. Beautiful view of the sea."

"But we're only here for four days," the man said, looking downcast.

I plastered my largest, most cheery smile on. "And we'll try to make your stay as welcoming and comfortable as we can."

"Not much chance of that if we have to put on our climbing boots and crampons every time we need to go to the bathroom."

I was wrong about them. Not as sweet as they seemed. The man may look like a Pekinese, but he had the jaws of a Rottweiler. Stronger measures were called for.

"Tell you what, Sir. We'd be pleased if you would accept some complimentary drinks at the bar. A small token from the management," I said, "along with this voucher for a bottle of wine to go with your evening meal." I scribbled on the comp-slip and slid it across the counter. "Just hand it to your table waiter." A bottle of house-wine would hardly break the bank.

The man looked as if might argue, but his wife nudged him in the ribs. I wished all of the Hotel Royal's problems could be fixed as easily.

I'd been wrong about Harry's fancy investors. They hadn't been used car salesmen. They ran a launderette in Hackney and had been looking to expand, they said. Take on a wider, business portfolio. Bollocks! Not only did they *not* invest any money in the hotel, but had tried to sell Harry some reconditioned industrial machines. I was glad he hadn't weakened and bought the things. But Harry wasn't stupid, just blinkered by these 'friends of friends' who'd held out their promise of a life belt to a drowning man. And make no mistake, Harry was drowning. Everybody said so. And some of the staff without the guts for a fight had already scurried off.

But my vein of optimism wanted to cling on to the last minute, waiting for a miracle. Harry had taken out a second mortgage on his house and it was a thin, anorexic drip-feed for the hotel right now. Enough to give the business a breathing space until summer bookings kicked in. Only *I* knew about the mortgage thing and I'd promised not to talk. The Staff was already demoralized enough. And, unlike Joe, I could keep a secret. You might think it half-baked, the idea of him re-mortgaging the one safe asset he had, but I say *Go Harry*! I'm a cheerleader. I'm rooting for Harry Evans and the good old Royal.

*

Monday morning, and I've got the day off. Normally I *never* get a full day off - officially yes, but living in the hotel means I often get dragged in to some panic or other. But Harry is trying to stay on my good side right now - the honeymoon.

And I'm about to be adventurous. I've hired a car, and I'm driving down to Newlyn where we get our wet fish deliveries from. I want to surprise Nigel, maybe drag him out to lunch. For surely he can't be delivering fish *all* the time.

Believe me, it's purely coincidental that today is the last day of February (in a leap year). I have no intention of leaping. My self esteem couldn't deal with any more rejections.

I hadn't heard from him since we went to St Ives, no phone calls, no letters, no flowers, no poems. It's not that I want to chase him. I definitely wouldn't chase a man. I've got my dignity. But I need to know if we are *on* or if we are *off*. I've already been fielding comments like - "are you and fish-face still an item?" Admittedly this came from the barman who, as you know, I'm not that keen on. Even so, it only underscored my own thoughts. And I'd rather know for sure, one way or the other.

It was a beautiful day for a drive. The sun was out and I had the C.D. blaring away and was singing along to the album *Crazy Love*. I screeched out the lyrics to *Just Haven't Met You Yet* and although I'm not a brilliant singer, what I lack in technique, I make up for in enthusiasm. Plus, it's not every day you get to sing with Michael Bublé. The search for perfect love, for your soulmate, that's what the song was about, and I guess we're all on the lookout for one of those.

But how will you recognise this perfect mate – they don't come with a label. I had an uneasy feeling that I'd never find mine, that Nigel wasn't the one. There were no sirens going off, no cannons firing, no champagne corks popping. He was an okay guy, though maybe not all the time. And the thought of seeing him again gave me mixed feelings. I *wanted* to see him, for it felt good to be part of a couple, but I *didn't* want to see him in case he confirmed my worst fears that I had somehow managed to drive away yet another man. I don't do it on purpose. I'm just me. And I can't see anything wrong with that. Being me, that is – obviously not driving men away.

Some of my friends at the hotel think we are a mismatch, the fish-man and I. That we are total opposites. But isn't that supposed to work?

"Hey, you can't park there. Not unless you're buying fish."

I'd done the last part of the journey on auto pilot, blindly following my Sat Nav. It didn't always work. Sat Navs didn't know everything. But it had taken me to the part of Newlyn Coombe that I needed.

"We buy fish from here," I said.

"Good for you."

Everyone's a comedian.

"And I'm looking for someone."

"Aren't we all," said the guy, a smirk on his face.

"Nigel. He works here."

The man rubbed his chin as if he was thinking seriously about stuff. "Nope, doesn't ring a bell. Try Jameson's over there. Maybe he's one of theirs."

"That's *him*," I said. "That's his name, Nigel Jameson."

"Your lucky day then."

"Yeah, but I don't get it. Our fish merchant is Newlyn Fish Supplies."

The guy looked at me like I'd failed some sort of basic I.Q. test. "Told you already," he said, "that's them, over there." He walked back to whatever he'd been doing before I'd interrupted.

He wasn't wrong; the long, low complex housed a fish supplier. I headed for the building that looked as if it might contain an office – the only concrete structure there, for all the rest were weathered wooden sheds, and the smell of fish coming from them was overpowering. It stung my nostrils and I could taste it at the back of my throat. I *like* fish. But I prefer them with lemon and butter or some sort of sauce.

"Yes? Can I help you?"

The voice was clipped and sharp. It implied that the last thing the woman really wanted to do was help me. She was one of those terrifyingly efficient looking people whose stare could cut through forged steel. But I can be pretty scary myself at times, so she could have saved her energy. She seemed to be a receptionist but I suspected that, like me, she was expected to be a general dogsbody as well.

I countered with my most charming smile. "I hope so. I need to speak to your delivery driver."

The woman's expression didn't change. "And *you* would be?"

"One of your regular customers. The Hotel Royal." I left it at that. I'd thought about adding Newquay, but how many of them could there be? I wondered if Harry had paid our bill yet.

Her face softened. "I hope nothing's wrong."

And I knew I had her. The balance of power had shifted. She was worried that I'd come to make a complaint, maybe she'd already had several to fend off. I knew the feeling. She was a fire fighter, fixing stuff others had managed to balls-up. I was a fire fighter too.

"No, everything's fine," I said. "Just something I need to see the man about."

Her face slipped into a sympathetic expression. I have several like that for dealing with awkward customers, so I got it.

"I'm sorry, but I think he's on his round right now." She shouted to some unseen worker bee, slaving away in the back office. "Seen Bill lately?"

A man's voice shouted back. "Out on his rounds, I think."

"Thanks, James, that's what I figured."

She twisted her head back to me, the apologetic smile already in place. "Sorry. Anything I can help with?"

"Bill?" I said. "Have you changed your van driver, then?"

The woman looked confused. "Lord no. Bill's been here from the year dot. Customers know the punch lines to his corny jokes by heart now."

"But what about Nigel?"

She only flinched for a second and then she was right back on course. The woman was to be admired. She was a professional. "Of course. You're in Newquay, aren't you? When Bill's busy, Mr Jameson does that run. Right. Haven't seen him this morning, though. You might try the sheds." She nodded vaguely in the direction I'd seen the ramshackle buildings. "Like me to phone for you?"

"That would be great," I said, thinking about the queasiness in my stomach the fish stench had caused, even from this distance. I didn't fancy getting any closer. I began to wish that Nigel had picked a different trade.

"Fred? That you?" The receptionist automatically shouted into the phone. The noise in the processing plant, she explained, as if some sort of explanation was called for. "Don't know how they're not all deaf down there."

I wondered if Fred was married. And what his wife thought about the pervasive smell of fish he brought home with him every night. What detergent she used.

"No, nothing wrong," she said. "Wondered if the boss man was down there with you. Somebody looking for him. Okay, cheers Fred. See you at the game."

The look of disbelief on my face must have done it. Made her take me into her confidence. "The game," she said. "The Pirates. Always follow the rugby. Penzance and Newlyn Rugby Club," she explained, like I'd just landed from Mars and had never heard of The Pirates.

"The boss?"

"Yeah, sorry, he's not down there. Fred thinks he's gone home for lunch. He sometimes does that when Emily has the afternoon off."

"Nigel Jameson is the *boss*," I repeated, like a robot. "Not the delivery driver. You sure?"

The woman give me a worried look. "Sure, I'm sure. He pays my wages."

"Good looking man, dark hair, swarthy features, 'bout yeh high?" I held out my hand to just above my own head to demonstrate.

"That's him," she said. "Although we never mention the height thing. He's sensitive about it. Not that Emily seems to mind. She's not that tall herself.

"Emily?"

"His wife. Emily works here part time. Does the accounts. It's a family affair. Mr Jameson's dad still works in the processing plant. Fish in the blood." She laughed.

"His *wife*?"

"Look, is something wrong? Do you want me to give him a message when he gets back?"

"No. No message," I said and fled for the door, felt my knees weaken beneath me but managed to make it as far as my car. I threw up on the tarmac.

Chapter 12

"You ask me, the guy wants his goolies cut off. Two-timing bastard."

I didn't disagree with Doris. Nigel Jameson was a two timing bastard. And, without his balls, like she'd suggested, his sex life would be limited. I'm guessing he'd need medical help.

Conservative, *dull* Nigel was not as boring as he pretended. He was intrepid. An adventurer who'd been leading a double life. But that didn't make him a good person. I wished I'd never met the guy, hadn't gone to bed with him. But the thing was done. I'd picked another dud.

"I've never been *the other woman*, before," I said miserably.

"Not your fault, babe. The man's a louse. You wanna go down there," she said. "Make him face it."

I was still thinking about that. I don't like arguments. Not the personal ones, anyway; the emotional confrontations where everyone tries to score points. They always leave me feeling ragged. Not that I'm a wimp. I'm fine with the business stuff; I'll go head-to-head with anyone. And Harry often sends me out onto the frontline to deliver the bullets he's made, but is too idle to fire himself.

But this was different. The fish-man had made me angry. He deserved some sort of payback. He hadn't even had the nerve to call me. To try and explain – but what could he say? How could he justify it?

I wanted to go down to his office and drag him out, cause a scene and embarrass him. Confront his wife. But then it wasn't his wife's fault; he'd used her, like he'd used me. We were both just goods on his inventory. Was it up to me to tell her? Ruin her life. Play God? I thought about the stench of the fish packing plant down in Newlyn and felt sick. I wouldn't go.

"I'll send him a text," I said.

*

"Something's gone wrong with the flush in number eight." Doris had her 'work' voice on. "Want me to get our Morris to pop down and take a look?"

Morris was Doris's husband and he always struck me as a Jack or a Fred rather than a Morris. He was ancient, and stick-thin, looked like he'd blow away at any minute, wore old shabby navy-blue overalls, and had a permanent drip hanging from the tip of his long nose. It's my belief that these old geezers generally have dripping noses. They were an unlikely looking couple – him: tall and brittle, her: plump and short.

He was our unofficial handyman. If there was something easy to fix that wouldn't take too long, he was your man. Harry only ever paid him for materials, not his time. (Other than giving him the odd bottle of booze. But then Harry got his booze cheap.) Morris didn't seem to mind. Said it gave him something to do. I'd have thought he'd have enough to do living in a house with Doris, for the man was as hen-pecked as you could get without actually moving into the chicken coup.

"Okay, that'd be great," I said.

But Doris didn't make a move. Just folded her arms across her chest and moved in closer, her tone confidential. "You notice our Joseph?"

I hadn't noticed much lately. Been too wrapped up in my own despair.

"What about him?"

"Not his usual, happy self. Just sniped at me," she said.

To be fair, sometimes it wasn't that hard to snipe at Doris.

"None of our business," I said, trying to cut her off at the pass.

"Thought he was your mate."

"He is. A *good* mate. But if he wants us to know, he'll tell us."

"Sometimes, Stevie, you can be a real tight-arse."

"Ta! Just call Morris, will you?"

She flounced off, and I went down to the kitchen to get a coffee for Joe. Maybe she was right. Could be that he and Wilbur had had a fight. I'd been wallowing in my own misery lately, too busy to notice anyone else's.

Alfie had been experimenting with pastries. He wasn't what you'd call a *natural* pastry chef and he'd been ambitious. But he hadn't quite pulled it off, for his profiteroles were misshapen, had spread outwards in the oven. I expect there's a knack to them. He put a few on a plate, shoved them in my direction.

"You can have these, can't give them to guests. The bastards would only complain."

"Fit for human consumption are they?"

"'Course they bloody are. If you don't want them, I'll take them home. Or the lad here will." He nodded at the K.P. "Take one to Joe," he said, pointing at the coffee I'd just poured out. "Cheer him up. Bloke's got a face on him like a smacked arse."

After that I was anxious to get back and see Joe. He was going off duty soon, and usually had a smile on his face the closer he got to the end of his shift. But not now. He looked like a different man, brow furrowed; anger sparking in his eyes.

"Cook sent these up for you. Thought you might like them."

"Our insurance cover food poisoning, does it?"

"He was trying to be nice."

"Alfie?"

"Even Alfie has his moments," I said. "You okay, Joe?"

"Just peachy. Wilbur's gone off to Cardiff for a job interview. Better money, good prospects. We had a fight about it before he left."

"Oh? Maybe Cardiff's nice."

"You'll be wearing out that bloody word."

"Eh?"

"Since when has 'nice' been something to shoot for?"

"I'm on your side, Joe. You don't want to go to Cardiff, just tell him. Talk about it. You guys are cool; you can talk about stuff like that, can't you?"

"I used to think so, but he came over all Prima Donna on me. Said if he gets the job he'll take it - whether I like it or not."

"He doesn't mean it. You guys have something special. He wouldn't wreck that."

"Maybe. Anyway, thanks for the coffee, but I'll pass on the . . ." he pointed disdainfully at the pastry languishing on the plate.

"Profiteroles," I said. "Alfie's been practising."

"He'll need to keep at it then," said Joe, and smiled. He sipped the coffee. "Thanks, Stevie, you're a pal. You decided what to do about Nigel?"

"Who?"

"Ah. I get it," he said cynically. "Drained the old brain-box of any memory of the man, eh?"

"Like he never existed."

"Pull the other one, Stevie. I know you."

"Yeah, okay. But I'm working on it."

"Good. Put it down to experience."

"Sure," I said. "I'm no worse off now than before I met him, and there's a lot to be said for being a singleton."

"Gotcha. Think this means we'll have a new fish-guy?" he asked.

"Wouldn't be surprised. According to Doris, at least, Nigel Jameson won't have the balls for it anymore."

*

The mourning period's over. I've put the man behind me and decided to move on with my life. Any man comes within a mile of me now will have to jump through so many hoops, that he probably won't bother. And being an old maid can't be that bad, can it? Some of them seem perfectly happy. I felt like a loser at first, until I reasoned the whole thing out. He's the one in the wrong, right? You know what I mean. So, get over it, I told myself. And I have.

Something else has filled the emotional space, a kind of sacred mission. 'Operation Sister', they're calling it in the staff room. I've thrown myself into the search for my sister, Sophie, with all my mental and physical resources. The physical ones aren't that promising, but you work with the materials to hand, and I don't have money to pay for expensive investigators. So, I went off for a day trip to Plymouth to see my mother. At the very least I figured it was a train ride and a day out. But all I got from her was a weak cup of own-brand coffee, a rich tea biscuit and another denial that any sister ever existed. It had been disappointing, but not unexpected. You try all avenues.

My mental resources were less limited. I'd gone on websites that promised to reunite friends and missing relatives. I'd also been sending emails to organisations that traced missing loved ones. The Red Cross, the Salvation Army - they were both on the case. But neither wanted to give me 'false hope', for their funding was drying up in these cash-strapped times and I didn't have a lot of information to go on. My mother wouldn't answer their letters and my grandmother was dead.

Even though there seemed no evidence at the moment to back it up, something deep inside my DNA told me that Sophie Anderson was out there waiting to be discovered. My mother still said it was wishful thinking, and that my grandmother was a daft old woman who'd made the whole thing up. That was when I'd re-read my grandmother's letter. It didn't sound as if the woman was senile. Her wits were sharp and she'd been first in line when they'd handed out the humour. I liked her.

The in-house phone rang and dragged me from my thoughts.

"Hey Stevie, reckon Chef would be okay with Coq au Vin?"

"Who knows? Ask him."

"You do it," said Harry. "I'm up to my balls in stuff here."

"Special occasion?"

"What?"

"The Coq au Vin."

"Nah. Bunch of Masons want to book a dinner-dance. Trying to give them a good price. We could use the business."

In my humble opinion - not that anyone would ask it - this was unwise. I remembered the last time we'd put on a *special do* as Harry called it. We'd had so many complaints about food (stingy portions, cold when it reached the table) that we'd had to give several refunds. That sort of thing makes Harry's wallet twitch and gives him a flare up of nervous eczema.

"I'll have a word with cook," I said. "Might be okay. He seems to be raising his game to a new level. Been practising with pastries." That didn't mean a lot, of course. Alfie's game level was still way off Cordon Bleu.

"Tell him I'll need costings for fifty. Remind him to keep the price down, Stevie. We're not running a charity here."

"Sure, Harry."

Chapter 13

"Harry's thinking of booking a dinner-dance," I said.

"Remind me to get the patent leather shoes out." Alfie laughed. It was more like a guffaw.

"You're in a good mood. Something happen?"

"Bit of luck on the gee gees," he said.

I should have known. It would hardly be because he'd finished writing his thesis.

"Wants you to do costings for fifty people. Three courses. Keep it cheap. You know the idea."

"Sure. The man's a skinflint. But I'll pull a few rabbits out of the hat. Long as he knows he'll need to pay me overtime. And for Smithy too." He smiled benignly at the young lad who was up to his armpits peeling spuds over in a corner of the kitchen. Either Alfie was *on something* or his bit of luck at the betting shop must have been substantial.

"I'll pass it on," I said. "Oh, and he seems keen on Coq au Vin. Got that in your repertoire?"

Alfie looked puzzled, but it was hard to tell if it was the word *repertoire* or the name of the dish that caused the slackness in his jawline.

"Sure. Tell him no need to sweat." *Harry sweated as a natural phenomenon.* "Coq au Vin's only a poxy chicken stew, ain't it?"

I looked it up when I got back to my computer. You could never be too sure with Alfie. And I suppose he was right as long as you flung in the odd bottle of Beaujolais, bacon, mushrooms, garlic, bay leaves and cooked it slowly for hours. I wondered how close our cook would get to the real thing.

Harry wandered over, looking flustered.

"You hear any more from that solicitor, of yours?" he said.

The question threw me, especially from him. His suit jacket was missing and he was rolling the sleeves of his shirt down, like he'd just finished doing some kind of hard, physical labour. Harry rarely did anything physical. It left him puffing and the trade mark sweat that wafted from his arm pits could be overwhelming, so he usually got someone else to do the heavy stuff.

"What's wrong?" I asked, alarmed, for his face had gone an unusual shade. Somewhere between purple and puce.

"Toilet in room eight's packed up. Something to do with the flush. Had to take the top of the cistern off."

"You *fixed* it?"

"Don't look so bloody surprised. I'm not useless."

He leaned on the counter, a triumphant expression on his face. "So, what about this stuff with your grandmother? Any updates?"

Joe must have told him about the will, for I hadn't said a word to anyone else.

So far, I hadn't heard a thing. They'd promised faithfully to send the documentation on to me, but nothing had arrived. This was the first time I'd really thought about it. Not that I was worried either way, for the search for Sophie had taken over the number one slot in my brain.

"Haven't heard anything, yet," I said.

"That seem strange, to you?" said Harry.

"I wouldn't know. Haven't had much to do with solicitors. Must be about three weeks now."

"Well, nothing's arrived here, obviously. Not even when you were on your sabbatical." *We'd both agreed to call my break from the hotel a sabbatical. It sounded better than saying I'd resigned.* "And this would be the address they have for you, I guess?"

That's when it hit me. And I heard the voice of Clarence Adams in my head: "Now that we're sure of your address, the will can be forwarded to you along with the letter your grandmother wanted you to have."

"I've given them the wrong address," I said.

*

"No bloody loyalty. You give the man a break when he's looking for a job and he repays you by soddin' off to some place in Torquay when you need him."

Our so called Maitre d' had cleared off. Taken his wages for the month and left Harry in the lurch. He'd had the overblown title of 'banqueting manager' as well. But we'd never had a banquet as long as I could remember. We'd had several functions, two of which had dubious outcomes; (the cold food/stingy portions fiasco) and one where several bottles of house wine that had been billed to *The Ancient Order of Foresters* had mysteriously gone missing. I still say they went home with our Maitre d' stroke banquet manager - now apparently ex!

"So. This mean we're hiring?" I asked him.

I'd be surprised if we were. More likely Harry would see the man's disappearance as a chance to trim some more fat from the wages bill. There was about as much fat on there right now as an anorexic, size-zero model on a diet of rice cakes.

His look of outrage couldn't have been topped if I'd suggested he lose weight and stop drinking Betty Stogs.

"I strike you as bloody simple?"

"You? Never."

"Right, then." He rubbed his hands together vigorously and, despite his previous rant about staff and their lack of loyalty, seemed to be enjoying himself. "I've just been watching the lunch traffic in the restaurant. Maximum covers in there today."

It was raining, so maybe guests had stayed in and chanced the delights of Alfie's kitchen rather than getting wet to go somewhere cheaper with better food. "And no problem with service – even without our Maitre d' - restaurant staff seemed to cope," said Harry.

I hadn't been in the restaurant, but I expect Harry's "seemed to cope" could be translated as: the remaining waiters flew around like blue arsed flies.

"Not hiring then."

"*Promoting.* That way we save a bit on the wages bill. I'm sure we've got enough bodies in there to cover dinner."

Dinner was our busiest time. Guests usually paid for bed, breakfast and evening meal. Anything else was icing on the cake for the restaurant. Breakfast was easy. A DIY affair, where people had to go up and serve themselves from a hot and cold buffet. So there were never as many waiters needed on that shift.

"So, who's this lucky stiff you're promoting?"

"That's the pure genius of it," he rubbed his hands together once more. *Glee* wouldn't be too strong a word here. And Fagin from Oliver Twist came to mind, although Harry's generous bulk would have barred him from the role.

I ran a quick inventory of the restaurant staff through my head. None of them struck me as particularly enterprising or natural management material. They were mostly jaded middle-aged guys on the minimum wage and women in the Doris-mould trying to earn a bit of extra cash to eke out the family budget. Not a mover or a shaker amongst them, unless you counted the Polish girl who'd been working there for a few months, and whose work ethic was almost a cliché. She was faster than the others, smiled more than they did, and seemed interested in delivering some kind of half decent customer service. No! He wouldn't do that, would he? Surely even *Harry* wouldn't resort to that.

"You wouldn't do that." I said, appalled. "The woman's still learning English."

"She's got a lot going for her," he said.

"Fair enough. But what about the resentment she'd face from the others. Foreigner coming in taking their jobs, getting promoted, more money."

"Not *much* more money," he said. "And we'd be saving on one wage bill."

"Sure, Harry. But you wouldn't throw her to the wolves. She'd have to liaise with Alfie."

"Reckon she could hold her own."

"You even know her name?"

"You know me and names. I'm paying her wages, and now an increase. Good enough wouldn't you say?"

"Agata," I said.

"What?"

"Her name's Agata something." I felt bad that I didn't even know her full name. She was married to a

Cornishman, a local man, so it could be one of those long standing Cornish family names. I made a mental note to find out. "You spoken to her?"

"Not yet, but she'll hardly refuse, will she. Strikes me as somebody who wants to move up in the world, has ambition."

Maybe Harry was right. But if that was true, then she'd hardly be staying at the Hotel Royal for long.

*

The smell of rich, aromatic coffee filled the kitchen. I cupped the generous porcelain mug in my hands, hugged it to me like a life raft. It felt secure. Something sure in a situation where I was out of my depth. I was not a marriage guidance counsellor.

"Want one of these?" asked Joe.

It was a chocolate digestive. Normally I could have eaten my way through a packet, but I'd noticed my clothes tightening up on me lately. Decided to take measures before any more weight crept on. And strangely, it wasn't because I was worried about staying slim to attract a man - I'd given up on the whole man-thing - it was my own vanity. For what if my sister Sophie was this incredibly beautiful, tall, willowy, creature? Someone I'd have to crane my neck up to speak to and who fitted into a size ten. So I shook my head. Refused the digestive. Edged away from the plate like it was something from the black arts.

Joe and Wilbur's kitchen was an impressive place. It was massive, contemporary, paid homage to modern design and those expensive granite tops that other people manage to afford, never you. Its gadgetry and gleaming cookware were better looking than anything in the hotel's kitchen. A whole rack of cookery books stretched the length of one wall, evidence that someone in the place had a passion for food. I wondered who it was.

Joe saw me looking at the recipe books. Said "Wilbur's a bit of an amateur chef. Took a course at Le Cordon Bleu."

"He'd get on well with Alfie, then."

"Sure. Who wouldn't?" Joe wasn't above using the odd bit of irony himself.

He shrugged; a defeated gesture and nothing to do with this stupid, default topic of conversation of mine. But I was putting off the crunch time, for like I said, I'm not someone who can hand out advice about relationships. My own hardly qualify me.

"Thought the three of us were supposed to be here?" I said.

Joe had phoned me in a panic. Wanted me over right away and Harry had agreed to man the reception desk for an hour. He might be more of a hindrance than a help, though, for he didn't fully understand our systems or booking software. But the worst was that he would expect something in return for 'the favour'. Still, Joe had sounded desperate.

"Wilbur's gone. Got cold feet, even though it was his idea."

"What, that I come?"

"Well, at least that we have another eye on the subject. Somebody we can trust."

"Look, I'm flattered and all that, but shouldn't you guys be doing this with a professional?"

"I already suggested that, but he won't go to *Relate*."

"I thought you pair were pretty cool. Had the whole thing pinned down."

"Yeah, but Wilbur's got some bee in his bonnet about us being stuck in a rut. Figures life's too short to vegetate."

Is that what *I'd* been doing – vegetating? Put like that it sounded pretty lame. But I was happy with my life, my job, the odd bit of surfing when there was time.

"And are you?" I asked.

"What, in a rut?"

"Yeah."

"Our lives follow a pattern, sure," Joe said. "And if that's what it means, then I guess we are. But doesn't everybody end up doing the same things? You work, you eat, you sleep, have fun."

"Enough fun?" *God, this felt creepy now. Like I was some kind of agony aunt.*

"I thought so," he said. "But Wilbur's definitely been restless lately. Like he's got a bucket list in his head that we're not getting round to."

"Midlife crisis? He's quite a bit older than you, right?" *In for a penny, in for a pound.*

"Jesus, Stevie. I never thought about that. Sure. He's about to hit the big five-o!"

"Could be it."

"Wow! '*Course* that's it. He's been rattling on about not wanting cards with the number on. Anybody ever tell you you're a genius, Stevie?"

"Never. But then a prophet is often underrated in his own land." *What the crap was that? But he'd embarrassed me and that's when I resort to waffle.*

Joe covered my hand with his large one and gave me a small peck on the cheek. A bolt of electricity fired through me and I stared at him in confusion. He stared back as if the same lightning bolt had missed him by a thousand miles.

"I'm lucky to have a friend like you," he said, and smiled the smile of the innocent.

And my insides curdled, like I'd just crossed over some invisible boundary marker, into a foreign land – or at least my head had. And I wanted to run. Like Wilbur.

Chapter 14

"That's it!" Harry looked pleased with himself. A Cheshire Cat on a particularly good run of luck. "Finalised," he said. "Done and dusted. The Masons are coming."

"I won't tell anybody if you don't," I said.

"Stevie, you're an ass."

"Ta." *A genius or an ass. Opinion seemed divided.*

"That new girl's going to talk to Alfie about the menu. And the Masons are booking their own band and disco, so saved us a bit of trouble there."

"Great," I said. *Let's hope so.* Nothing was ever as simple as it looked on the drawing board, but that was probably just me going through my pessimistic, glass half-empty stage.

"Get your mail problem sorted yet?"

"Can't get hold of the landlord," I said.

"Get yourself round to the flat. Bet you'll find a shit-load of your stuff in the hall."

"But he'd *return to sender* wouldn't he?"

Harry gave me one of those old fashioned looks, cynical, world-weary. And for a minute he reminded me of a male version of Doris. He cocked an eyebrow, said: "Think that landlord of yours would take the trouble?"

"You've only got to write on the bloody thing."

"Exactly."

"Yeah, okay. Next spare minute I get, I'll trek over there; see if my letters are piling up."

"You being smartarsed? Think I'm working you too hard?"

Life can be unfair, for I wasn't. Just thinking out loud.

I'd been meaning to sort this mail thing for ages. I'd given the solicitor my new address, the bedsit, which by now was my *old* address. *Is life always this complicated? Or is it just me?* And when I first realized that Harding and Willis had probably sent the will there by now, I'd immediately phoned the post office. They'd shuffled me from one department to another until a bored voice finally told me that any undeliverable post ended up in a dead letter office. This turned out to be a warehouse in Belfast, where workers sorted through 60 million items a year, forwarding them to the right address or returning them to sender.

My hopes hadn't been high that I'd ever be reunited with my mail. And the last thing I wanted to do was phone Clarence Adams again. He'd keep calling me Ma'am - which made me feel ancient - and it could cost me thirty quid. Plus, I'd have to admit he had the wrong address, and he'd think I was an incompetent imbecile. I wasn't.

So, exactly like I'd told Harry, the next time I had a morning off, (it was a Sunday), I hightailed it over to bedsit-land. It's a depressing sort of place, even though you get the occasional, distant glimpse of sea through the pockmarked, run-down buildings.

There's something to be said for having a car. I hadn't owned one for two years now. I'd given up the uneven battle of juggling cash for the road tax, insurance, MOT, the price of petrol, new tires. I'd thought about buying a second hand bike, but hadn't got around to it yet.

Anyway, walking was better for you and fitted right in with my new healthy living regime - that so far was mostly in my head. Walking was also free. The bedsit was all the way across town, but I made it inside twenty minutes. So maybe I should start thinking about running marathons.

Déjà vu. The place hadn't improved and it brought back some dodgy memories. Sitting outside in a refrigerated fish van. Nigel helping me in with my stuff. I looked up at the flaking paintwork and rang the bell. There hadn't been a bell when I'd lived here. Somebody must have complained.

"You like ringing doorbells?"

I'd only rung twice.

"I used to live in the ground floor flat," I told the woman.

"Good for you. You want a medal?"

"Not really. Just want to collect my mail."

Why do people have to be so angry? Life's tough at times, sure. But I'd never even met this woman before; if I'd stayed she would have been my neighbour. But I'm easy to get along with and it's unlikely I would have coveted either her house, her goods, her manservant, her maidservant, her ox, her ass, or anything else belonging to her. *My mother had sent me to Sunday school classes; a baby-sitting device.* And it's true; I wanted nothing belonging to this unhappy, angry woman. All I needed was to get to the hall table and see if someone had sent me mail. If it was still there. For this was the kind of place where things went missing.

"Knock yourself out," she said.

*

I knew it! I had a sister. Someone to go shopping with. Share jokes with. Eat pizza with. Have girlie nights in -

when you dyed each other's hair experimental colours and painted your toenails.

Her name was right there in black and white on an impressive looking document drawn up by *Harding and Willis, Solicitors*, and informing both my sister Sophie and I that we were the two main beneficiaries named by my grandmother (*our* grandmother) to equally share her remaining worldly possessions – which seemed to be varied; bricks and mortar, and shares. I'd never met anyone who owned shares before, and definitely not been related to one.

The whole thing was unreal. My head felt like this weird, alien thing perched on top of my body, huge; at least the size of an overgrown watermelon. And it was about to either burst, or simply detach itself and float off into space. This must be what it feels like when you're on drugs. I don't know. I've never taken any. Honest!

I lay back on my bed hugging the paper to my chest. Reliving the second that my eye had captured the important words: Sophie Anderson. My mother had lied. And now another emotion fought for a foothold - regret. Why couldn't she be like a real mother? Thinking about her children first, before herself. Children! She had children, not just a child. It was official, I wasn't alone anymore.

The theme from The Good, The Bad and The Ugly reverberated loudly around my room (it's a small room) and my shattered nerves felt as if someone had taken a cricket bat to them. I groped for the mobile to silence the ring tone.

"Yeah?"

"Stevie, I know it's your day off, but you need to get your butt down here quick as you like."

"Sure, Harry. Someone have a death in the family?" I'd told him not to disturb me unless somebody died.

"No, but *you* will. Unless you get your bleedin' ass down here right now."

Back to his charming self. The new management style forgotten. The honeymoon over.

"What's up? And give it to me in one sentence with no swearing."

There was a short silence. Either he was considering the implications of firing me, or trying to summarise the situation.

"Joseph's threatening to walk out on me."

"God, Harry. What is it with you and staff? What did you say to him?"

An exaggerated sigh blasted its way into my ear. "You saying this is *my* fault?"

"Only that you can be insensitive at times."

"Christ, woman, I'm trying to run a business here. And all I said was he'd have to polish up his act if he wanted to carry on working here. He's been moping around on the front desk like some bloody great fairy.

"You never said *that* to him?"

"What?"

"The fairy thing."

"Sure I did. I pay the man's wages. Least he can do is smile for the guests and look interested."

"I'm coming down," I said, and pushed my copy of the will under a pillow, along with the special instructions that my grandmother had left for me. I hadn't opened that letter yet. I'd been leaving it to the end – to savour it. The way you do when you eat the fried eggs first from your plate and leave the chips to last.

Chips are my favourite. But I haven't had any lately. I've been trying to be good.

I beat my own record. Uniform on, hair sorted - admitted my hair doesn't take half as long as it used to now that it's short - quick check in the mirror, door locked, one flight of stairs and then down in the lift. It was an emergency, so I resorted to the lift, although I've been using the stairs lately. Every little helps on the calorie busting front.

I'd never seen Joe so upset. I hustled him into the back office. It wasn't sound proofed, but at least it was better than having him break down in public, like some sort of freak show.

"Harry's a bastard."

"I know," I said. "But he's often a good-hearted bastard."

"I'm surprised he didn't call me a faggot." His piercing blue eyes latched onto mine. "You tell him?"

"Never! I wouldn't do that. You told me in confidence."

"So, how come he called me a fairy?"

"He doesn't have a wide vocabulary," I said.

Despite himself, a smile tugged at Joe's mouth. "No. That's true."

"Now what's up?"

"Other than me watching my life flush into the sewers?" he said.

"They're always looking for people in my Am Dram group. Looks like you wouldn't need to audition."

"You calling me a drama queen?"

"Well, aren't you? It can't be that bad."

"We're having a trial separation. *Himself* has gone up to Scotland to find his bloody inner self. How much worse you want it to get?"

"Jesus, Joe! I'm sorry. But maybe that's good. A break. Give you both time to think."

"I don't need time to think." He thumped my desktop with the flat of his hand and I jumped, but then my nerves aren't as solid as they were this time a year ago.

"But your problem is that *Wilbur* does. Give him some space. Let him breathe some wholesome Scottish air, do a bit of skiing."

"Him? Ski?" Joe's voice was bitter.

"He might surprise you."

"He already has," said Joe, miserably.

"Why don't you head off home? I'll cover your shift."

"What? And sit in the house by myself?"

"Go for a walk then. Or a drive. Redecorate. You've got two days off."

A light bulb seemed to come on in Joe's head and for the first time in days, he beamed. The full face job. Like he was really happy. "Sure," he said. "Why not?"

Chapter 15

"Hi. Can I speak to Sophie Anderson, please?"

"Do you have a room number for her?"

I didn't. "No, but if you could just check your register."

"I'll put you through to Reception. Might take a while though, they're busy out there. We've just had a large influx of students from Germany. They're still milling around."

I imagined the woman at the other end of the line. Pictured her connecting me to Reception. Saw the excited students in my mind's eye. *They were here. They'd arrived. London. The heart of the city. A Bayswater Road backpacking hostel.* I was glad it wasn't me facing them. Answering their questions, taking details, checking passports, getting them assigned to dormitories, trying to get them 'processed'. Like pushing jelly through a sieve.

"I don't mind waiting," I said, as cheerfully as I could." But of course I did. For now that I knew where Sophie had gone, I could hardly keep my impatience at bay. But you didn't get anywhere by being rude. A good attitude and people might actually *want* to help you. I knew about such things.

It took a long time and I was tempted to try again later in the day, but by that time my own Reception would be a whole lot busier. We were expecting a coach in from Huddersfield at five. It wasn't even a full bus, only twenty people, which was why Harry had been growling at any staff unfortunate enough to cross his path. But it was hardly our fault that the two coaches had melted away, and turned into a measly twenty people. They still deserved their short break and not somebody surly barking at them. Harry was supposed to be helping me book them in, but at this rate, he'd be as much use as a chocolate fireguard.

"Hello. Reception - can I help?"

"Ah." I attempted to bring my brain back into line. (Sophie!) It didn't take more than a second, for brains are amazing things. "I'd like to speak to my sister, please - if she's in. I don't know her room number."

"Sure. What's the name? I'll check the register." The receptionist was Australian.

"Sophie. Sophie Anderson. Oh and thank you."

"Not a problem." The woman sounded competent *and* cheerful, even though she'd just had a horde of German students passing through her hands.

It took a long time and the silence made me wonder if she'd gone off for a coffee break. I started to lose faith.

"No. Sorry. No one of that name currently registered with us. Either in the larger dorms or any of the single rooms."

"But she must be there." Even I could hear the desperation in my voice. "That's the address she left us." (Or at least my grandmother. Sophie had sent a postcard back with the address on it and my grandmother had included it in the *letter of special instructions* that came with her will.)

"Look, I'm sorry, but we have thousands of people through our doors every year. Most of them only stay a few days. That's the sort of place we are. And there's no one here registered in that name. I've looked back through two weeks."

"I hate to be a pain, but it's absolutely crucial we find my sister." *Why had I said we? Who was this 'we'?* "She left Canada before Christmas," I said. "Does anyone stay there for extended periods?"

"Some people do and I suppose I could always ask one of the full-time receptionists. They might remember. Canadian, you said? The woman's Canadian? What was the name again?"

"Sophie Anderson."

There was a silence as if she was writing something down.

"Okay. I'll have a word with one of the others."

"Brilliant. Thanks a lot. I'll hold on."

"Not *now*." The woman sounded surprised. "We're far too busy now. But if you could call back in a day or two."

"A day or two's too late," I said, frantic. The woman would forget all about it and I'd have to start from scratch again.

"Well, I'm afraid it's the best I can do." Her tone became frosty and I knew I'd blown it.

"Fine," I said. "I'll call back."

*

"Excuse me, are you busy?"

It was Agata, our new Maitre d' come waitress come Jack-of-all-trades - like the rest of us. And she'd managed to turn 'excuse' into 'eggscuse' with her accent, which came across as cute. Her second name was Truscott, a Cornish family name with weight and history behind it.

A Maitre d' was implicitly male. If you wanted a female one, even the French didn't have a name for it. But stuff like that wouldn't bother Harry. And it certainly didn't bother me. For I figured that Agata Truscott, a mere female, had already been worth two of the guy she'd replaced, the one who'd run off to Torquay - taking several bottles of Harry's extra special brandy with him. Harry hadn't reported the theft to the police. So I figured that the brandy had come from the same dodgy source that most of our alcohol came from. Skelly's shadowy boss and the back of a van somewhere.

Agata Truscott coughed. She was a polite woman, who wouldn't complain, as Harry did, that I'd "gone off on one". A simple, polite cough, that wasn't judgmental, but designed to remind me she needed something.

"Sorry, Agata. Mind if I call you Agata?"

"I pleased with that," she said – and looked as if she really was. Maybe some of the waiters were already giving her a hard time. Could be she needed a friend.

She was a tall woman - I'd say six feet - with coal black hair, styled into a trim bob, and had that efficient look that some people manage to carry around with them, even when they're not doing anything. But she had a nice smile. And I liked her.

"Okay – how can I help?"

"Mr Evans tells me to come see you if I have problem. Deputy Manager knows *everything* about hotel, he says."

"Deputy Manager, eh?" Maybe I should ask for a pay raise. *Hilarious*!

"Is okay?"

"Sure. What's the problem?"

"I need to get menus printed for big night. Maysons," she explained, when I looked vague. *I had my moments – of looking vague. Right then I'd still been thinking about how to tackle getting my sister's new address.* "I take them to printers today or is too late."

"Ah. The function."

"Yes, and the cook won't tell me what he cooks."

I was up-to-speed. I can do it when I have to. "Right, two things, Agata. First – we don't have special menus printed for functions." Good God, Harry would have a coronary if we did. "We type up the menus and put them inside plastic wallets that we use for Christmas. I'll show you where they are."

I wasn't surprised that Harry hadn't told her where we keep them. He didn't know. "Second, I'll have a word with Alfie. But for future reference, if you call him *Chef* and take him the odd pack of cigarettes, it often oils the wheels."

"Oils wheels?"

"Bribery," I said.

Agata smiled. "Ah." It seemed a word she was familiar with.

"Works with Alfie."

"Stevie – I call you Stevie?"

"Sure, why not?"

"England not so different from Poland. Oils wheels the same."

"Yep. But don't let anyone Cornish hear you say that. This is *Cornwall*, definitely *not* England. England stops at the Tamar far as they're concerned."

Agata laughed. And even though she was at least six inches taller than me and slim as a pin, I knew we were going to get along.

*

Our coach from Huddersfield was late. The driver had called an hour ago. They'd had a puncture and he was making sure that when they finally arrived, the guests would still be able to have dinner. "Some of them are cranky as hell," he'd told me, "don't know what sort of trouble they'll cause you if they don't get fed."

Shit. Nothing new there, though. I've been fending off disgruntled guests for years. But I could do without it tonight. Joe and I would have been able to glide through, but Harry wouldn't be much help. And he wouldn't be in the best of moods, for it would mean paying out at least some overtime, a word that would send Harry and his wallet into a deep trough of depression. The late arrivals would back everything up: booking in, getting luggage up to their rooms, Alfie staying on late, overtime for the kitchen, overtime for the waiters.

Doris lumbered past Reception. It looked like she'd had a bad day as well.

"Not here yet, then?" she said.

"Had a puncture on the A30," I told her, "shouldn't be long now."

"That'll please his nibs. Still, he'll be happy we're almost at capacity."

I hadn't told Doris about the cancelled booking of the other coach. The company hadn't told *us* until it was too late, until Doris and the other chambermaid had gone around making beds, hanging up fresh towels, putting loo rolls in and folding back the ends of them into professional looking arrow points. They'd had a busy day. I would tell her tomorrow. The rooms would be ready for some later occupants; they wouldn't be wasted. But I didn't think Doris would let the chance for a moan go by. And who could blame her? It was a lot of work for her and it was hardly fair if it was all for nothing. But life wasn't always ideal. She'd know that by now.

Chapter 16

Harry had left me to get on with it. In the middle of booking in the pensioner's express, we'd had a call from Joe. He'd wanted an extra day off. He was in Scotland. He'd sent us a postcard, he said.

A part of me said *well done, Joe* - for there he was, fighting for what he wanted. Like I'd suggested. But that didn't help us - by us, I mean me – for Harry had given up on face to face encounters with grumbling guests and hidden himself away in his office saying he had important paperwork to catch up on.

"I didn't sign up for this," complained the barman.

"If you couldn't take a joke, you shouldn't have joined," I told him.

Harry wasn't the only unhappy bunny. Our 'cocktail' barman, Christopher Newly, had been drafted in to help get luggage up to the rooms. And the lift had broken down. He wasn't taking it well.

The news of the broken lift had spread like wildfire and I'd had to hand out complimentary drinks slips. And once word got around that there was something free to be had for 'inconvenience', everyone magically seemed to be inconvenienced. There was a run on Reception similar to the Californian gold-rush.

It wasn't a good start. But dinner went well. The restaurant service ran smoothly, thanks to our new Maitre d' and a couple of guests actually came up to Reception to thank me. For the way I'd handled a tight situation (the coach being late) for the quality of food from the kitchen, *eh*? And the prompt service in the restaurant. Most of that would have been down to Agata, for compliments about service had been rare before she'd taken over the room. And as for the food, well either Harry had agreed to pay cook overtime, or Agata had taken my advice and thrown a couple of packs of Marlborough Alfie's way.

"Excuse me." The old man was hanging onto his wife's arm as if the pair had been welded together, and my heart gave a tiny lurch. Growing old together, it was a bitter-sweet thought for me. I doubted I'd ever find anyone to stand beside me through life's trials, hold me up when I wobbled with age.

"Yes, Sir?"

The old boy smiled, maybe to signal that he wasn't about to complain. "I was just wondering – *we* were just wondering, he nodded at his wife - if you had any kind of entertainment on tonight."

Depends on your definition of entertainment. I wouldn't label Harry's karaoke nights as entertaining, or his version of stand-up. And I couldn't see Mr and Mrs Watson feeling at home with it. But you could never tell. I'd been proved wrong about people before.

"I'll check and get back to you," I said. "Normally we have karaoke in the cabaret lounge tonight, but everything's backed up a bit. Room twenty-one isn't it?"

"Yes," he smiled at the woman beside him. "My wife's age."

She poked him in the side, "Albert!" protested Mrs Watson. But she seemed pleased all the same.

*

We got by last night without Harry setting up his karaoke equipment or telling embarrassing jokes. It was late by the time everyone had finished dinner and for the first time ever, Harry himself didn't seem that keen. Thoughts of the lift and paying out to have it fixed had put a dampener on his spirits. And now that breakfast was over, and most guests had gone out on a coach tour to Mevagissey, it was quiet. So, I stuck up a sign on the front desk and got myself a coffee from the kitchen.

"All ready for Saturday night?" I asked.

"Who rattled your cage?" said Alfie, a look like thunder on his face. "You sound far too chirpy for your own good. You know something we don't?"

"The Masonic dinner," I said.

"And that means *what* to me? Lot of overfed arses patting each other on the back. Not gonna change the world, is it?"

I looked at my watch. Eleven o'clock in the morning. Bit early in the day for much to have gone wrong. You'd think! Unless cook had been out on the booze last night and had a hangover.

"What's up, doc?" I said, in the Bugs Bunny voice that has taken me years to perfect. Laughter conquers most things, I've found, except maybe Alfie on a bad day.

"Who else but an idiot would book a bloody function a week before Easter? We got enough work on in here with all the hot-cross buns and crap he expects me to make."

"God's sake, Alfie! Only trying to be friendly - *and* cheerful," I said, as an afterthought.

"Take your feckin' cheerfulness somewhere else. Some of us got work to do."

I was about to say something pithy back, when I looked at the young K.P. He shook his head slightly and drew a finger across his neck in a dramatic mime. Either he wanted me to shut up or somebody had just had their throat cut. I took the hint and left.

Doris was waiting in the office for me. I prepared myself for an onslaught. Yesterday she'd pulled her trolley around corridors on three different floors, dashed about, cleaned, polished, vacuumed, and changed linen. Doris was good at her job, quicker than most of the younger chambermaids we'd had over the years, but it helped to know you were doing it for a reason. I figured she'd be pissed off and I'd be first in the firing line. She could hardly have a go at Harry.

She didn't look pissed. "You hear about poor old Alfie?"

"What?"

"His dog got run over, spent the night at the emergency vets, and then the poor bloody thing had to be put down."

"No! But I just been down there, he never said."

"He wouldn't, would he?" Doris looked at me pityingly, like I didn't get it and very likely never would. "Bloke's a Judas Priest fan, his knuckles got tattoos on them and Smithy says he's got *just try it, mate* tattooed across the top of his arse as well. Though I ain't never seen that one, mind."

"Interesting."

Doris ignored the interruption. "Somebody like that, he ain't likely to cry like no little girl, is he?"

"But he told *you*."

"No he didn't. Smithy said."

Doris left as soon as she'd delivered her news. She seemed happy about it. Not the dog's death, obviously, but the fact that she could spread word of the tragedy around. Some people are like that, I've noticed. They seem to relish being able to pass on news, good or bad. I don't suppose it made them bad citizens, but I guess a psychiatrist might make something of it.

I was glad when she left for it gave me a breathing space, time to think about Sophie and the next stage in my campaign to find her. I tried the Bayswater Hotel again. What could they do? Kill me?

"Ah, you must be the woman Mel was talking about."

"Mel?" I said.

"Aussie, works here part time. She spoke to you a few days ago."

"Yes," I said. "She was helpful, but we couldn't find my sister."

"She told me. And something rang a bell, so I looked her up in last year's register. Sophie, wasn't it? I remember her. Not too many people stay here for a month."

"A month?"

"Sure. She was here for Christmas. We had a drink together in the bar."

"You did?" I stopped breathing.

"Yeah. Nice lady, but something sad about her. She was on her own for New Year's Eve. Nobody should be on their own at New Year," she said.

"That's pretty sad," I agreed. I didn't tell her I'd been on *my* own. Me and Sophie. Two peas in a sad little pod.

"Yeah." I could sense some impatience now in the woman on the other end of the phone.

"Well, thanks for taking the time to look for her," I said. "It was good of you. I'll leave you to it, expect you're busy. "

"Don't you want her address?"

"You've got an address?"

"Sure. She left us a forwarding address. Some place in Bristol. Hang on, won't take a minute to get it."

Ecstatic! That about covered how I felt. Columbus couldn't have been more thrilled when he discovered America. Though to my mind, America had always been there, already inhabited by people. Columbus had been a late comer to the party.

I spent the next ten minutes on Google Earth looking at maps of the place. For it really existed. It wasn't just a post office box. It wasn't a figment of my imagination or anyone else's, but a real place, a house opposite St Andrew's park.

There was no phone number, though. But maybe that wasn't such a bad thing. I would have been tempted to phone her straight away. It could be an awkward call; maybe a letter would be better. I'd waited thirty-four and a bit years. I could wait a few more days.

Chapter 17

I wasn't the only one waiting. Harry had been waiting as well. For a miracle. For the lift to miraculously cure itself, and for the thin drip-feed of money that he'd managed to siphon into the Hotel Royal to last till Easter. We were expecting great things from the Easter 'rush'.

So far, he'd been paying bills strategically. Some were filed in the bin - or shoved under his mattress for all I knew. Food suppliers were being paid and we were all still getting our wages. The man was a gifted juggler. He was wasted in the hotel business. He should have been performing in the Cirque du Soleil.

Joe was back. He was looking a lot happier than when he'd left. Right now he was whistling cheerfully and it was getting on my nerves. He couldn't hold a tune.

"You still here?" he said.

Like I had somewhere else to go.

"Joe, when they excavate this place in some distant future, they'll find me under one of those pillars."

"Gruesome. You should get out more."

"Sure, but right now I'm waiting for the lift guy."

"Lift guy? New man in your life?"

"Sworn off men for Lent."

"You celebrate Lent?"

"It's a joke, Joe" I said. "What about you? New guy in your life?"

"Nothing wrong with the old one," he said and beamed.

I was glad somebody around here was happy. I'd started off the day upbeat, but Alfie had growled at me again, like a lion with a thorn in its paw and Harry had imitated a bear with a bad headache. No need to go to the Zoo, this place brought it to your doorstep.

Harry's lift-maintenance agreement had run out, he said. For my money, it was dubious he ever had one. Though I suppose there are rules about that sort of thing. Health and Safety stuff, insurance you need to have if you're dealing with the public. But then Harry Evans didn't always follow rules. The back door was a door he was familiar with.

"Right. I'll be out back having a quick ciggy," I said. "Give me a shout when somebody who looks like a lift mechanic arrives, will you Joe? Bloke's coming down from Surrey."

"What? The lift's broken?" Joe shouted at the back of my head, and I smirked. It was good to have him back, but I wasn't sorry that somebody else would be taking flak because the lift still wasn't running.

*

I wanted to leave for Bristol right now. Right this minute. Leave the whole bloody lot of them behind. Everybody seemed to be angry: Harry, Doris, Alfie, the K.P. several of the guests. There must be something in the air. Or maybe last night had been a full moon. I'd have to look it up – not that I had the time. I was far too busy dealing with complaints about the heating, for the boiler had broken down again, but at least the lift was fixed now (you win some, you lose some) and the creaky and infirm didn't have to walk up two flights.

The coach party was about to leave this morning, and if I were honest, I'd say some of them looked relieved.

They'd asked for an early breakfast, another thing that hadn't pleased cook much. But I couldn't see what his problem was; we knew when they booked in that they'd be making an early start. Though of course Harry hadn't specified exactly how early *early* would be. At times I think he's frightened to go head-to-head with Alfie. They'd all wanted a cooked breakfast at six o'clock, so maybe cook couldn't be blamed for throwing his dummy out of the pram.

The barman was in a foul mood as well, for he'd been drafted in to collect suitcases from outside bedroom doors and help load them into the coach's baggage hold. He threw me a scowl as he passed and I countered with a smile. My contrary-bone is the biggest one in my body. I've found that around Christopher Newly, my 'happiness measure' rises in direct proportion to his grumpiness. For some reason it wound the man up when I grinned at him. So I did it a lot.

"What goes around comes around," he snapped, and tapped the side of his nose with a finger.

But I'd no idea what he meant by that.

Everyone seemed to relax once the coach had been waved off and Harry even felt brave enough to venture out of his office.

"You see all that bunting and crap?" He pointed vaguely in the direction of the *cabaret lounge*. "Tell that Aga woman to see the place's decorated for tomorrow night."

"An Aga's a cooker. Her name's Agata."

"Close enough," he said. And he was right, for Harry didn't usually come that close with people's names. "Might as well do it now. There'll be loads to do tomorrow."

"She'll be busy, couldn't the barman sort it?" I asked.

"Sent him home. He's been in since early this morning."

"He's not alone, is he? We've *all* been at it since the crack of dawn."

"We need him," he said. "He can make cocktails."

He said it with a sense of reverence, like the man had just invented the wheel or produced penicillin.

"So, you want Agata to decorate the room?" I said.

"Sure, and tell her to crack on with it." He seemed to have an afterthought - which was worrying, for Harry's afterthoughts usually meant more work for me. "You can help her; get the thing done twice as quick. Joseph's out front, right?"

"Yeah, but he was going home. He only came in to help out."

"Bloke's just come back after three days off. We're not running a soddin' holiday camp, Stevie. He can type up the menu for tomorrow night while he's there."

"Thought that was done already."

"See where thought got you, then."

Harry was right; it didn't pay to think sometimes. Go where they pointed you, do what they told you, leave the thinking to others. Do the job they paid you to do and no more. "So, *you'll* tell Joe, then."

"Course," he said, like he always did his own dirty work. And I went off to look for Agata.

I found her out back where banished smokers formed compliant little knots of lesser beings, pariahs who polluted the air, dismissed from civilized society. And I'd joined them. I'd tried to give up again, but it wasn't the right time.

"Hey, didn't know you smoked," I said.

"Sure," said Agata and took out her rolling tobacco. "You like me make you a roll up?"

"Nah. I'm good." I slipped a packet from my blazer pocket, lit up and gratefully inhaled a lungful of smoke, blissfully sucking down the carcinogenic chemicals. I knew about the tar, seventy per cent of it sticking doggedly to your lungs. But it was easy to ignore that when the feeling of well being rushed through your veins. Carbon monoxide, nicotine, cyanide, formaldehyde, ammonia, nobody talked much about those. Anyway, you had to die of something, right?

"You busy?"

"Always busy," she said.

She didn't look busy, but then again neither did I. "Harry wants us both to decorate the night club for tomorrow's hoo-ha."

"Night club?"

"Cabaret lounge," I said.

"Oh, *the bar*," she said. She smiled. Like she'd just been initiated into some sort of secret society where members were exclusively hand-picked.

"He wants it decked out like a whore's bedroom. Should see the stuff he's put in there. I'm sure the Masons will love it."

"You think so?"

I'd have to remember Agata's tendency to take everything literally in future.

"No, Agata. I *don't* think so, but then we're in charge. We'll try and make it tasteful. It's a concept Harry hasn't got to grips with yet."

"What about menus? Mr Evans ripped up other ones I printed off. Chef and he have big fight."

"Oh?"

"Chef wants to use wine in Coq au Vin, but Mr Evans says too expensive. So Chef says we call it chicken stew. I type that and both of them shout at me."

"Life's a bitch," I said. "But don't worry, Agata. Harry's told Joe to type up the menu. Let them all shout at each other. We'll go and pretend that it's Christmas in the bar and that the dance floor in there isn't like two large table-clothes sewn together."

"Oh, I just remember. Orchestra for tomorrow."

"Band," I said, helpfully. "We call it a band."

"Okay, band want you to call them."

"Me?"

"Keyboard man. He want to talk to you."

What next? "Okay, get me the number and I'll call him and then you and I can get the room done."

"Sure."

But she didn't sound a bit sure.

*

Joe was grumbling under his breath, but I ignored him and dialled the number for *The Syncopated City Slickers*. God, I hope they'd put more thought into their music than their name.

"Hi," I said when the phone was finally answered. It had taken forever. Hadn't these people ever heard of answering machines? It was still early for someone who called themselves musicians to be up and around, I guess. Musicians and actors, they turned the clock on its head - that's what I've heard.

"Hi," said the sleepy voice on the other end. "What can I do for you?"

"No idea," I said. *Lazy bastard, didn't he know some of us had been up since five this morning?* "I was told to phone this number. I'm calling from the Hotel Royal. Someone wanted to talk to me about the function tomorrow night."

"Oh, hi Miss Anderson. Yeah, right. Just wondering what time would be good to bring the equipment in. Speakers, amps, P.A. - decks for the disco."

Once they got that lot in, there wouldn't be much room for the audience. But it wasn't my problem, of course, for the band had been booked directly by the Masons. *Who was I kidding? Everything eventually became my problem.*

"Come around ten tomorrow. Cleaners should have finished by then."

"Ten in the morning?" the voice said, appalled.

"Sure. It comes round twice a day, you know."

"I'll hardly have got to bed by then," said the guy.

"Then I guess tomorrow's your lucky day."

I put the phone down and took perverse pleasure in the guy's parting groan. Something about the voice was familiar, but I didn't linger over the thought. I had enough other stuff already fighting for space in my head.

"Ready?" asked Agata. She'd been waiting patiently, a box balanced in her hands. She held it like the crown jewels were inside.

I nodded. And we headed for the bar "What's that?"

"Tea-lights," she explained, like I'd never heard of the idea before. "And candle holders, crystal," she said proudly. "I find them in the store room."

Yeah, and Skelly 'found' them somewhere dodgy as I recall, so we'd never used them. But Agata seemed remarkably pleased with her discovery, so I never mentioned their provenance. We put them out on a few tables and I crossed my fingers that none of the Masons would recognise them as missing stock. Harry's often told me I worry too much. So, I've decided to stop worrying and just let life roll right on over me.

The phone rang on the bar. "Call for you, Stevie. Put it through, shall I?"

Joe sounded excited. I'd told him about tracking my sister down and I swear he was as keyed-up as I was. "Young woman," he said, "sounds cute."

"'*Course* you put it through," I said, trying to picture Sophie in my head. I'd given her all my numbers in the letter, hoping against hope she'd phone, or at least write back.

"Hello, Stevie Anderson?"

"Hi, speaking. That *you* Sophie?"

I could hear laboured breathing. "It's me," the voice said. A voice that reminded me of my own."

I wanted to scream and cry and whoop hysterically, but I just waited for her to carry on. She didn't.

"Sophie, this is brilliant. God, I can't believe it's you. Can we meet? Can you come down to the hotel? Should I come up there?"

"It's no good. I can't do this," she said. I could hear a muffled sob and the voice retreated back into the ether, like it had never been. *Disconnect*.

I got through to Reception. "Joe, find out that number for me?"

"Sure," he said. "Anything else you'd like me to do while I'm at it? Juggle? Serve afternoon tea? Book people in? I'm busy out here."

"I'll come out," I said.

I got the number. It was a mobile, but when I phoned it, it went over to voice mail. I tried again and again and each time I left the same frantic message. "Look Sophie. I need to see you. We have to meet. We're all we've got now." But nothing happened. No one phoned me back, either on the hotel line, or my mobile. And I gave it up in the end. I had to get back to work. I had to think about real life. Life without a sister. My little sister Sophie didn't want me. I'd tried to reconnect to some sort of family tree, but the tree had turned into a withered bush.

I wondered if I'd swamped her with all my excited questions, my expectations. But on the other hand, could be that the only remaining member of my family, the one I'd been pinning all my hopes on, had been disappointed in me; had simply been underwhelmed.

Chapter 18

"Room looks great, Stevie. You did a good job, there."

Harry was getting on like an expectant father. He'd been all over the place this morning, beaming, rallying the troops. But there was a nervousness to him that only someone who'd known the man, seen his many moods, could have picked up.

"Agata did most of it," I said. I'd abandoned her in the middle of it.

"Can I pick staff, or what?"

"Sure, Harry. You can pick staff," I said. I didn't know if he was talking about me or Agata Truscott, but either way it didn't matter. Life marched along its own pre-destined path whatever you tried to do. I'd become a fatalist overnight. For it didn't seem to matter what I did in my life, some outside force came along to sod the whole thing up.

"What's that mean?" An angry looking young man in a cheap suit pointed vaguely at the guest notice board. The thing was a work of art in its own right with a beautiful Maple frame around it that had been lovingly handcrafted by Morris. I looked over at the board. There were several notices up there.

"Which one?" I asked, more politely than the guy deserved, for his tone had been bullying and he'd interrupted a conversation. Hadn't anyone told him that was rude?

"That stuff about today's lunch," he snapped.

The man was a rep for an agricultural machinery manufacturer. Maybe things hadn't been going well for him. But there was no need to take it out on innocent bystanders.

"We have a function tonight, Sir - so our kitchen is quite busy. We'll be serving dinner as usual for residents in one designated part of the restaurant, but I'm afraid lunch will be limited to a choice of soup and sandwiches."

Alfie would have to perform some delicate acrobatics to manage even that lot together. He'd dragged in both Kitchen Porters and we'd got an extra dish-washer for the day, and a Sous, a friend of Alfie's. Hard to think of him as having friends.

The man sidled off, grumbling under his breath about being a regular guest who'd be taking his business elsewhere in future.

"Pillock! Don't know how you keep that smile on your face sometimes," said Harry.

"It's plastic," I said. "And if he's a *regular*, they've just moved the Taj Mahal to Bolton."

"They have," he said. "I've been."

"The real one, Harry - not the curry house."

He laughed. And I laughed. Sometimes, it helped

"Can I've a word?"

Harry got off side, didn't want to get involved in anything else.

"It's you! You get around, don't you?"

"Cornwall's a small place," he said.

My brain took a giant leap. Matthew Barry must be a *Syncopated City Slicker*. He had what seemed to be a keyboard in a black plastic gig bag slung by a strap over his shoulder. It looked heavy.

"So, how can I help?"

"Where can I put this?"

I was tempted to tell him, but I don't always go for the obvious. Instead, I smiled at him. He was an easy man to smile at. Easy on the eye, too. Tall, good looking, short blond hair, (cliché territory) clean cut, someone you could happily introduce to your grandmother. Not the type you'd immediately tag as a musician. If he was a boozer or took drugs, he looked well on it. His green eyes had some kind of fleck running through them that I hadn't noticed before. He looked about seventeen, but according to his website he was twenty-nine. Five years younger than me – *toy boy*. Just as well I'd gone off men. The last thing I needed in my life was a toy boy who didn't get up till noon.

"You can set up in the far corner of the cabaret lounge. Be a tight squeeze, though." Agata had said there were five of them.

"Tell me something new," he said. "The band's always the last thing they think about when they plan these things. You'd think the word dinner-*dance* would give them a clue. But it never does."

"Bitter, eh?"

"Just knackered. Early start."

I looked at my watch. It was eleven o'clock. "Sure," I sympathised. "Try five. Right, I'll leave you to it."

"Sure thing. But I still need to know where you want me in the restaurant with this thing." He patted the gig-bag affectionately.

"The restaurant?"

"Yep. I'm booked to play background music for the meal. My other keys and synth will already be in the night club."

"So, you're a moving target, eh?"

"Sure. Harder to hit one of those."

I went to get Agata. The restaurant was her baby and I was glad. It meant I could sidestep, let someone else take the flak for a change, and there was sure to be flak. There'd already been grumbles from the waiting staff about how the extra tables brought in to cater for both hotel guests and the Masonic Lodge had eaten up space. It would be like negotiating an obstacle course and some of the waiters in there weren't exactly Olympic material. Agata had put screens up to segregate the ordinary diners from the function, but they weren't a work of art. I pictured her trying to find room for a man and his piano.

*

"Take over, Joe. I'm going out for lunch."

I needed some air and to escape. I'd been cooped up in the place since five this morning; its delights had paled.

"Harry know?"

"He's not my bleedin' mother. I've given him enough free overtime to take a thirty minute lunch break."

I hadn't had a plan. Walk into town; grab a sandwich; that was about it. But once I started walking I just kept on going, like I was walking to the end of the world. Freedom. No thinking about what to do with my life, or men, or missing branches from my family tree. I'd reached a Zen-like state when I heard a loud shout from behind. I turned, the mood broken, my head forced to reconnect with my body. I saw Skelly charging to catch up. But I saw something else as well and the image, frozen in my mind, forced the breath from my mouth as if someone had landed a brutal punch in my gut. Jesus! It couldn't be. Skelly grabbed my arm, fastened onto it with a grip that was sure to leave bruises. I tried to shake him off, but he wouldn't let go.

"No, you don't," he said.

I dragged him along in the opposite direction, back the way we'd come. But the figure had disappeared.

"Leave me alone," I said, angry with him. "That's my sister. I need to get to her."

"And I need you to deliver a message, a serious message. Got it?"

"Skelly, let me go. She's gone now and it's down to you."

"Forget your fuckin' sister. Tell Harry he'd better come across with the readies or my boss will have no alternative. You got that?"

"*No alternative?*" I said.

"Yeah, he'll understand." And he let go.

I ran as fast as I could through the shopping precinct, looking in doorways, looking for the familiar flash of red hair. *Long red hair*, just like mine before I'd had it cut. And the face. God, the face. It couldn't be. It couldn't possibly be.

I peeled off from the main drag, searched in shops, went into a church. Ran on through the town as fast as I could. Maybe she'd gone back to the hotel looking for me. But that didn't make sense, for if she wanted to talk to me, surely she'd have stayed and not run. Even so, I ran the rest of the way, past hotels, past Tolcarne beach stretching below, looking at the back of every head, searching for a glimpse of red hair. I crossed the road and ran up the steps to the hotel. Flung myself up to the reception counter.

"You in training for something?" said Joe.

"Anyone come in, ask for me?"

"What's wrong?"

"Joe, did my sister come in?" I grabbed hold of his hand.

"Your sister?"

"What are you – a parrot?"

"What the hell happened? You look awful."

I couldn't help it. I couldn't hold the tears back for another second. "My sister," I said between sobs. She's here. She just followed me."

"You sure?"

"'Course I'm sure."

"What did she say?"

"She didn't. She just ran away."

"Why would she do that?"

"How the hell should I know?"

"Maybe it wasn't her."

"You saying I made this up?"

"No, but I'm saying you could be mistaken. That maybe you want it too much."

"Joe, I'm not stupid. I'm not mistaken and I'm not crazy. I just saw my sister. She was following me."

"Okay, calm down. I believe you."

"Joe?"

"What?"

"We're twins."

Chapter 19

They were laughing in the kitchen, Doris and Alfie. I couldn't see what they had to laugh about. The world had turned into a pale, grey place. Maybe not for everybody, but for me.

"What the hell's wrong with you two?" I said.

"It's the silver-service in the restaurant," explained Alfie in between bouts of laughter, "Doris has never done it before."

"So?"

Doris had been drafted in as a waitress for the night. I didn't even want to think about how she'd manage. She'd never as much as served a guest before, never mind silver-service, which was a complicated business and called for a certain amount of dexterity.

Silver-service meant serving food from platters at the table to the guest's plate. You had to hold both a serving fork and a spoon in your right hand and, in a sort of pincer movement, pick up and transfer the food. It looked cool when it was done properly, but in the hands of an amateur could be lethal. It was a technique that needed a lot of practice.

"I'm left-handed," she said.

"Doris is left-handed," confirmed Alfie. He seemed to find something funny in that.

"And?"

"The waiter is meant to stand behind the guest . . ."

"Waitress," butted in Doris.

"Yeah, okay! The waitress is supposed to stand to the guest's left," said Alfie, "hold the tray with their left hand

and serve with their right. Silver-service *has* to done right-handed."

"Sure," I said. "I can see where that would be *hilarious*."

"You had to be there," said Doris. "I'm left-handed. I can't do sod-all with my right."

They both looked at each other and sniggered again.

"Those spuds were hot, I made sure of it," said Alfie. "Don't want no more feckin' complaints. And Doris dropped at least three of them in some pretentious prick's lap."

They both laughed again. *Funny stuff!*

"*Four* of them!" she said.

I left the kitchen and went back up the stairs to Reception. I didn't feel in the mood for humour, which was unfortunate, because everybody around me seemed to have caught some kind of happiness bug. Harry wandered over, a king-size grin on his face.

"Shit, Stevie, couldn't have gone better if we'd planned it."

"We *did* plan it, Harry." I shot him a look that said: *go away and stop bothering me. Take your happiness somewhere else; spread it around people who appreciate it.*

But he wouldn't give up. Harry was happy, could hear the cash registers ringing. "And guess what?" he said, as if I was a mind reader with a degree in Psychology.

"No idea."

"They're downing that cheap plonk like it was Champagne."

"You should make a few bob tonight then, between that and the stuff they down in the bar." Even *I* could hear the bitterness in my voice.

"What the fuck's wrong with you?"

"She's lost her sister," said Joe, trying to contribute something to the conversation.

"Sorry for your loss," said Harry. And he looked sad. As if he really meant it. And I felt like a silly little kid who'd been allowed to mix with the grown-ups.

I was a fraud. I'd always tried to show that I was independent, could stand on my own two feet; that nothing bothered me, short of world peace, famines, and the way we were sodding up our planet.

"It's all right, Harry," I said. "I'm glad it's going well. And I'm sorry I'm a pain, but sometimes you don't know what you've got until it's snatched away from you."

"Right," he said, and coughed. An embarrassed noise that said he'd done his bit of communicating for the night. He nodded at Joe. "I'll leave you both to get on with it. Check on the bar later will you, Stevie? Tell Christopher to push the brandy if he can."

"Sure," I said and thought about Skelly and whoever was planning to rearrange Harry's anatomy. Our illustrious leader would need to pedal a lot of cheap brandy to start paying off his dodgy debts. But maybe there was a miracle out there waiting to happen. Life can sometimes surprise you.

*

"Stevie, you busy? Can we talk?"

It was Agata and she looked worried. "Sure, come into the office, I said.

"This barman. You know him?"

"Not really," I said, cautiously. I didn't like talking about colleagues behind their backs - even when I *didn't* like them.

The man had been recruited as a wine waiter in the restaurant for the dinner part of tonight's dinner-dance. Maybe he didn't fancy the idea.

"I think he's . . ." Agata searched for the right words, but made do with a mime instead. She raised her hand to her lips, and tipped it up, like she was knocking back the contents of an invisible glass.

"Drinking? You think he's drinking?"

"Yes."

"What? Taking the stuff the guests have ordered."

She nodded her head. "One for them, one for him, I think. And when I tell him, he gets angry."

"You got someone else in there knows *anything* about wine?"

She shrugged.

"Got another waiter knows how to open a bottle?" I asked.

"Sure."

"Okay. Send the barman out to the office. I'll warn Harry he's coming. Oh and Agata."

"Yes."

"Do it discreetly."

"Of course, I do," she said.

I warned Harry about Agata's fear that the barman was getting drunk, was pilfering. He waved an airy hand and I wondered if he would believe her, or if he'd take the barman's side. *The man could make cocktails.*

I went back to help Joe. He'd been trying to make up bills for guests who were leaving in the morning and man the desk at the same time.

"So, you really think she's your twin? That's cool," he said.

It all made sense now, the letter from my grandmother, the photograph. It hadn't been my grandmother, it had been Sophie. And no wonder I'd always felt there was something out there, someone tugging at me. It was the whole twin thing in action. I was sure of it now. Not that it mattered, for the woman had rejected me.

"If you'd seen her, Joe. Same face, same height, same colour hair, same age."

"And you couldn't be mistaken? I mean they say everybody has a double, Stevie - this doppelganger thing."

"I'm not mistaken," I said, "but it hardly matters now, does it? She doesn't want to meet me."

"Then why would she bother travelling down from Bristol? Why would she follow you?"

"Search me."

"I reckon she wanted to see you. She feels the same as you. You're twins, right? But she just got cold feet. Could be her life's complicated. You never know."

"Think so?"

"I think you should take a couple of days off before Easter kicks in. Go up to Bristol, find her and have the whole thing out. You'll never forgive yourself if you don't. That's what your grandmother wanted as well, wasn't it?"

"Sure." I thought back to my grandmother's letter, her 'special instructions' that had been included with the will. Her last wish had been that I try to find Sophie. *Try and reunite the family again, Stephanie. It's up to you now to find your sister and talk some sense into that mother of yours. It's time she forgave me. I was only doing what I thought was best.*

So, it was all down to me. And it seemed unfair. Why had my grandmother placed such a burden on me? She didn't know me, or anything about me. She knew Sophie. Maybe Sophie wasn't up to it. Maybe Sophie was weak. But something told me she wasn't. The twin thing again. I just felt it. Felt I would like her, this twin sister of mine. Felt she was in some kind of trouble. It might sound fanciful and that's what my mother would say, but it was a feeling that was growing stronger by the minute.

"I'll go," I said.

"Great. You won't regret it. It'll only bug you till you meet her."

"I'll tell Harry in the morning. He should be in a good mood then. He'll know how much he's made out of this little lot."

"Some things you just need to sort," said Joe with feeling, "otherwise they fester away."

"*Fester*? That's a horrible word."

"Okay then, rankle, irritate, make you bitter, *whatever*," he said.

"You got something like that, Joe?"

"Sure, you know . . ."

"What?"

"I've got to hide who I really am. The world's a cruel place when you're different, Stevie. What would happen if this lot knew about me and Wilbur?"

"Maybe it's time to find out. You might be surprised how people rally round. You got loads of friends here Joe."

"And *him*?" Joe threw a hand out in the direction of Harry's office. "You think he'd be thrilled to find he's been harbouring 'a fruit' under his roof?" Joe gave a cynical snort.

"Harry might be a step too far. Why not just start with some of your friends. Test the water. You know I'll be here for you, whatever you decide."

Joe stepped over and hugged me, fiercely. And when he finally let go, there were tears in his eyes.

"Fancy a coffee?" he said.

"Love one."

"Sounds like they've moved onto coffee and speeches in there." He nodded at the restaurant, cuffed his wet eyes with his sleeve. "I'll go get us a cup."

He came back with two large mugs, not the tiny coffee cups that the guests were being served with. It was sweet and strong and gave us both the boost we needed.

Joe didn't mention Wilbur again, or coming out, or how unfair the world was. But his face had changed; his expression was set, more defiant.

"Christopher's surly tonight," he said.

"What, the waiter?" I asked.

"No, the barman. He's in there making Irish Coffees, practically slinging them at guests.

"He's still there? But Harry was supposed to pull him; Agata reckons he's been drinking."

"Could be."

"That's great. How's he gonna run the bar?"

"Don't look at me," said Joe. "I only work here."

Chapter 20

"Will this lot be making a racket all night?"

"Sorry, Sir?"

It was the rep from the machine company. He always had some sort of problem. I wouldn't be sad to see him go.

"The band playing in there. What time do they stop making that racket?"

"I believe they finish playing at twelve, Sir."

He grunted something I couldn't make out, and looked at his watch. I could have told him it was eleven thirty, for I'd just looked at the massive clock in Reception. It was there for guests who didn't want to wear out their watches.

"Is everything okay, Sir?"

"So, another half hour, then?"

"They have a disco for an hour after that, I believe. We have a late licence until one."

It was never going to be easy, keeping both residents and Masons happy. They were on opposite teams. I'd warned Harry about the noise and asked the band to keep it down to ear-splitting, but things were never going to be simple. I'd known that.

"What! How'd you expect me to sleep with all that going on?"

I couldn't have slept through it either, but then I didn't have that luxury. I wasn't expecting to get to bed until at least two - conservative estimate. Harry had asked me to stay on until the last function guest had left. It was sometimes a little *too* convenient when you lived in the same place that you worked.

"That's why we've put most of our guests in the East Wing, Sir," I said, "well away from the party. Only the function guests who have booked rooms with us and are staying over for breakfast are in the rooms *above* the bar."

I'd already checked. You couldn't hear the band where this guy's bedroom was, unless you counted the slight vibration of the bass through the floor in the outside corridor. But then a bass can be penetrating at the best of times. I figured he'd be fine, but maybe he was angling for some money off his bill.

Then I'd gone to the kitchen to get a last coffee for me and Joe. He would be going home soon. Lucky for some. The coffee was stewed. So were some of the Masons, for the bar had been doing good business.

"How's it going with your grandmother's will?" Joe asked. "You a millionaire yet?"

"This time next year," I laughed. "The solicitor says disposing of the property will take time."

"She own her own house then?" asked Joe. "That'll give you something to keep the wolf from the door."

"Yeah."

I didn't tell Joe what the will had said. He was a friend, I know. But I didn't want to think about it, or get my hopes up. Sometimes, when you did that, you were disappointed. I'd already been disappointed in life; in love, in my family. My grandmother had owned a property, described as her *residence*. It didn't specify what kind of residence, but I don't think I'd ever have called one of the places I'd lived in a residence. And then there was something called The Holiday Apartments Rental Agency in Ottawa. Did that mean that she'd *owned* the agency? Or the apartments? I pictured some of the places I'd rented that called themselves holiday flats, and shuddered. It was hard to believe that anyone in my family owned a single brick. My mother had always scratched around for money, had always rented. It seemed strange that my grandmother hadn't helped her, but then families are complicated things (according to my mother). My mother would be happy now, for the will settled a gift of 5,000 pounds on her. Maybe that was why she'd phoned me.

But even though it was written in black and white, the whole thing seemed unreal. My sister was real. And all I wanted was to find her, talk to her, shop with her, walk along the beach, both of us eating ice cream. I knew she'd like ice cream. I did.

"I've finished those bills for the morning. Sure it's okay for me to head off? I hate to leave you with this lot, Stevie. Some of them are drunk."

"Forget it, Joe. You've done your bit. Harry's still here if anything kicks off."

"Okay, if you're sure. And don't forget what I said. Ask for a couple of days off. You've bloody earned them."

"Sure," I said. And I meant it. It was a good idea. I'd book a train to Bristol tomorrow; get things straight in my head. Maybe my sister had just got cold feet, like Joe said. But I still couldn't shake off the feeling that it was more than that. That Sophie really *did* want to see me, but that something bad was happening to her, maybe something she didn't want to drag me into.

*

Agata had left an hour ago, shortly after the waiting staff. Joe had dropped her back home; turns out she and her husband live on the other side of the boating lake, opposite Joe. Though unlike Joe's upmarket place, Agata was in one of the tiny shoeboxes that perched precariously on the side of a hill, had no garden or parking space, but could claim a lakeside view. I had my own view. *A back alley and a fire escape*.

The night was petering to an end. The kitchen had closed long ago, so apart from a few scattered Masons, there was just me, Harry who was helping the barman cash up, and the musicians packing their kit. The only sound coming from the bar now was a half-hearted drunken chorus of *The White Rose*. The song was a default setting for patriotic Cornishmen when they were hammered. I took the opportunity to nip out back and have a last cigarette before going up to bed.

It felt good, not all cigarettes taste as good as the promise they hold out, but this one did. And as I sucked it in contentedly, watched the smoke drift lazily into the night sky, a feeling of serenity overtook me. I thought about what I might say to my sister when I spoke to her tomorrow. I'd go to Bristol even if Harry *didn't* like it.

"Hiding out here, eh?"

The voice was slurred and there was a strange look in the barman's eye.

"Why would I need to hide?" I said.

"I know it was you."

"What?"

"Dobbed me in to the boss."

"Why? Did you do something?" I asked.

"Don't play the innocent with me, you stuck-up little bitch. I said you'd get yours, and you know what? Tonight's the night."

I backed up to the door, but the guy pulled me back into the alley. He breathed into my face and my head reeled from the sour smell of his breath, the stink of brandy fumes. He grabbed me by the hair, pulled my head towards him and covered my mouth with his own, probing deep with his disgusting, slimy tongue. I stamped down hard on his foot with my four inch stiletto. He howled in pain but still managed to push me back into the wall, pin me there, while his filthy hands groped my breasts. He forced his knee up between my thighs, and his hands followed. I screamed at the top of my lungs.

The noise surprised me, for I was so scared that I didn't think any sound would come out. The ferocity of it took him off balance and he smacked me hard across the face. The metallic taste of blood filled my mouth and my lips stung where his ring had caught me. The bastard. I brought my knee up and lashed out towards his groin. He shrieked in pain, but wouldn't let go. I screamed louder, a wailing, banshee-sound full of anger and fear. Surely someone could hear me. They weren't all deaf in there. The screaming enraged him even more and he put his hand over my mouth. I bit it.

The door was flung open and someone carrying a black bag over his shoulder rammed my attacker with it. Then he hit him in the face. Hard. Square on, with a ferocity that must have broken bone, for there was a sickening crunch. And Christopher Newly slid to the concrete. I hoped he was dead.

Events got fuzzy in my mind after that. I remember being helped back into the lounge, covered up with someone's coat. But I'd no idea what happened to the barman. He'd said I'd get mine. I started to shake when I remembered his words and somebody poured a brandy, forced it down me. I felt like throwing up.

"Where's that bastard?" I said. It was hard to form the words. My lips had swollen like blubber.

"Don't worry about him. Harry and Joe have him in the office; they're waiting for the cops."

"Joe? Joe came back?" I said.

Matthew Barry looked at me, confused. "Joe - my drummer," he said. "The big guy; he works out."

I looked up at my rescuer. Not a natural for the role, for he didn't look as if *he* worked out.

"Matthew, you're bleeding!"

"Smacked him one," he said, pride in his voice. It was only then he noticed his skinned knuckles, his swollen hand.

"You're a musician, you need those hands," I said. "Get some ice on it."

"Never mind that, how are you? That bastard. He didn't, *you know*…?" He couldn't say it.

Rape. That's what he meant. And I was sick just turning the word over in my mind. I shook my head.

Harry came in with a black look on his face. "Police have got him. They need to talk to you, Stevie. Need to get a statement. And . . . they've brought a doctor with them."

"I don't need a doctor," I said. "Tell the doctor I'm fine. Good night's sleep, that's all I want." I felt ridiculously tired; the sort of tired where your limbs feel like lead and can't remember how to do the job they were designed for.

"Better if you do, Stevie." Harry patted me on the hand. He'd never done *that* before. He looked embarrassed, like he couldn't find the words. "It's procedure," he said.

A tall man came over to me. "In these sorts of cases, Miss," he said "it's better if you have an examination right away. It won't take long and Dr Whitely is an understanding sort of bloke. He'll make it as user-friendly as he can in the circumstances."

It hit me then, exactly what kind of an examination they meant. "No, I won't do it. I won't be mauled about any more. Leave me alone. I want to go to bed. I want my sister. I want my mum."

Harry grabbed hold of me and didn't let go, even when I punched him in the arm and shook and sobbed. He ruffled my hair and tried a smile. But he didn't pull it off. It didn't reach his eyes. "Thought you didn't like your mum," he said. And that's when I knew. Harry was more than a boss.

Chapter 21

"It's like a bloody funeral home in here," I said. "Wish everybody would cheer up and stop treating me like some kind of invalid."

"People find it hard, babe. Not sure what to say."

"But not you, Doris."

"No, not me. You're like the daughter I never had. Three lads. Me and Morris - we could only manage to make boys, though we always wanted a girl. So you're me surrogate daughter."

I sniffed, tried to hold back the tears. Tears overtook me at all sorts of unlikely times now. They all said I should go to counselling, but that's the kind of head-stuff I'd always run a mile from.

The policewoman who'd spoken to me afterwards, made me a cup of scalding, sweet tea, said I shouldn't blame myself, or lose my self-esteem. Blame myself? For what that bastard had done? Before she'd said that - I hadn't. But then I'd started going over things in my head. I hadn't liked the bloke, had been taunting him. Every time he'd come near me with that pained look on his face, I'd made it my business to grin at him. So maybe it *was* my fault.

Apart from the crying thing, I figured I was getting on okay. There were the nightmares, of course, but I sensed that those were normal, that my subconscious was working its way through all the toxic stuff on its own – without my help. So, I'd just let the thing get on with it.

That bastard Christopher Newly was out on bail. The police had warned me it might take some time for the case to come to court. They were talking about charging him with indecent assault. 'Inappropriate touching', the policewoman had told me. *Indecent assault?* I wondered when assault could ever be called *decent*.

At first, it had been like a tidal wave crashing over me. Trying to suffocate me. The police took my statement, took photographs of my face where the bastard had punched me, the doctor gave me an internal examination. That was the worst bit. Then he gave me a pill. Told me to sleep. And I'd gone to bed like it was any other night. I'd spent the whole of the next day there, under the duvet, trying to sleep it off. As if it was the flu or something 'normal' and that a day in bed would make it all go away.

But then reality had kicked in and I knew that March the 19th would be a date seared into my brain with a branding iron and that dinner-dances and Masons and cheap brandy fumes would be memories I would need to wrestle with. But strangely, recognising that, owning up to it, was helpful. Maybe even healing. I came to the decision that this animal was not going to ruin my life. I wouldn't allow him to do that.

He wasn't going to plead guilty. And it was just my word against his, for although Matthew had seen me pushed against the wall and heard my screams; he hadn't seen the actual assault. So, I would have to be a witness.

I didn't feel brave, but knew I had to do it. Go to court, have people pawing over my private life; maybe even say I'd led the creep on. I know how these things work. I've watched enough T.V. But it had to be done; for me, my self respect and for all my sisters out there. Hey! You see. I really have become a Feminist. He couldn't be allowed to get away with it. For next time, maybe he'd rape someone.

"You planning on changing that pillowcase any day, now?"

"Sorry, Doris. I went off on one."

"Yeah, I know," she said gruffly. "But we need to get on. Big holiday push coming up. Easter's nearly here."

Doris was good at this. She should be a psychiatrist. Unlike the others, she didn't treat me differently from normal, didn't give me a chance to wallow in self-pity. They made them tough and full of common-sense in Mabe where Doris had been born and brought up.

It must have been her idea for me to help out with the rooms. That way she could keep an eye on me. The other chambermaid was ill, but they could easily have drafted in one of the waitresses who might have been more of a help than I was. Still, I guess Harry figured Doris being a mother figure and all, it would make sense. Better for me to start crying making up somebody's bed than out there in Reception. Not that I did it often. But I'd had my moments.

"That's it. Where next?" I asked.

"Room twenty-one," she said.

I smiled. It reminded me of the elderly couple from the last coach. The one from Huddersfield. The wife had been ancient, wrinkled, but with the life-force behind her eyes – and a man by her side who still imagined her as a twenty-one year old. Where would I ever find a man like that?

"Room twenty-one?" I said. "That's a nice room."

"There'll *all* good rooms," said Doris with the air of someone who owned the bedrooms rather than cleaned them. "We work hard to keep them like that."

When we finished the final room, I went out to lunch. I felt like a stranger in my own land, wearing a track suit (an *old* tracksuit) and the maid's blue tabard on top, instead of my normal uniform. I couldn't sit in the staffroom with its edgy atmosphere and even worse, the looks of pity. Instead, Alfie made me a sandwich and I took it across the road, sat on a bench opposite the hotel, gazed out to sea.

I'd promised Harry I wouldn't make any rash decisions. Wouldn't go up to Bristol right away, but that had been three days ago. I hadn't been ready then, knew I couldn't face my sister. But now, something clicked into place in my head. I got out my mobile, checked the train times, looked for a cheap hotel. I thought about the backpacking hostel my sister had gone to. Sure. They must have such things in Bristol too. Or a youth hostel.

Maybe my sister, Sophie would be pleased to see me. Maybe she wouldn't. Fifty-fifty chance, better than the lottery. I could live with that.

*

"Can I buy you a coffee?" the man asked.

I didn't answer. Figured he was a creep. A creep with an expensive three-piece-suit and a serious looking tie. Perv! Otherwise, why would you ask a stranger on a train if you could buy them a coffee - unless you were looking for something else?

I got up and walked away from my seat and the guy looked puzzled. I could buy my own bloody coffee. I asked myself if I'd have felt the same before someone had assaulted me. I couldn't answer. And maybe from here on all men would be suspect. All except the ones I knew and trusted. Joe, Harry, and now - Matthew Barry; a man who'd taken the skin off his knuckles to defend my honour.

He'd sent me flowers, and an instinct told me it was something he rarely did. I mean the guy didn't get up until noon, so he'd hardly be one of those organised people who thought about things like sending roses. And roses, they were a signal. They meant something. But these were white, not red. So, not romance then, but purity. I'd meant to phone him, say thanks. Maybe I'd send him a postcard from Bristol.

I sipped the coffee. It wasn't as good as Smithy makes, but this was a buffet car. I bought an over-priced cereal bar that was advertised as a flapjack, was like rubber and had little taste in it, or perhaps that was just me. Most food tasted bland now.

The buffet car seemed as good a place as any to spend the rest of the journey, so I sat looking out of the window, watching the world go by. It was better than going back to my seat with the man opposite me watching every move. Or pretending to read the newspaper I'd picked up in Truro Station.

We arrived at six thirty and I grabbed my small holdall and made my way towards the taxi rank outside Temple Meads. The station was fizzing with activity, colour, excitement – people buzzing with it as they rushed to meet arriving passengers. Sweethearts, friends, mothers, fathers, brothers – sisters. I didn't feel part of it. No one rushed to meet me.

"Where to, love?"

It was a question I'd been mulling over on the train. Did I head straight for Sophie's house in St Andrews or to the place I'd booked and paid for already? Maybe Sophie worked shifts. I knew nothing about her or her life.

"The YHA place," I said.

"What? The one over at Harbourside?"

"I don't know. It's a youth hostel about a mile from the railway station."

"That'll be it, then," the taxi driver said. "Next to the Arnolfini – on the quay."

He was right. It was on the quay in a fancy area of Bristol, at the heart of the tourist district. £22 a night for a private room. I could have paid even less and had a bunk bed in one of the dormitories, but somehow I felt my dorm days were over.

I took a shower, spent time over my make up and looked at the result in the mirror. It wasn't bad, not for someone who'd been smacked in the mouth a few days earlier. I put on a decent pair of jeans and a black roll neck sweater along with my black corduroy jacket and grey Wrangler ankle boots - I'd bought them in a charity shop for a fiver. I got them cheap, because I have small feet. Size three. I figured the result was okay. I wasn't out to win any fashion awards, but I was meeting my sister for the first time, I reckoned she was worth the effort.

The woman on the front desk seemed surprised when I asked if she'd mind ringing for a taxi.

"Don't get much call for that with our usual guests," she said. "They normally walk into town and save their money for drink."

"I'm going over to St Andrews."

"Ah. Bit of a walk, then."

"And I don't drink." I don't know why I said that and I don't think the woman believed me. Obviously I *do* drink, just not very often, and when I do, the outcome is predictable. I get hammered with very little effort.

The drive across town didn't seem to take long, but maybe that was because I was busy writing all these different scripts in my head. What would Sophie say? What would I say? How it would be. Now that the time had arrived, I felt nervous as hell. And I understood why my sister had got cold feet when she'd come down to Cornwall. It wasn't easy.

I stood outside the huge front door, feeling small, and wanted to change my mind. Felt like running, the way Sophie had.

The house was big and old fashioned, but one of those that look as if they might be comfortable to live in. The white and grey paintwork had seen better times and there was no bell, just one large, brass knocker that someone had lovingly polished. So – there was little money here for upkeep, but there was pride. Someone still cared, tried to go against the economic grain. It was a sentiment I recognised.

"I've come to see my sister Sophie," I told the woman who pulled open the huge front door. She was elderly but held herself erect, with the poise of a ballerina, and she had a strange smile; almost angelic.

"Well, don't stand outside in the cold, me dear, come on in. She lives on the next floor up. Best tenant I ever had. Lovely girl. But then you'd know that already."

"Yes," I said. And somehow I knew it was true.

"Must be lovely to have somebody close like that," she said. "I've never had any siblings. Always wanted a sister."

Me too.

"Go on up then, dear. She's there. Heard her come in a while ago."

Could it be that simple? I just knock on her door and she invites me in.

The look on Sophie's face wasn't shock, just a weary acceptance as she stepped aside to let me in.

"I knew you were coming," she said. She sounded neither happy, nor sad, just resigned. "The twin thing, I guess."

"You too?" I said. "You get that?"

"Sure, we came from the same egg." She smiled. "Shared a womb. Though Gran tells me you were greedy and took most of the grub."

I was confused.

"You weighed in a whole pound heavier," Sophie explained.

"I only just found out you existed," I told her. And even to me, it sounded lame.

"Me too. Gran told me before Christmas. Hell of a great present."

"Yeah? But then why . . .?"

"Did I run away? I wanted to meet you sooo much, Stevie."

"You *did*?"

"I was being cruel to be kind. Didn't want to find you and have to lose you again."

"You won't lose me. I won't leave, I promise. Never! Is that what people have done to you, Sophie? Left?" I was thinking about my grandmother. First my mother, then my grandmother. It must have been devastating for my sister.

"No, I was thinking more of me leaving *you*. There's no good way to say this, Stevie. I've got cancer."

Chapter 22

My eyelids were gummed shut and my head was clamped in some kind of heavy vice affair where pygmies with massive hammers took turns pounding it. Even my teeth hurt. I ran my tongue along them, checking, taking inventory. None missing, but they were coated with a sticky goo and my tongue had an acre of fur on it. I tried to lift my head up, but it was too heavy for my neck to move. My mouth was desert-dry. I could drink a gallon of water and still feel thirsty.

"You too?" a voice said. It was weak and croaky.

I finally prised my eyelids open with an effort that seemed far too great for such a trivial result.

"Me too *what*?" I asked the voice.

"Hangover," said my sister.

"Ah. Now it makes sense."

"We shifted two bottles of wine, last night. I don't usually buy more than a bottle," she said, "but it was a Bogof."

"Bogof?"

"Buy one get one free – at Tesco."

I laughed. It hurt my head even more.

"What?" asked Sophie.

"*Tesco*. We even do our shoplifting in the same place."

"Sure," she said. "We're twins. I'll make coffee." She nodded towards the kitchen. It was at the end of the hall.

I figured she could hold her booze better than me. I couldn't even get off the couch.

Bits of last night came back to me. The laughing, the crying. Throwing our arms around each other, clinging on tight and sobbing for ages. She'd made us spaghetti and we'd got drunk. It seemed like a great idea at the time.

She'd told me about her life in Canada. About her grandmother - *my* grandmother. I was surprised that Sophie hadn't known about me until now. But our grandmother had kept her word that she wouldn't say anything about me. My sister had only recently found out who her mother was and had tried to meet her.

I wasn't surprised that mother hadn't even replied to the letter. She wouldn't want to come face to face with her mistakes. And it *was* a mistake. I've tried not to judge her, but it's too hard not to. I'd never had children of course, but I don't think I could have given one away, no matter how desperate the situation. Surprisingly, Sophie didn't seem to blame the woman, or hold anything against her. But then maybe having cancer does that to you. Gives you a different perspective. Shows you what's important, what isn't.

I felt cheated. I'd only just found her and now I could lose her again. But I wouldn't let that happen. We'd fight this together. Sophie had been diagnosed with breast cancer. She'd only found the lump when she was in London, maybe that was why she hadn't been in touch with her grandmother. Didn't want to worry the old woman when she was ill herself. Although Sophie had already told me that, as badly as she'd wanted to find me, if she'd known just how sick the old lady was, she'd never have left Canada.

It gave me another insight into the character of my grandmother and I wished I'd known her. She seemed like a selfless old lady, concerned only for the happiness of the pair of us - and even her daughter who came out as a villain in the piece. But what did I know? My mother's motives may well have been pure and she was doing the best she could.

"Hope that's okay. Coffee's a bit weak, had to make it stretch to two. I haven't been shopping lately."

"Tastes like nectar," I said. And it did, for it had been made by my sister.

"I'll have to keep you around," she laughed. "Most people say I'm useless in the kitchen."

"You too, eh? I still can't believe you're my older sister," I said.

"Hey! Less of the old. There's only ten minutes in it. And that's because you sent me out first to recce the joint, make sure there was enough grub for both of us."

We fell into a contented silence after that, drinking our coffee, each busy with our thoughts. For the first time in my life, I could truly say that I felt whole. The other half of the jigsaw had been slotted into place – and it was a perfect fit. Except for one thing. Sophie was ill.

"What's next?" I asked her.

"Don't let's spoil the day. It's a beautiful morning out there," said Sophie. "Let's go to the park and have breakfast."

"But we need to talk about this. You can't ignore it."

She raised a hand to stop me. "Let's just enjoy a day together. Relax in the sun. Do a bit of sightseeing. We'll talk later, I promise," she said.

And I believed her. She was my big sister. I felt like I'd finally come home.

*

The optimistic feeling of spring was everywhere; in the mild weather and the cheerful shafts of sunlight filtering through the trees like golden lattice work in the park opposite Sophie's house. Carpets of daffodils and narcissi were spread out lavishly under the tree canopy. It was a riot of shades and shapes; and strings of colourful bunting tied to the mobile café flapped gently in the small breeze, giving the whole place a carnival atmosphere. People were decorating trees with yellow and purple sashes, for Easter. There were others rolling painted eggs down a hill. It was a rural idyll in the middle of a city.

I couldn't have been happier. I looked at my sister and smiled. She was smiling too. An onlooker might think we were both on some form of medication.

"Cake?" she asked. "They have great home made cake here. And ice cream. Cake's no good without ice cream. I love ice cream. Don't you?"

"I do," I said. "But I thought you said breakfast. Ice cream for *breakfast*?"

"Sure. I have it all the time, beats toast any day."

She was right. It was the best breakfast I'd ever tasted. Maybe we'd hit on a hangover cure.

The excited shouts of small children drifted over from the playground behind us. It was a happy, innocent sound that would drag a smile from the most cynical of lips, but it seemed to have the opposite effect on my sister. Her face was sad and pensive, and when she turned to look at me, there was an echo of loss that sent a shiver through me. It made me want to cry for her.

"Have you got a special man in your life?" she asked.

"I seem to repel them."

"Maybe only the bad ones," she said. "The right one is still out there, waiting."

"Think so? Maybe I'm just like mother. Can't find a decent man who wants to stay. How about you?"

"I was married once. He left." Her voice was flat.

"Shit, Sophie. I'm sorry."

"Yeah. So was I. He was a good man, but he couldn't take the pain anymore."

"The pain?"

Sophie's eyes held a depth of sorrow that I hadn't seen before and I shook my head. Wanted her to know that she didn't need to rake through it, whatever it was. Not for me. She seemed to understand.

"It's okay. I want you to know everything about me. I feel like you're one half of me."

"Same here," I said and I found it difficult to breathe. This must be what it's like to have a family, I thought. A *real* family.

"We had a daughter. Emily she was called. An angel." Sophie gave a small sigh. "Everybody thinks their kids are angels, right? But she truly was. You know?"

"I know." And somehow I did, for I could see it there in my sister. The love. The hurt. "What happened?"

"She got sick. She was only five when she died." Sophie automatically looked at the kids behind us - laughing, whooping with joy. The way only kids can. No worries. No mortgage. No fear of losing your job. Still untouched by life's insanity.

"God, Sophie. I'm so, so, sorry."

"I know." She reached over and held my hand, like I was the one who needed comfort. "I wish you'd been there, Stevie. Things might have been different. I drove my lovely man away. I mourned forever and he never seemed to start. We just drifted away from each other."

"Maybe there's still a chance."

"No." My sister shrugged her shoulders. "All boats burned behind me. He got married again. He seems happy. I think it was easier for him. Men don't carry their kids around for nine months or have to push them through the birth canal, do they? Maybe it's not so hard for them."

"Maybe not," I said. But then I'd never met a man I considered husband-material, never mind one who'd be safe in charge of small children. I couldn't even picture myself as a mother. This maternal stuff was complicated. I had never been tempted to coo at small babies belonging to friends, or brave enough to lift up the tiny bundles in their baby-grows. But I could see that Sophie must have been a lovely Mum.

"Emily," I said. "You have any photos of her?"

"Loads. We can look at them later, if you like."

"Yes, I'd like that." I said.

*

The next day we went shopping. I went window shopping, but Sophie actually bought stuff. Like the beautiful, bead-encrusted top from an exclusive boutique. It was turquoise. I thought then how daring she was – and brave. She didn't give a hoot about playing it safe with her red hair. She loved vibrant colours and to hell with what experts said about skin tones, or conventional wisdom suggested you should wear with hair the colour of deep-mahogany. She was like me; people accused her of dying her hair. And we'd both been called carrot-top and ginger-head, even though our natural colour looked nothing like either of those.

I suddenly felt drab beside this woman who took chances, who went against the grain. Me in my black jeans and top. I wasn't a fashion victim, but I'd always gone for safety, for colours that blended in with my hair; olive greens, dark browns and blacks. Oh, and white was good. White was a safety net. And *gold*, I guess, if you were going somewhere special - but I rarely went anywhere special.

"I love purple," she said, as if she'd picked up on my thoughts.

"I do too. But on other people."

"It'd look great on you, Stevie. On both of us. Let's make a pact."

"What?"

"We'll celebrate. When I beat this bloody cancer thing, we'll go out bold as brass. We'll both wear purple and eat cake and ice cream again."

"Shit, Sophie. You'll make me cry." It was the one jarring note in a perfect day, but I suppose we had to think about it sometime.

"Never mind all that. Just promise me we'll do it."

"I promise," I said. And it was a promise I was going to keep.

*

I made several promises to my sister. That I would go home which meant going back to work. She didn't want me staying around, visiting her in hospital, watching her throw up and lose her hair. She said she couldn't stand that.

They were brutal promises to extract from me, and we spent three days debating them and I fell into a dark, depressive mood, which she ended up dragging me out of. It should have been *me* comforting *her*, looking after her. Cleaning up when she puked and helping her pick out a wig. But she would have none of it.

These promises she dragged from me were non-negotiable, more like demands. But in the end I gave in. It was her disease, not ours, she told me. She was happy to have found me and if things got so bad that she couldn't cope she'd come down to Cornwall for a break in between chemo-cycles. I tried to talk her into letting me stay while we fought the bastard thing together, but there was no shifting her. She was the most pig-headed, single-minded, quietly courageous person I had ever met. And she was my sister.

We said our goodbyes at the station and both of us cried. It must have looked weird, two redheads, same faces, same size, same age, red-rimmed eyes, clinging onto each other as if it was the last time we'd do it.

I texted her from the train to tell her I was missing her already and she sent me one straight back. "Me too. Luv u lots. C u soon. LOL. Look in yr bag, Sis".

"Ee, that's gorgeous, duck."

The woman sitting opposite me was from somewhere in the Midlands. I can't remember where exactly she'd said, for I was thinking about other stuff, but she was a friendly old girl and had already called me 'duck' several times, so I guessed she did it to everyone. And she was right, it was completely gorgeous. The top was smothered in luscious, crystal beading that shone when the light hit it and the turquoise colour was glorious.

The card with it read: "I bought it for YOU. Enjoy it. And don't just look at it; find somewhere special to wear it. See you soon. Your loving sister, Sophie."

Chapter 23

"Don't just stand there like a fart in a thunderstorm; we've got people expecting cream teas in the restaurant."

Agata looked upset. I don't think her English-to-Polish dictionary catered for Harry's vocabulary, which was limited in certain areas, but creative in others.

"It's okay, Agata," I tried to reassure her. "Mr Evans understands that the problem with the scones isn't your fault," I said. "Just carry on setting-up and I'll get Smithy to run them into you as soon as he gets back from the bakery."

Harry looked flabbergasted. "We're buying scones from the bakery? Why are we buying them in, when we've got a perfectly good kitchen of our own?"

I took Harry gently by the arm (he had a broken hand) and steered him away from our Maitre d'. She had enough problems. So did Harry, of course, but some of them were of his own making. Buying cheap booze from bootleggers and not paying them off when they threatened to break your hand might be seen as a bad business decision in some places.

"So? he asked, when we were out of earshot of both Agata and Joe. "Why aren't we making our own cream teas?"

"We are," I assured him. "Just not the scones." I raised my hand to hold back a torrent of swearing. "Cock-up on the catering front."

"What is wrong with that bloody chef?"

"Not his fault, this time," I said. "Your damn dog got into the kitchen and snaffled the lot. Time Alfie and Smithy got to him, there were only crumbs left."

Harry looked as if he wanted to add something, but for once seemed lost for words. Ask a philosopher about life; the meaning of it, where it's heading and why we're all even bothering. *Ask several, take a sampling.* You'll likely get a different reply from each of them. Life can fluctuate between the stars and the deepest, blackest pit, depending on what it gives you and most important, I guess, on how you deal with the sort of crap that it throws at you.

Right now I can't complain. I'm doing the job I love. I've found my sister. I could lose her. So, my life is good in parts, bad in others. My sister Sophie is battling away up in Bristol – *without me*. She told me not to worry; said it wasn't that bad. I didn't believe her. She'd lost a breast and lymph nodes from under her arm, so how easy could that be?

She'd been in hospital for five days. It sounded barbaric. How could they throw you out after only five days and expect you to pick up your normal life? She said things were fine. I tried to imagine it, but couldn't, and Sophie didn't want to talk about it. One day she'd tell me, she said, but not now; it was too soon. *Having a breast taken off.* I shuddered. Wondered how they did it. Was it just a quick slice and that was it? I felt sick thinking about it. I wanted to cry and scream and tell the world what an unfair place it was.

At least Sophie was being looked after. She'd hired a nurse/companion to help, for she couldn't lift her arm. *I* could have been her nurse. *I* could have helped her. But her latest text said that this was the way she wanted it and when she felt well enough, maybe I could come up. She'd had her hair cut into the same short, spiky style as mine. Easier to watch your hair fall out when it's already short, she'd said. Shit!

Harry's fortunes had also been mixed. The Good, the Bad and the Ugly, according to Doris. She reckons the ugly speaks for itself, but then she's always been irreverent about our heroic leader, never been tempted to sing *Hail to the Chief*. And he's not that bad. He's using a new deodorant now which seems to be doing the trick. And he's still a fair advert for Betty Stogs. Harry reckons "good old *Betty*" is the finest of Cornish ales and the only woman he would want in his life.

Then there's the broken right hand. That's the bad. He still maintains that he broke it putting the empties out back, but we've got a new barman now who's keen to impress, so I can't see Harry putting the crates out himself. It smacks too much of physical labour.

The good – and this is the really great bit – is that Harry Evans, for all his faults, has never been one to give up easily. He's known for his stubbornness, something that Doris claims we *both* have in common. Thank God that's all we've got in common. Well maybe that and our love for the hotel.

The Royal is full right now. One hundred per cent occupancy! You might think there's been some sort of miraculous intervention, but mostly it's down to a convention of real ale enthusiasts in town and the West Country Football Cup - a competition for kids, being hosted by Newquay this year. Harry advertised in a footy magazine and now we're swamped with miniature David Beckhams and their families, as well as weird looking blokes with strange tee-shirts that don't quite fit over their beer bellies - discussing the finer points of secondary fermentation, mashing in, and the virtues of different flavoured hops.

But my job is the same whoever the customers. Smiley face, fire-fighting when things go wrong; when the guests in our few rooms that are still awaiting a makeover discover that the delights of *an intimate family hotel with old fashioned values* also means old fashioned plumbing.

"Phone call for you, Stevie." Joe's normal voice was what you might call refined, but right now he sounded like a cross between a drill sergeant and Genghis Kahn.

"I'm not deaf," I said.

"Sorry, Stevie. Thought you were out back."

"Right. Good. Now who's on the phone?"

"Some crazy woman asking if you'd like to be a nun." Joe screwed his face up.

"Shit, Joe. Do I look like nun-material?"

*

I'm the first to admit that as a singer goes, I can just about hold a tune in a paper bag and only then if someone else is holding the bag. And that singing 'Maria' in *The Sound of Music* would be a step too far - even for an Amateur Dramatic Production. But I think my lot were desperate. They couldn't think of anyone else. I was the right size. I was the right age. *Really*? I was in the company. I had a pulse. But I couldn't reach the sort of high notes that Richard Rodgers had envisaged when he wrote the score.

I said NO. It was an emphatic no. But Gloria Endersley, the Chairperson of our group is a formidable force. She's five foot nothing, even shorter than I am, wears all kinds of flamboyant headgear and long, flowing robes. Her width is roughly the same as her height. Her voice is deep and dramatic. Someone unkind might call it affected, but I don't think she'd mind, for she sees it as part of the arsenal of a 'thespian'. Real actors, of course, are nothing like this, but no one would have the nerve to say that to Gloria, she's not the sort of person you pick an argument with.

She doesn't recognise the intrinsic properties of the word *no*. So, after ten exhausting minutes on the phone with her, I found myself agreeing to take a couple of singing lessons to help me hit the high notes. The group would pay for them, she said cheerfully. And I wouldn't have to worry, because she would be with me all the way, for she was playing Mother Superior. *God preserve us all.*

Chapter 24

"I'm coming up," I said.

"No, you're not. I just wanted to hear your voice. I'll be fine. I've got a *very* attractive elastic sleeve on. It's black and quite sexy."

"A what?"

"Compression sleeve. Fits from my shoulder to my wrist. Supposed to reduce the swelling of the Lymphedema."

"And has it?"

"Early days yet," said Sophie.

And I could tell from her voice that she was struggling, that she must be in some kind of serious pain. It was late at night, and she wasn't sleeping.

"So, tell me about this Lymphedema thing," I said. "Sounds a right swine."

"I phoned so you could cheer me up. Not to give you a blow by blow account of the dodgy flow of my lymphatic system. It's a bugger, Stevie. Okay? But I need to forget all that."

"Sure," I said, feeling feeble and guilty that I'd been more interested in putting my own mind at rest than Sophie's. But hey – nobody's perfect and the word *cancer* does things to you. "So, on a scale of 1 to 10," I asked her "how attractive and sexy *do* you look in this black, elastic sleeve?"

"Easily a twelve. Got an arm like a Sumo wrestler."

"Always a good look," I said.

And she laughed. "Now what's new with you? You got a man yet?"

"All those worth getting have already been got. I've decided to become a nun."

I told her about the couple of singing lessons I'd had. With two different teachers. The first woman had encouraged me to pinch the cheeks of my bum in, although I failed to see the connection between pulling in my arse and trying to work my way through all my vocal registers to find the clever and powerful falsetto that I'd heard other people produce. Mine only came out as this pathetic head-voice that was weak and cracked in the middle of notes.

"You'll get it, girl. Keep at it. I've got faith in you and I can't wait to see you in a wimple. When's the show?"

"You're not thinking of coming?"

"'Course I am. Give me something to shoot for."

"In three months," I said. "Last week in June first week in July."

"Perfect. My chemo cycles should be just about finished by then. Save me a seat."

She blew me a dramatic goodnight kiss down the phone.

Stuffed! I was totally stuffed. I couldn't let my sister down, so I'd have to go back to the singing lessons. I could already feel Richard Rodgers and Oscar Hammerstein convulsing in their graves. And I cursed Gloria Endersley for dragging me into it and for being so ambitious. Why hadn't she picked Oklahoma? I could probably have coped with that.

I fell asleep, and in my dream, nuns with angry faces threw rotten fruit at me and Sophie sat in the front row laughing. My mother hovered overhead, her face grim, and her black dress in tatters. She looked like a giant black crow. I forgot my lines. But Sophie didn't seem to mind. She was my sister, after all. She just grinned as she ate her ice cream.

*

Joe stepped into my tiny office at the back of Reception and he looked as if somebody had died.

"Christ, Joe. What?" I immediately thought about Sophie.

"Don't shoot the messenger, will you?"

"I'll strangle the bloody messenger if he doesn't hurry up and tell me what's up."

"There's a call for you from the police, Stevie. Just giving you a head's up before I put it through."

You always think the worst, don't you? And I was terrified it was something to do with Sophie. It never crossed my mind that it could be about me. So, hearing the policeman's familiar voice sent a jolt through my nervous system.

"Miss Anderson?"

"Yes."

"It's D.C. Alan Winter. I wondered if it would be convenient to come and see you. Explain a few things. Better in person than over the phone."

"Sure," I said. "I'll get the kettle on. I don't suppose a couple of Kit-Kats would amount to police bribery, would they," I giggled. I don't know why I giggled, except I was nervous and I do daft things when I'm nervous.

"Kit-Kats would be lovely, Miss Anderson. Shall we say twenty minutes?"

We said twenty minutes. And it was the longest twenty minutes of my life. Plenty of time for my stomach to churn up a whole bunch of acid and my head to produce a full-blown migraine and my imagination to scare the shit out of me. But that was the easy bit.

The hard bit was seeing the policeman's face again and remembering that night, the assault that I'd tried to put behind me, bury under a blanket of concern for my sister. But I guess I'd always known it was only a matter of time before it resurfaced and I would need to go to court, would have to see the guy again. I know you can go behind a screen, at least that's what I'd imagined. But I didn't want to do that. I wanted him to have to look in my eyes. The way I would look in his. I wasn't in the wrong here, it was Christopher Newly.

Detective Constable Winter struggled to make himself comfortable on one of our tatty staffroom sofas. The guts had been knocked out of it by the pressure of lots of backsides – skinny ones, heavy ones – so that you sometimes ended up sliding off the thing. He was a tall man with long gangling legs that stretched out awkwardly in front of him.

"Sorry to break into your day," he said.

"That's okay; I've got somebody covering for me. Is everything all right?"

"Thought you better know about the new situation right away."

"Situation? Has something changed?" I said. "I thought the Crown Prosecution Service was busy forming their case against him."

"The CPS were – *are*. But something's happened you should be aware of."

He sipped his tea, like he was filling in time, like he wasn't keen to get to the bad bit. And I guessed there *was* a bad bit. It was written in his face.

"So . . .?"

"So – it's a condition of his bail that he reports in once a week to a police station. And he hasn't done that for two weeks now."

"What! Didn't anybody notice? Don't they keep a record of these things?"

"Well of course they do. But there's a lot of stuff going on in the county right now. Manpower's spread thin. I'm sorry."

"So am I." I said. "Where does that leave me? Can I walk down the street without worrying about him coming for me? And he knows where I live. God Almighty!"

"I'm sure you'll be fine. I don't think he has any notion of coming after you."

"You don't, eh? Well, what else would he do?"

"He knows he's due in court any day now. I think he's hoofing it as far away from here as he can get. I'd put money on it - that he's not even in the county any more."

"Well I hope it's not your own money," I said, angrily. *You trust the police. You trust the system to get you some kind of payback. Some kind of justice.*

"I know it's hard."

"You reckon?" *Of course it's bloody hard. It was bad enough before, when I knew I'd have to go and face him and all the sleazy questioning from some poxy defence barrister. But this was worse.* "The bastard's going to get away with it, isn't he?"

"He'll have a warrant out against him for skipping bail and non-appearance in court."

"Terrific."

"Look, I realise you're worried. And that's why I came round to see you. But the slightest hint anything's wrong – I'm here. Just pick up the phone."

He gave me his number - Detective Constable Alan Winter - both at the station and his mobile. So I figured that he got the idea I was terrified, and took it seriously. What else could he do? It wasn't like the movies, this was Cornwall. He could hardly station a man outside my door.

Joe was just as frightened as I was. Violence isn't in his nature, but he said he'd look out for me. I was to come and get him if anything weird happened. I loved him for that, but I knew he wouldn't be much of a deterrent against somebody like Christopher Newly.

Harry was the same. He said that if the bastard as much as set foot inside his hotel again, he'd sort it. Or he knew people who could. I didn't doubt that for a minute – that Harry knew all kinds of people. You only had to look at the plaster on his broken hand.

Chapter 25

Aaaaaah Aaaaaah Aaaaaah Aaaaaah Aaaaaah Aaaaaah Aaaaaah Aaaaaah

Aaaaaah Aaaaaah Aaaaaah Aaaaaah Aaaaaah Aaaaaah Aaaaaah Aaaaaah

Flah flah nee *ah* nee nee ah. Flee flee flee *na* nee nee na.

"Stevie. Stevie! What the hell's going on in there?"

The pounding on my door was loud enough to filter through the headphones. I opened up, figuring the fire alarm had gone off and I hadn't noticed. The massive fists trying to hammer my door down belonged to Doris.

"What the hell's happening?" I asked.

Doris was flushed, her face covered in red blotches and she was puffing out gouts of air through strained lips like she'd run the 100 metres.

"That's what I'm asking *you*," she said - a bit accusingly, I felt. "I've just run up every bloody floor. We thought somebody was attacking you. What was all that screaming about?"

"Screaming? Oh, you mean this?" I tried another of my vocal warm-ups, a single arpeggio this time.

"God, Stevie. You're not expecting people to pay money to listen to that, are you? It's like some sort of animal in pain."

"Thanks for the support. It's not the finished product yet - *obviously"* I said, a bit miffed. "It's only a warm-up exercise."

I'd been pleased with the progress I'd made, but not everybody seemed to appreciate how much work went into it, or the finer points of voice training.

"This ain't just from *me*. I been sent up to ask you to stop. Guests are complaining. 'Spect you can't get the full blast of it with those on." Doris nodded at the headphones that I'd been following my vocal tutorial on. "Pregnant woman in number twenty said she nearly had the baby scared out of her. It's coming down through the pipes."

"What, the baby?"

"Don't be daft. The *singing*. It's coming through the plumbing. You can hear it on every floor, Stevie. Up to me - I'd say go for it, but Harry told me to come up and shut you up."

"That's what he said?"

"That's the only bit I could repeat."

"Bastard!"

"Yeah, well. You know Harry. He's all for encouraging culture an all." She laughed.

"So, you're an emissary," I said.

"A what?"

"Doesn't matter." Doris had drawn the short straw. Harry would hardly come all the way up himself. He gets nosebleeds when he goes above the second floor. "Cup of tea, Auntie D? You look done in."

"That'd be great," said Doris, making herself at home on the end of my bed. She patted it. "This one of them memory-foam things?"

I gave her a cynical look. "Do I look like somebody could afford a memory-foam mattress?"

Doris blew a bead of sweat from the end of her nose. "I swear somebody keeps adding more stairs to that little lot when my back's turned."

"Should've taken the lift."

"Lift's out again," she said.

"Aw, shit! One step forward and two steps back in this place."

"Harry wants you in his office."

"Doesn't want much, does he? This is supposed to be my day off. And why didn't he phone if he needed me?"

"Think his nibs already tried that." She looked pointedly at the headphones."

"Yeah, okay. But we'll have our tea first."

"Suits me," said Doris. She'd have made a fine union-rep.

*

"You're joking! The lift's out of order? If you put this in a script nobody would believe it." The man didn't smile, so I assumed it wasn't a compliment.

"I'm sorry, Sir. But these things happen."

"Seems they all happen here. Should've listened to my wife and booked in at The Headland."

I wanted to ask him why he hadn't. If I had the money for a 4-star luxury hotel, I'd have gone there. And the guy looked as if he had the money. And he certainly had the attitude. But I just swallowed hard and smiled. Harry wouldn't thank me if I bad-mouthed one of the guests.

The guy must have picked up on my thoughts. "All my son's friends in the team are staying here." His expression said that this showed a lack of taste on the part of the organisers.

"I see," I said, *neutral replies being something I've cultivated over years in the hotel industry*.

The miniature hooligans from the football tournament hadn't been easy guests. Doris had been within an inch of cuffing one of them who'd stolen toilet rolls from her trolley and decorated the corridor. *High spirits* was the verdict of the sociopathic parents belonging to this ten year old vandal. But he was no different from the rest of his team mates. They'd been running round the place like trainee Al Capones firing water pistols at each other and frightening an eighty-four year old widow from Grantham who'd threatened to sue us.

"And when might the lift be fixed, do you think?" The man's tone was dripping with sarcasm, but I refused to let him rile me; acted like he was a valued customer and not a pompous, conceited arse who thought the rest of us were beneath him.

"The lift engineer is on his way from Penzance, Sir," I said and smiled sweetly.

"Let's hope he has a map."

It was a fair enough exit line, I suppose - if you were a creep who got cheap laughs at the expense of hotel receptionists. Hotel receptionists who couldn't answer back because of some customer-service-code that said customers were always right. They weren't.

Joe sent out another one of his heavy, pissed-off sighs, a signal that he wasn't enjoying himself. He'd been making out bills before Changeover-Day. I gave him my five-minute-fag-break signal and nodded towards the backdoor. He hit save on the computer and with a look of relief took over from me behind the desk. Joe wasn't keen on admin. But it was part of the job and at least we both still had a job, something that a few months ago would have seemed unlikely.

Guests had a special outdoor smoking area at the front of the hotel with some tables and chairs and a cheerful-looking canvas awning. Nothing luxurious, but better than the alley out back among the empty beer crates where staff polluters were forced to go. The alley had a darker meaning for me now, but I'd been trying to work my way through that.

I pulled hard on the cigarette and thought about Harry. He was a chancer in many ways, not the ideal hotelier if you were to list all the qualities needed for the job. But he was fighting tooth and nail to keep the place open, to keep us all in a job. He'd done his best to attract extra cash, even put his house on the market and was living in a room at the hotel, hoping that the house sale would go through quickly and give him a breathing space until the next miracle happened along. Or the country's economy came off life-support.

According to Harry, 'banks hoard cash'. He said this with a bitter, reproachful tone and called his own bank a whorehouse, like his animosity was on a deep, personal level. Banks won't part with cash, he told me – especially not to small businesses that could be affected by bad weather and changes in people's holidaying habits.

If you had *working capital problems* that needed *cash flow solutions*, he reckoned the banks had one slogan for people like him. One they wouldn't dare use in all those fancy T.V. adverts of theirs. I didn't ask him what it was, but I figured it would rely heavily on the Anglo Saxon words for body parts. And take profanity to a whole new level.

Harry had bored me to death with his business speak. Banks were given a rating on some kind of mumbo jumbo formula that included 'capital safety levels', the strength of their 'loan portfolio' and how they met their commitments. But when I'd asked our noble leader what that meant in plain English, his translation was more or less what I expected. "You're up shit creek," he said.

After that in-depth analysis of the banking system, I hadn't asked anything else. But I now understood why Harry and his bank manager weren't on first name terms.

"Stevie, you out here?" It was Agata. "You're needed on Reception."

"God's sake. I only just got here," I shouted and looked wistfully at the cigarette that still had a couple of decent drags left in it.

"Man with lift is here."

Chapter 26

This lift-guy was different from the last one, at least thirty years younger, a couple of stone lighter and a whole lot more attractive. He had on one of those tee-shirts with the logo of the company across it. His pecs were bursting through the thin material and his substantial biceps pushed the tee-shirt to its limits. He carried a heavy toolkit in one hand, swung it like it was a kid's toy. He was an impressive sight if you were into that sort of thing.

Joe called him slutty. But both Doris and Maureen - our other chambermaid - said they wouldn't step over him to get to Harry. *Me*? Well, I've given up on men, as you know.

He did a great job with the lift, although it was hard to get volunteers to join him for the trial run. I suppose disaster movies with people hurtling through the lift shaft to a gruesome death wouldn't have helped his cause.

He'd travelled down from Newcastle and ours was the second lift he'd tackled today after a posh hotel in Penzance. It was comforting to know we were in such hallowed company. The up-market hotel, not the bloke.

When he'd finished, he changed from his working gear into an impressive suit and had dinner in the restaurant. He invited me for a drink in the bar when my shift was over, but there was something about him that set my teeth on edge. Too much perfection in one package seemed too good to be true. Doris said I was an idiot. Joe said I was a sage. And I wondered if I'd ever be brave enough to date again.

Watching the lift man go through his paces had rung a distant bell with Joe, and he retrieved an ancient postit-note that he'd written out for me when I'd been in Bristol with Sophie. He was apologetic. But I understood. Some things get put on the back burner in this hectic cookhouse of life. Still, Joe wrung his hands in remorse.

"He'll think I did it on *purpose*," he fretted, "and I didn't."

"Joe, it's okay. I'll call the man. I'll explain. In the great scheme of things it doesn't matter."

But it mattered to Joe that he hadn't passed along the message from Matthew Barry. For Joe was a perfectionist, one of those people whose high ideals often mean they shoot themselves in the foot.

"It *does* matter. He's a decent guy. And he likes you – I can tell."

"I'm not interested."

"Call him," he said. "He's not like the fish-man or that asshole barman. He'll look after you, Stevie. He'll respect you."

"And how do you know?"

"Because I see things other people are too busy to see."

"Yeah?"

"And I love you, Stevie. I'm the mother you wish you had." He laughed. "And maybe he can give you a few pointers about your singing."

"You don't like my singing?"

"Life's a search for perfection."

"What's that mean?" I said. But I guess I already knew.

"There's room for improvement." Joe slapped the postit-note into my hand. "Just ring him, what can you lose?"

Getting involved with a man who didn't get up till noon, couldn't be sure where his next gig was coming from, and played music in an outfit called The Syncopated City Slickers, might put some people off. Then I remembered how he'd taken the skin off his knuckles to defend me. Maybe Joe was right. What could I lose?

I gave Matthew Barry a call. It had a déjà vu feel to it, but like Joe said – he was nothing like the fish-man. I was relieved when it went over to voice mail and I didn't have to speak to the guy in person. His answering machine wouldn't mind that I had taken so long to return the call. I tried to be cool and sophisticated, but I think I gabbled. But hell, it was a lost cause anyway. The man and I had nothing in common. He wore tuxedos and I slopped around in trackies when I wasn't wearing a blazer with the naff logo H.R. emblazoned on the pocket.

*

"Stevie, can you swing a day off?"

"What's wrong?"

"Nothing's wrong. I just want to do something," said Sophie, "and I want you to come with me."

"Anything!"

"Really? Even if it means going to see mother?"

"Why would you want to see *her*?"

"Why? She's my flesh and blood. She gave me life and I've never even met her. I need to see her in case . . ."

"You're not . . . ?" I couldn't say it. I wasn't brave enough.

"Dying? We're all dying, Stevie. Dying is as sure as being born, except they can work out when someone's going to give birth, give or take. But death? That's the real lottery."

"God, Soph."

"You on personal terms with the Maker? For you're always bringing his name up."

I couldn't answer. I just wanted to cry. Sophie's call had taken me by surprise and I wasn't ready for another confrontation with my mother. And how bad would that be with my sister in tow.

"Look, girl, I want to go and see her. *Before* I start this damn chemo. I don't want her feeling sorry for me."

"Sure. I get it."

"She doesn't need to know about my cancer. I want your promise that you won't tell her."

"But Soph . . ."

"Stevie! I need your word on this. It's important. She's got to accept me for myself. Not because she thinks I'm going to peg out any minute and she's got no choice."

"Yeah, but . . ."

"No buts. You coming or not? I could do it on my own, but I want you there. We're a double act, remember."

"Sure."

"Sure we're a double act – or sure, you'll come?"

"Both."

"Brill. So, think the slave driver will give you a day off?"

"Just say when."

"What about tomorrow? Thought I might stay overnight in a place I've heard about in Newquay. Seems the plumbing sucks and the food's not that great, but some of the staff are pretty cool."

"You're coming *here*?"

"Just booked. I told Joe not to tell you. Wanted it to be a surprise. It's okay, isn't it?"

"Okay? It's bloody brilliant. When you arriving?"

"Five minutes too soon? I'm down the road at the station. Wanted to make sure it was okay with you first."

I put the phone down and went into a strange Zen-like state. I could feel a smile tugging at my face and my mind found this peaceful place that I didn't know existed. Amazing! Instead of stressing about what might happen when Sophie went on her crusade to find a missing mother, a feeling of quiet optimism nudged its way into my head. It didn't make sense, but I went with it anyway. And who knew? Maybe our mother would welcome us both with arms wide open. Would get out the best china and the chocolate digestives.

"Wow! Hold that look," said Joe.

And I felt my face redden. "What?"

"An improvement on the one you had this morning."

"Yeah, well. One of those stupid little football brats ambushed me outside the restaurant and squirted water in my eye," I said.

"She's here, eh?" Joe grinned.

"You kept that quiet."

"Sure," he said. "I can keep a secret when I have to, when do I get to meet her?"

"How about now?"

The voice sounded strong, but the face was a shock. I suppose I'd been expecting some sort of change in my sister. But her face had lost weight and found extra lines from somewhere. Lines that were proof of the battle she'd fought, was still fighting. But she could still smile and I guess that's what stopped me from crying.

"Hey, you gorgeous red head," I said and hugged her close. She felt brittle.

"You like it?" She ran a hand through her tufts of hair.

"You never told me you had such a ravishing sister," said Joe. But I could see it in his eyes, the shock.

The reaction of the two of them was automatic. They were like a jigsaw that fitted together naturally without any kind of hesitation.

"Thought you said he was a first class pain-in-the-arse and could do with a nose job," said Sophie – "when he turns out to be the most fabulous man on the planet."

"Nose job?" Joe looked at me like he'd been betrayed and put a hand up to his nose.

"Shit, Joe. It was a metaphor. Just that you keep sticking your nose in – in the nicest way of course."

He went over to Sophie and gave her one of those theatrical hugs and kissed her on both cheeks. *"Fabulous, eh?"*

"Sure," she said. "Now where can I get a coffee in this hell hole? And is the chef having a good day, for I haven't eaten since breakfast."

Chapter 27

"I know *why* you did it," said Sophie. Her smile was serene.

I've never been able to smile at my mother like that, but then we have a history. We've rubbed and chaffed against each other since my teenage years. I wasn't an easy teenager; I'm the first to tell you that. Still, I don't think my mother could have written a book on child psychology either. We both had our faults, but she was supposed to be the adult, wasn't she?

I balanced the cup and saucer on my knee, felt awkward. It wasn't my mother's fault, I suppose, that she only had one side table and she'd given it to Sophie. Mother had dragged out the fatted calf for her long lost daughter. This turned out to be custard creams and her best teacups, but the principle was the same. And why didn't the woman use mugs, everybody normal did.

Her silence didn't phase my sister. "I understand why you sent me away," Sophie said again.

"I didn't send you away. *She* took you. You think I wanted you to go? You were my daughter and no matter how hard life would have been bringing up the two of you (my mother had the decency to look at me at this point) my heart wanted you to stay."

"But Gran said you did it to keep me safe," said Sophie.

"You cried a lot. I couldn't figure out why. Believe me, I tried to understand. To pacify you. Get you to stop. I tried everything." My mother's eyes filled up with tears.

"It's okay," said Sophie and reached for her hand.

"No it isn't. But it was the only way out. You were a cranky baby, not like Stevie here." She actually smiled at me. A wistful smile. "Stevie was a cutie, always gurgling, always content. A sweet baby, like one of those perfect ones that look out at you from the pages of magazines. He didn't mind her. Could put up with her, he said. But *you*, Sophie . . . He threatened to do something violent to shut you up."

"Who threatened Sophie?" I said.

My mother rubbed the side of her face with the heel of her hand, her eyes far away. Like she was remembering. And the memory wasn't a happy one.

"Did he hit you?" asked Sophie.

"He broke my jaw. I didn't want him hurting you, Sophie. Can you understand?"

"Who? What are you pair talking about?"

"Our father," said Sophie. "He was a drunk."

"And a psycho," said my mother. "But a good looking psycho." She gave a short, bitter laugh.

"But why didn't you tell us. What was wrong with the truth? We'd have understood," I said.

"Would you?" She gave me an odd look. "You can be judgemental at times, Stevie. It's one of your weaknesses."

"And you haven't got any, I suppose?"

"Look, you guys. Don't let's argue," said Sophie. *My sister the peacemaker.*

They went into the kitchen together. I could hear waves of soft laughter drifting through. Cups chinking. Water running, as they washed up. The sound of cupboard doors opening and closing. Normal, everyday sounds. Cosy domesticity.

I couldn't remember the last time I'd heard my mother laugh, if I ever had. Or maybe I hadn't listened enough. But she hadn't listened to me either. Not when I told her I wanted to make something of my life. When I'd taken on a job to pay my own way through college. Where had she been then? What had she been doing?

I'd always assumed that not only didn't she love me, but that she hadn't even liked me. Was I wrong? When she'd said just now that I'd been a sweet baby, was it true? My mother and I had a huge gap to bridge. But maybe Sophie could help us. My sister Sophie. *The bridge builder.*

Those were the same words my grandmother had used in her letter to me. The one that arrived with the will. The letter of special instructions. She'd asked two things of me, things that when I'd first read them seemed impossible. One: I was to find my sister. And two: to build bridges. I was to reunite the family; my mother, Sophie and I. It wasn't rocket science the old woman had said. But I knew it was.

My grandmother had guessed at the coldness between mother and me. Had used the word reconciliation. She wanted the two of us to become 'real friends', for us all to be a proper family. That was my grandmother's dying wish. If I could find Sophie, she said, she thought that might help. *A proper family*? My sister would need to be a miracle worker, but first, we had to get her well.

*

"Must have been bloody good coffee."
"Eh?"

"Our friendly neighbourhood musician – saw him drop you off in his van," said Joe. "You said he invited you for coffee."

"He did."

"Just saying – looks like he makes good coffee. Haven't seen you beam like that in a while."

"His coffee's lousy," I said and couldn't stop myself smirking.

"Ah . . ."

"Ah *nothing*! He seems like a decent bloke, that's all. And he's got a sense of humour."

"Always helps."

"Sure, but don't put the flags out too soon, Joe. Maybe he's only looking for a mother-figure."

"What? Somebody to cook for him, do his laundry, you mean?" Joe cocked a cynical eyebrow.

"Okay. So I'm not the most domesticated – and I can't cook. That stuff's overrated anyway."

"So what is he? Twenty? Twenty-one?"

"Twenty-nine."

"Cradle robber."

"You like him then?"

Joe pursed his lips in an exaggerated mime of a sloppy kiss. "If you don't want him, I'll have him." He reached over and poked me in the ribs. I giggled. We both giggled.

Harry walked by, scowling. "We running a hotel here, or what?" he snapped. "You're worse than those bloody kids we had last week. Go and do something useful for a change." He stared malevolently at Joe. "Get me a coffee from the kitchen. Black, two sugars."

"Shift change. I'm off duty."

"Then why the hell are you cluttering up my Reception? Sod off home and wear out your own carpet," said Harry, his face tight with anger.

Joe looked crestfallen and I thought he'd bite back, but he didn't. He still had his mortgage to pay. He sloped out the front door without a word.

"What was that about?" I asked. "You eat something from Alfie's kitchen?"

"The workings of my digestive system have got sod all to do with you, Stevie. Just do what I pay you for. That doesn't include larking about like some bloody juvenile delinquent in front of the guests."

"It was only a joke, nobody died. Just a bit of fun and there were no guests around."

"You're not paid to have fun," he barked, and stomped off in the direction of the kitchen.

Doris appeared like a genie. "You too, eh?"

"Me too what?"

"'E just gave me a mouthful. Said I should learn me place. You believe that, Stevie? After all these years cleaning his bloody toilets for him without a word of complaint."

"Bad day, maybe."

"Visit from his bank manager. The guy just left. Didn't sound good, babe."

Chapter 28

Don't know if Harry still has the stomach for a fight. But then I guess he doesn't have much choice. He's dropped the price of his fancy beachside house by five thousand and still no one wants to buy it.

He offloads onto me. I reckon he thinks I'm an easy target. Or else he trusts me to keep schtum. Maybe I have an honest face. I heard all about the bank manager's visit, how Harry offered to 'open up a vein' for the man. But the bank wants more than blood. It wants cash. And right now poor old Harry doesn't have it. He's been given to the end of the summer season to drag the Royal out of trouble. Nobody else knows, and now that I do, it's a burden to carry rather than a blessing.

The man's done me no favours, for I'm having nightmares about it. I had one last night. The hotel was sinking into quicksand and I flung a flimsy rope around it and pulled. I don't know if the place sank – and me with it. It was a nightmare; you rarely get to see the end of those things. Maybe tonight I'll get to watch the second reel. It's not something I'm looking forward to. I'm thinking of turning to drink.

"Quick, call the Fire Brigade!" The woman in front of my reception desk looked frantic.

"What?" I sniffed the air. Usually my nose is a refined instrument. It can certainly smell smoke and burning. There'd been a few times when strange smells came out of Alfie's kitchen, but right now I couldn't detect even a whiff of smoke.

"Call this a proper hotel?" she said.

Well yes, I do. We may have a few shortcomings, but on the whole we end up with mostly satisfied customers.

"Don't just stand there. You retarded or something? I said to get the Fire Brigade."

At times, manning Reception was like being put in the stocks without any of the benefits - at least they threw fruit at you there.

I thought about Harry's reaction if I went off half-cocked and called the Fire Brigade out on a false alarm. Not too good for repeat business.

"I don't understand," I said. Which I didn't. "We've got fire sensors. We test them every month along with the fire alarm. They should have kicked in by now."

"What?" The woman's eyes bulged and her face had the strained look that I'd seen lately on Harry's.

"When there's a fire," I said, "we have drills. We're well prepared. And the Fire Brigade comes out automatically." I felt like I was losing touch with reality for the woman's face moved menacingly closer to mine and she thumped the top of the reception counter. A blow that must have hurt her hand.

"There's no bloody fire, but there will be if you don't move your arse."

No call for it, was there? I mean just because I'm on the customer-service side of the counter, why should I have to put up with abuse like that?

"Is there a problem?" Harry didn't usually get stuck into problems with guests. His territory was the theoretical rather than the practical. The sharp end where people might complain and hurl abuse at you was not top of his list of favourite hotelier's activities. But the woman's voice had risen and she was pulling in strange looks from other customers who'd collected in a knot hoping for some sort of excitement.

"Problem? Sure there's a problem," she said. "The staff in this place are all idiots. I'm trying to get this woman to call the Fire Brigade."

This woman? You ask me, that sort of language was unnecessary.

Harry looked worried. "Where's the fire?" he asked her, "our sensors should have picked up on that. And the Fire Service should be here by now. The alarm rings automatically in the station." His confused gaze moved from her face to mine. A shrug was all I could manage. He was covering ground I'd already walked over.

"Are you *all* imbeciles?" The woman's voice was dramatically loud now and she'd moved alarmingly close to Harry, invading his personal space in a way that I could tell was making him jumpy. And I suppose he didn't relish being called an imbecile. He could join the rest of the gang. But at least there was a reception counter between me and the madwoman from room fifteen. Harry didn't have the luxury of a safety barrier.

"Madam, if you could just calm down . . ."

"Don't you bloody 'Madam' me. Get on that phone and call them. My daughter's trapped in the toilet. She's terrified."

Turns out it wasn't any deficiency in our bathroom suites that was responsible for the woman's 2-year-old being stuck in the toilet. And would you leave a kid that young to go to the loo by themselves? I'm not an expert on toilet-training but a kid that size who decides to sit on an adult toilet – *with the seat pulled up* – is just asking for trouble.

Lulabelle Adams (and who names their poor kid Lulabelle for starters?) had fallen to the bottom of the pan. The resulting vibration had then caused the toilet seat to come down heavily, trapping her shoulders and arms, effectively imprisoning her.

It was hard not to laugh. The kid was distressed and Mrs Adams was a frantic-eyed harridan threatening to sue, even though the accident was as much her fault as anyone else's. It could hardly be laid at the door of the Royal or its hard pressed staff. But it was down to US to deal with it.

Obviously Harry didn't call the Fire Brigade. He called Morris instead – who took the screws out of the toilet seat. But even then, the unfortunate Lulabelle, who was by this time screeching quite animatedly, could not be removed.

The seat, minus screws, wouldn't budge. After ten minutes of strenuous work by Morris, the kid's arse was still stuck firmly in the toilet bowl, her arms dangling down inside the seat, her shoulders jammed tight. And - to speak frankly - her shoulders were decidedly chubby. Lulabelle's face might have been described as cherubic, but only by a family member who didn't want to insult the kid. Like the rest of Lulabelle's body, it was round and fat. Rolls of fat made up the construction of this wailing infant.

What sort of language skills could you expect from a two-year-old? I didn't know. I haven't had many dealings with them. But this one didn't strike me as any kind of infant prodigy, for – other than screaming – she couldn't string an articulate sentence together.

Her mother looked straight at me. Screamed like a maniac. "Well bloody do something!"

Why me? Why not, I suppose. But I just stood there like an idiot. It wasn't a situation I was familiar with, more an engineering puzzle.

The solution presented itself in the form of Doris. Practical, down-to-earth Doris who'd had kids of her own.

"Grease her with butter," said Doris knowingly. "Works with wedding rings when they get stuck." She grinned at Morris, a private joke.

It was a solution that didn't go down well with the hysterical Mrs Adams. But Harry still refused to call the Fire Brigade until we'd explored every avenue. Smithy was summoned from the kitchen with a pack of softened butter and Doris took charge.

"Right, Stevie – you got thin fingers. Take a slab of butter and see if you can ease a finger between her shoulders and the seat rim. Lather her shoulders in grease."

I can't say it was a happy experience for either me or Lulabelle. The poor kid was screeching the whole time and her mother was leaning over my shoulder, breathing down my neck, threatening police action if I as much as harmed a hair on Lulabelle's precious head. I wondered why I was the designated greaser. I turned my head to look at the mother. She had fat fingers.

I gave one final, desperate tug and went flying backwards, taking Mrs Adams with me in an ungainly rugby tackle, the white plastic toilet seat triumphantly in my hands. The kid cried, Mrs Adams pulled the remainder of the butter-basted infant from the toilet bowl and hugged her.

Harry thumped Doris on the back. A gesture of appreciation and relief. A job well done. He just ignored me, but if you were expecting justice in this life, I suppose you'd landed on the wrong planet. It's simply an observation. I wasn't bitter.

Chapter 29

I've had the luscious bead-encrusted top that my sister gave me hanging up on my wardrobe door today. Admiring it, thinking how great it would look on a model with long flowing blonde hair. Wondering if I'll have the nerve to wear it tomorrow night.

Sophie's pleased, because I'm finally going somewhere special. It's some kind of charity ball and I wasn't keen at first. But Matthew made such an effort to talk me into it that I've tried to overcome my natural aversion to anything that smacks of pretentious bullshit. Maybe I'll be surprised, and the evening will turn into a magical Cinderella thing.

I've promised my sister I'll get pictures of me in the turquoise top and long black skirt and Matt in his tux. But as you see, I have reservations. This is not a fairy tale but real life.

Joe is dead excited for me, but then he's into the whole dressing up bit. Maybe he should go instead; for I'm not that thrilled about eating mass produced plastic chicken and fighting for your share of overcooked vegetables on a table with complete strangers.

It has overtones of the Masons for me and Coq-au-Vin that turned into chicken stew. And that awful man who assaulted me. I've tried to delete him from my memory, at least until I finally see him in court. But although my brain is only the size of a medium head of cauliflower, I suspect it's still capable of excellent feats of memory and will be able to dredge up his face when I'm off-guard. In my dreams, when my subconscious sneaks in to take advantage.

It may sound ungrateful, and that I'm bringing all sorts of low expectations to tomorrow night's Mayoral Ball. But that's not so. I truly am excited that Matt has invited me out, but a trip to the cinema or the local pizza place would have been great. I don't feel comfortable around people whose ambition is to sit at the Mayor's top-table and are networking – all in the name of charity. It's sanctimonious twaddle. Dishonest.

Matt knows how I feel, and he feels the same, so I'm not sure why he's going. Or why he's bringing me. But at least Sophie is happy I'll finally be wearing something that isn't just *camouflage* as she calls it. "Enjoy being Cinderella," she'd said, "although I don't see you as a downtrodden kitchen skivvy."

My sister's back in Bristol now for she starts her chemo soon. And I'm trying to forget the look on her face when I waved her off at the station. She was being brave, but the fear slipped through and I guess she was remembering all those negative things you hear about chemo; how having toxic chemicals doing battle in your body can make you feel.

Harry passed by Reception. He was humming a tune from South Pacific. *Some Enchanted Evening*, I believe it's called. It's one of Harry's favourites.

"You sound happy," I said.

"Why not? Positive thinking, Stevie. You should try it sometime."

Of all the nerve. I'd been a proper Polyanna lately, for Harry's sake rather than my own. Trying to pull him out of the sludge of his depression. Disgustingly cheerful, I was, chirpy even, and working overtime designing leaflets to attract new customers for him.

"Chance of a link up with a golfing holiday company. Steady flow of middle-aged golfers trying to escape the old ball-and-chain." Harry grinned, but thought better of it when he saw my face. "Not that all women are alike, Stevie. I ain't saying that. Just that blokes need the odd break away from the missus once in a while. Blow the cobwebs away."

"Yeah, Harry. My new advertising copy useful then?"

"Sure, Stevie. Give yourself a raise." He chuckled. *Harry enjoyed a good joke.*

"So, when can we expect all these blokes in tartan trousers and overpriced golfing sweaters, then?" I like a joke as much as the boss does.

"Don't be a cynic. They'll be here. Just going to a meeting with old George from the Tourist Board now." Harry gave me a wink.

He had his meeting-suit on. I should have noticed, but then I was preoccupied with Mayoral balls that I didn't want to go to.

"You look smart," I said.

"Yeah? The aftershave not too overpowering?" he asked, unsure.

"Just right." *Liar, liar, pants on fire.* Totally overpowering, of course. But Harry's aftershave needed to be industrial strength.

He leaned on the front of the counter. Looked up at the clock above Reception. "That right?"

"Sure. I always synchronise it with Big Ben." It was a smart aleck reply. But Harry believed me and looked down at his watch.

"Hate these bloody digital things. Happy to be a dinosaur. Always felt better just turning a knob."

"Yeah?" I didn't own a watch, didn't see the point, not when you had a mobile.

Harry started in humming again. Cheerful. Time on his hands, that's what I reckoned.

"Your appointment not for a bit, then?"

"Half an hour. Hey, Stevie? You still doing your nun thing in the summer? Haven't heard you practising lately."

"Matt's been working with me in his studio. Teaching me the finer points of falsetto."

"Matt?" Harry grinned. "You got a boyfriend?"

"Just a friend," I said. *A friend who was taking me out to a posh ball, that's who.* "The bloke with the tux, you remember?"

"The musician? The one who thumped the barman . . ." He sounded like he was going to say more. But even Harry can be sensitive when he tries.

"Yeah, Harry. That guy."

"Nice bloke."

Maybe.

*

Gloria Endersley was not a woman to be trifled with. Not that I'd done much in the way of trifling anyway, and if I had, she wouldn't be somebody I'd choose.

"It's imperative we rehearse this together. We'll be singing the number together on the night," said Gloria.

I was confused. I'm sometimes confused, but not about obvious stuff like this.

"Surely Maria sings this one with the children. In her bedroom. During the thunderstorm, when they're all scared." *Everybody knew that, didn't they?* My Favourite Things was one of those songs that even people who hated The Sound of Music remembered.

Gloria pulled herself up to her full height, which wasn't that statuesque. *This was the pot having a go at the kettle if I'm honest with you.*

"Anyone worth their salt knows that the Mother Abbess sings this song in her office, before she sends Maria off to work as a governess for Captain von Trapp."

"Are you sure?" I said.

Gloria linked her beefy arms across her breasts in a provocative way. She was cut from the same pattern as Doris, but in a wrestling match between those two I couldn't swear as to who would have the weight advantage. I would put money on Doris to win, though. But then I'm biased.

"If we are being totally true to our art," said Gloria, and her cheeks puffed out in a peculiar way, "I believe we have to trace the origins back to the original Broadway musical, before that fiend Ernest Lehman decimated the work in his film adaptation."

"What?"

"These Hollywood people are not to be trusted," said Gloria.

She spat these words out with the kind of venom one might use when describing mass murderers.

"I see." It was an extemporiser. Obviously I didn't see. I had never heard of Ernest Lehman.

"That's settled then. I'll sort out a couple of hours with the school, and we can rehearse the number together. So get yourself ready, Stephanie. We're expecting great things of you. All that money we've invested in lessons. Results, Stephanie. Results!"

The woman swept out the front door of the Royal as if she herself were royalty. As if an entourage was following on her heels. I didn't have time to answer. Or the energy.

Chapter 30

You know how I've decided to become an old maid and all, and sworn-off men for life? Well, lately I've come to rethink the decision. Not that I'd completely changed my mind, but my resolve to go quietly into old age with a cat by my side instead of a man, had weakened. Or maybe wobbled would be a better word. And it was all down to Matt.

He has become a friend. From friend to *boy*friend doesn't seem too big a leap right now. He's not perfect, but then neither am I, so maybe it could work. Why the sudden change? The man just sent me a corsage. It's beautiful, lots of delicate blue flowers all attached to this fancy wrist band, ready to wear with my princess of the ball outfit tonight. And I have to tell you I blubbed when the florist delivered it just now.

"Stevie, you come to kitchen?"

"What's wrong?"

Agata looked flustered and she had Smithy in tow, although the young K.P. was hanging back; he was never completely at ease front-of-house, confining his activities to the kitchen downstairs and the alleyway out back for fag breaks.

Agata raised her arms in a dramatic gesture. "You *see* - if you come to kitchen. Maybe he listens to you. Alfie likes you."

It was news to me. I didn't think Alfie liked anybody.

"Miss Anderson, you need to come *now*," said Smithy, "or we won't have no plates left."

"He's throwing plates? I said in horror. Our house-crockery was only cheap catering stuff that came as a job lot, hardly bone china, but Harry would have a fit if we had to pay out for more.

Nobody answered, either they were both too traumatised or it was a no-brainer. Agata grabbed the lapel of my blazer. I recoiled. That's when I knew it must be serious, for Agata was a mild mannered woman who respected other people's property and personal spaces.

I left Reception unmanned. It could have doubled for the *Mary Celeste*. I arrived outside the kitchen alone; both Agata and Smithy had miraculously melted away. I'm not stupid enough to go storming into a situation fraught with danger, for even the odd badly aimed flying plate could still wing you, so I looked in through the glass porthole of the swing doors. Alfie was nowhere to be seen and everything was quiet as the grave; maybe not a cheerful comparison, but you get my drift.

I decided to tough it out, and stepped slowly into the kitchen where the remnants of a battle covered the tiled floor. Jagged lumps of stoneware were scattered around, and the door to one of the ovens was wide open. He had his head placed dramatically inside it. It wouldn't help. You can't gas yourself in an electric oven.

Alfie's theatrics were laughable. Maybe I should introduce him to Gloria Endersley. He heard me and pulled his large, bald head and tattooed neck from inside the secondhand industrial oven that Harry swore was top-of-the-range.

"It's only *you*. I told them to get His Holiness."

"He's not here," I said.

"Well, you'd better find him quick, or he won't have no kitchen left."

"Look, Alfie – maybe I can help."

"Struggle with English do you?"

"That's hardly fair. I came to help. I could've stayed behind my desk. Safe!"

"*Life* ain't fair," he said. "You got ten minutes to get His Lordship in here, before I start redesigning his feckin' kitchen."

"Might take me a while," I said. "Think he's got another meeting with George. He's trying to get us some golfing guests."

"Tell him no sod goes in or out this place. And nobody gets no grub till he comes to meet *me*, never mind feckin' George. I been onto him for weeks about this, but he won't listen. Tell him I'm taking *direct action*."

I tried Harry's phone, but he had the bloody thing switched off. Joe was due to take over from me in an hour, for I'd had it all planned out. Take a long relaxing soak with lavender bath oil. (It was meant to be soothing, good for stress.) Then I'd spend some time painting my nails silver, and relax with a cup of herbal tea and a book, before getting dressed up and take my taxi to the Headland for tonight's hoedown. Matt was going to meet me there. I guess he didn't want me getting out of his van with my fancy gear on.

But plans have to be flexible in this place. You think I'd know that by now. Still, I took a couple of deep breaths and told myself that this emergency with Alfie, whatever it was, wasn't going to spoil my evening. Funny that. I hadn't been looking forward to it at first, but it's strange what the appearance of a beautiful blue corsage will do.

I couldn't find Harry anywhere. Both he and George had left the Tourist Board office an hour ago, but nobody could tell me where they'd gone. And when the ten minute deadline that Alfie had set drifted on by, there was nothing to mark it. No threatening phone call from the kitchen, no sound of breaking dishes, I wondered if he'd fallen asleep down there. Neither Agata nor Smithy would venture into the place; instead they were busying themselves folding serviettes in the restaurant. Pussies.

Harry collided with the front door jamb on his way in. His face had a red, polished glow.

Oh no. "You been drinking?" I said.

"You keeping tabs on me?"

"Nothing to me. Just that we've got a situation here."

"Oh?"

"Chef"s barricaded himself in the kitchen. Won't let anybody in there but you."

"Jesus, Stevie. I leave you for an hour and the whole place falls apart."

"Looks that way," I said. But it was wasted breath. Harry wouldn't recognise irony if it smacked him in the mouth.

Joe arrived.

I left.

The changing of the guard.

They could all get on with it. It was my night off.

*

It had a surreal feel to it. Going from our hotel to this one. This was beautiful, all midnight-blues and golds and chandeliers and massive gilt mirrors polished to a high shine. In the summer you could take a glass of wine out onto the terrace and sit watching the sunset. But this wasn't summer, not yet. And there was a chill in the air. Not just literally, but metaphorically.

Matt had said he'd meet me. He knew how I felt. I didn't know anyone here and I doubted they'd be my kind of people - laid back, happy to hang loose in trackies. He'd left a ticket for me in Reception, so I suppose it could have been worse. But he was nowhere to be seen.

The receptionist eyed me quizzically. An up and down assessment, like she was rating me on a one-to-ten. I knew the score, had done the same thing myself. She was wearing a burgundy blazer with thin gold trim around the lapels and cuffs. The uniform was well cut and fitted her exactly, for she was tall and willowy. She could have passed for a model. But the blazer made her look like a cinema usherette from the '60s.

"Maybe you'd like a drink in the bar," she said. "I believe the first couple are complimentary." The woman smiled. I got it. She was being friendly. Doing her job.

"Thanks," I said and returned her smile, even though I didn't like the emphasis she'd put on complimentary. Did I look like a freeloader?

"No problem. Dinner will be served in the function room in thirty minutes. After the speeches, there'll be dancing in the ballroom. But you'd know about that already."

"Pardon?"

"I expect Matt's given you the low down."

"Matt? You *know* Matt?"

"Well, yes." The receptionist looked uncomfortable. "He often plays here. He's set up in the ballroom if you want to go on through."

"He's *playing* tonight?"

"Of course. You didn't know?"

The embarrassing ring tone went off in my bag. One of those stupid little black evening bags, all beaded and with silver clasps. Doris had insisted I borrow it, had said it would go with the outfit. I went fishing into it to silence the thing, and wished I hadn't downloaded the Mission Impossible theme for my phone. The hotel receptionist smirked.

"Hey Stevie. You finished eating there yet?"

"Haven't started," I said.

"No chance you could get back?" asked Harry. "Things are looking bad."

He wasn't wrong. "I'm on my way."

Chapter 31

"Imagine I'm a five-year-old," I said. "Just give it to me simply."

It was a line Harry could have taken advantage of. The fact that he didn't, showed how rattled he was.

"Chef's got a grudge. Reckons I messed up his income tax. Says it's down to me that Her Majesty's Revenue and Customs have hit him for back taxes that he can't pay."

"Hardly your fault, is it? Just get on to Mrs Harris the bookkeeper," I said. "She'll sort it."

Harry looked at a scuff on his shoe. "It's all bollocks," he mumbled.

And when his eyes came back they veered off to the left. It seems that people making stuff up automatically look to the left (your left, so I guess it's their right). Things like body language were important when you were trying to catch people out in a lie.

"He's talking out of his ass," said Harry.

"You sure?"

"*Honestly.*"

That was it then. Harry was lying. People who bend the truth usually add something like 'truthfully' or 'sincerely' or 'honestly' to give some muscle to the lie.

"So what does Mrs Harris say?"

"Doesn't matter. She's not here is she? It's not her kitchen he's threatening to burn down." His eyes shot off to the left again.

It was then the truth hit me. He'd been saving money. Sorting out the wages himself. Shit! I expect Mrs Harris, the accountant, still did people's books from home, the way she always had, just not *ours*.

"So what's the bottom line?" I said. I felt sick. Not only because I hadn't eaten yet, but I was still in shock over the way Matt had manipulated me. And now this.

"Says I need to give him 900 quid for the Taxman 'cause he's been given the wrong tax coding. Not my fault, Stevie! Not if the Taxman screws up."

Something told me it *was*. But it didn't matter who was to blame. Now was the time for solutions, not for pointing fingers. "So, what about tonight's restaurant sitting?" I said.

"Restaurant's closed. Had to give fifteen guests a refund and they've gone into town. Chinese is probably making a killing," he said. His voice was bitter.

"So, he's still in there?"

"It's a siege. Like in the movies."

"Get the cops, then," I said. "Have him removed. It's your kitchen. You're entitled."

"Figured we could settle this without too much hassle. Negotiate."

"What? Offer him a couple of hundred?" I said.

"Sure and while we're at it, why don't I offer to wash his dirty kecks for him! I'm running a business here, Stevie."

"Not without a chef you're not."

"Yeah, okay. So I'll give him time-off in lieu. Spread it over a year. The K.P.s should be able to take up the slack."

"No money then?"

"Where would I get money from?"

"You tell *him* that?"

"He threw me out. I figured maybe you could be my messenger. Tell him about the time-off thing."

"They shoot messengers, Harry."

Harry laughed. But then he could afford to. He wasn't the one who'd have to face a cook with a tattoo that said game over and a set of catering knives.

"C'mon Stevie. *Please*. Chef likes you. He won't throw you out."

"That's what worries me."

Harry laughed again, but it had an edge of hysteria. "Wait a minute. Give him this."

He headed for the bar and came back with a carton of Marlborough and a cheap bottle of whiskey.

"He'll hardly be able to give those to the Taxman, will he?" I said.

Turns out that Harry's idea of the whiskey was a good one, for Alfie and I sat on the kitchen floor getting more hammered as the night went on. I told him about Harry's offer of *time off*. He gave a snort and called Harry a bastard. I didn't argue. The carving knives were within easy reach.

I came up with a plan. Got Harry on the in-house-phone. Gave him the news. If he wanted the kitchen to start running again, he'd have to hand over an extra hundred pounds a month. Nine months would do it. I'd told Alfie I'd negotiate a settlement with the tax people for him. Nine instalments of a hundred. I couldn't see them refusing.

"That's bloody extortion," fumed Harry.

"Best deal you'll get," I said. "If I were you, I'd take it."

"Frigg's sake, Stevie. Whose side you on?"

"Tell 'im I don't want none of his bouncing cheques neither," shouted Alfie. "Cash only. He hands me a ton and the kitchen opens for breakfast tomorrow morning."

"You hear that?" I said.

"They heard it in bloody Lands End," said Harry. He slammed the phone down. But an hour later, Smithy the young K.P. came down to the kitchen with an envelope. There were five twenty pound notes inside.

Chef smiled benignly at the lad. "Clear off home now, mate," he said. "But be here half an hour earlier in the morning. You got some clearing up to do."

Smithy looked confused. Maybe it was the unfairness of having to clear up crockery he hadn't broken. But working in Alfie's kitchen, he'd be used to injustice. More likely it was being called mate.

*

I suppose I should have felt good. The kitchen would be returning to normal and some of that was down to me. But the pain in my temples was vying with the sickness in my stomach, and the coffee that Joe had just forced me to drink wasn't making things any better. I tried to stop the room spinning by staring at a point above Joe's head and hoped I wouldn't throw up.

"Can't believe you drank that rotgut whiskey of Harry's."

"Me neither," I said.

"Closest that's been to Scotland is the label."

"I'm not a driskey winker."

Joe laughed. Maybe *I* would eventually, but not now. Not with all the fireworks going off in my head. I tried to focus on Joe's eyes and pulled myself up in the chair.

"Lost another man, Joe."

"Matt? He's been trying to get you on the phone."

"Know what he did?"

"He told me you got the wrong idea."

"What? This is *my* fault? Bloody men! Sod 'em all."

"He likes you, Stevie. Have a word with him – when you're sober."

"I hate him."

"Sure you do. You're angry. You got dressed like a princess and ended up sitting on the kitchen floor with a guy who weighs 250 pounds. But he's a good bloke."

"Who, Alfie?"

"You know *exactly* who. Matt's okay. Flesh and blood, sure. Like the rest of us. Human. Maybe he didn't handle this too well and maybe he's not perfect, but who is?"

"She any better?" Harry walked into my office and raised a quizzical eyebrow. He put a plate of sandwiches on the desk. "Get her to eat something."

"What am I? Wallpaper?" I said.

"Ah, she speaks. Thought it was too good to be true," said Harry.

"Harry carried you from the kitchen," explained Joe. "You were in a bit of a state."

"Ah shit! You'll never let me forget this, will you?"

"Just eat the sandwiches," said Harry. "Made them myself."

"*You* made them?"

"Sure. I'm not useless. Oh and Stevie?"

"What?"

"Thanks."

Joe put me to bed. Told me not to bother turning up for my shift in the morning, he'd cover it. I didn't argue, for I guessed I'd still be drunk then, judging by the way the room was fading in and out of focus. If the whiskey had been a *Skelly Special* it was closer to moonshine than anything you could buy over the counter. I wondered if my face would break out in spots. People went blind after drinking raw moonshine. As a drinker, I was a lightweight I guess. That was the last thought I remember before the blackness closed in.

People wandered in and out of my dreams. My sister, my mother, Matt, in his tux. He held me in a particularly sexy way and led me in a slow dance. I tried to hold on to that part of the dream, but it slipped away and I found myself in the kitchen throwing lobster after lobster into a massive pan of water at a 'fierce boil'. I picked them up by the tails and flung them in and I could hear them shrieking, a shrill frantic sound that wouldn't stop.

That's when I woke up to find my alarm clock's insistent bell punching its way through the silence of my tiny room. *The Penthouse.* I looked around the familiar space. My mouth was parched, my throat on fire, my head a massive concrete block set on a neck that would barely hold it up. But I smiled all the same. I was home. I loved this place. It might stagger from one crisis to another at times, but the Royal would make it through; I was sure of that. And despite the battering my body had taken last night, a feeling of optimism took hold of me. I had no idea where it came from. I didn't feel sick any more, just hungry.

I'd get dressed in my uniform and surprise them all. Then I'd go grab one of Alfie's famous breakfast specials. It was something he was good at. He called it his Hungryman's Feast: eggs, sausages, bacon, mushrooms, beans, tomatoes, Hogs Pudding, potato fritters, and thick slices of fried bread. Just think of the biggest fry-up you can imagine on the largest plate possible. Hopefully we'd still have a few plates left to serve them on. I found myself singing a tune. Raindrops on roses and whiskers on kittens. My Favourite Things.

Chapter 32

I ate breakfast in the staffroom. Doris came in to drink her morning tea. She had a special mug she kept in the kitchen, blue and white with the crest of Torquay United Football Club on it. It wasn't a subtle piece of china and I wondered if Morris was a fan or she'd got the thing at a boot sale. I'd never bothered to ask, not when there were so many other important questions that needed answers: Who are we? Where did we come from? When am I likely to get a raise?

Doris was a multi-tasker, for she balanced the tea and lit a cigarette, puffing away like the little-engine-that-could. We weren't allowed to smoke in the staffroom, but Doris applied her own rules to most stuff.

"Something happen yesterday?" she said.

"Like what?"

"Dunno. But something funny's going on. Joseph's in Reception for starters, and he don't belong to do mornings. And cook was humming went I went in to pour meself a tea. Cook ain't one for humming. And you - you ain't on duty but you got your uniform on."

"Life's a mystery, Auntie D."

"You don't say so." Doris shot me a cynical look, but I held my ground. "You get the note?" she asked.

"What note?"

"That weird woman with the turban from the Am Drams dropped it in. I put it on your desk."

"Thanks."

"How was the special do last night?"

"An education," I said.

"Yeah? But *good*, eh?"

I didn't answer. I was thinking about the note. Probably meant I couldn't put off the evil hour any more and would have to start rehearsing with Gloria.

Doris took the hump and left.

Good days and bad days, you get a mixture of both – in life and in the hotel business. I was about to have a good one. How did I know? Attitude. Seems to me that a lot of this stuff is down to how you approach it. So, I decided that whoever or whatever tried to screw up my day wouldn't get a foothold.

"Hey Stevie, you coming tonight?"

"I'm working. Something special on?" I asked Eli.

"I'm doing a spot at the Con Club." Eli Parker winked. "Get you in free if you fancy it. Come for a drink after work."

Eli was our new barman. Small, chunky, easy smile, good bloke. Middle-aged, hard worker - and an Elvis impersonator.

"I'm off the drink," I said.

"Have a coke."

"Maybe."

"It's not a date, like," he mumbled, and turned his head away, embarrassed. "Some of the others are coming – Joe, Aggie and her old man, couple of waiters. Be cool if you could make it."

"Rent a crowd?"

"Few friendly faces in the audience never hurt," he said.

"Okay, sign me up."

"You're a right diamond, Stevie."

"Yeah? I'll have that in writing." *I could show it to Matt if he had the nerve to turn up.*

I headed for my office. Joe was still working out in Reception, in the thick of a discussion with a sales rep for bathroom suites. Harry would have fobbed the guy off on him. But Joe didn't mind stuff like that. He'd string the bloke along for a while and it helped to relieve the boredom when things were quiet. And quiet was something we specialised in right now. The end of April, a time we should be picking up custom, not losing it.

The note from Gloria Endersley wasn't what I'd expected. It did mention that the two of us would be starting run-throughs any day now whenever she could find a decent rehearsal pianist. Mrs Andover, our usual pianist, had let her down, she said. Eventually most people gave up the unequal struggle, for Gloria was a hard taskmaster and single minded in her wants and dislikes.

The main thrust was that she needed to recruit a set designer. Someone 'funky' she wrote. Someone who understood the need to remain true to the traditional idea of the show, but could bring a fresh new eye to scenery design. And if I understood Gloria correctly, somebody who worked free, wouldn't mind taking orders, had time on their hands, and who could produce miracles on a shoestring. She'd fired the last guy.

She wanted me to think of somebody.

Harry stuck his head round the door, said "Need you to do something for me."

Tell me something new. Everybody wanted something from me. Except my sister, of course. Life is bloody weird. The very one I'd be happy to help, who could have done with my help, didn't want it.

"I'm a bit short this week," I said. "Boss is a tightwad. Still waiting for my Christmas bonus."

"Funny stuff, Stevie. You should do stand-up."

"So?"

"It ain't financial," he said. "It's medical. Nip round to my office in five minutes? I need to find some pliers or something first."

"What?"

"I'd ask Morris, only he ain't here."

"You need a plumber?"

"My office, five minutes, smartarse."

He left. And for the first time I started to worry that Harry had flipped. Maybe the hotel's troubles had finally been too much for him. He needed my help with a medical problem and had gone in search of a pair of pliers. I wouldn't feel happy touching any part of Harry's anatomy, but I couldn't deny it - the puzzle was intriguing. I smoked a quick fag in my office (if Doris could do it, then so could I) and made my way to Harry's den.

*

"C'mon, Stevie. Don't be so squeamish. Take a firm grip on them cutters and force your hand inside," said Harry. "It ain't that hard."

"I can't. It's bloody silly. Somebody at the hospital should be doing this. Somebody with experience. You could get an infection or something." I shuddered. Not just because I was in close proximity to Harry's 'bits', but I didn't relish the job.

"For God's sake, Stevie. It ain't brain surgery. Just get them cutters between the arm and the plaster and start bloody cutting."

Any normal person would go to hospital outpatients to have their cast removed. But Harry couldn't wait for the allotted time. He wanted the thing off now. And if I didn't do it, he said, he would try and get the bloody thing off himself. Except of course he couldn't hold the cutters in his left hand.

I forced the cutters between his arm and the plaster cast, squeezed hard and closed my eyes. The plaster made a disturbing cracking sound as the steel cutters bit their way through. I relaxed slightly, eased the tension out of my shoulders. Just another day at the Hotel Royal. Another skill I could write up on my C.V.

*

"You wanted to go?" I asked him. I didn't think so, but Harry had been a pain since he realised a bunch of us were headed off down the road to the Conservative Club.

"You know better than that. I don't fraternise with staff. Just don't stay all night is what I'm saying." His face had that sour look like he'd eaten something past its sell-by date.

"You're not my mother, Harry."

"Nope. Just the mug who pays your wages every month."

Which was hardly fair considering I'd just saved him a trip to the hospital to have his cast removed.

He wasn't pleased. Not because he hadn't been invited. Like he said, Harry didn't believe that meeting staff socially was a great idea. Either he thought it took away his credibility as a boss, or he'd have to fork out for a round of drinks. My money was on the latter, although the drinks at the Con Club were cheap. It's why customers went there, not because they were Conservatives.

He was grumbling because he'd be left on his own to deal with the few customers currently enjoying the delights of the Royal. He was a wuss, for most of them would be safely tucked up in bed by now.

Usually I got landed with the job of 'late night porter come receptionist'. It was convenient. I lived in the place. Harry saw my accommodation in the attic as some kind of generous perk from a bountiful benefactor, whereas I saw it as his excuse to lumber me with any after-hours customer complaints. So we were both mugs. Made us even, I guess. Except I didn't own a hotel, one that was mortgaged up to its armpits and had been given until the end of the season to live.

Chapter 33

Nobody else seemed to notice how Eli's jewelled jumpsuit strained at the seams. How he missed the cues on his Elvis backing track, and ended up still singing when the 'band' had long since finished playing. Everyone at our table clapped vigorously, which was just as well for the rest of the audience didn't.

Eli was a good bloke. Didn't mind helping out in the hotel when he got lumbered with something that was nothing to do with tending bar. He couldn't make cocktails. Which in my book made him okay.

"Look at that man gyrate."

I guess only Wilbur would have described what Eli was doing like that. Wilbur was a little tipsy, but he wasn't a nasty drunk, more of a cute one. He didn't normally drink, but tonight was a bit of a hurdle for him.

"It's a *wiggle*," said Joe. "They called it the Elvis wiggle, didn't they? Am I right, Stevie?" Joe looked at me.

"Don't drag me into a domestic, mate. And I'm too young to remember Elvis."

This was a special night for Joe. It was the first time he'd been brave enough to introduce Wilbur to the others. He'd paved the way in a long, painful discussion in the staff room, when he'd *come out* to the other staff. Most people had been great, but not everything's perfect. One waiter had pointedly moved seats. I guess so he wouldn't be contaminated. Who knows? The world's a weird place.

I didn't expect the evening to be fun. But it was. Agata and her husband enjoyed themselves, Wilbur and Joe enjoyed themselves, Eli enjoyed himself and *he* wasn't even drunk. And I enjoyed myself. At least until another guest arrived at our table. That's when the ice-water trickled its way down the back of my neck.

"Is this a conspiracy? Did you lot set this up?" I was glad I hadn't been drinking. My head was clear. I could let him have the lot, both barrels, fully loaded.

"Harry told me you'd be here," said Matt, dead sheepish.

He grabbed my hand. I pulled it free. We had a back and forth wrestling match with my hand as the prize. I heard sniggers coming from the others.

"Right, let's do this in private," he said. "That okay?"

"I've got nothing to say. At least nothing you'd want to hear," I said. I was proud of the way I said it. Quietly. Dignified. Head held high.

But I let myself be led away to another table all the same. It was better than making a scene.

It was closer to the bar and the smell of beer made my head reel, or maybe that was the way Matt had both my hands clasped in his.

"I did it for you," he said. "Thought you'd like it. You know – somewhere glamorous. Moonlight on the terrace, you in that special dress your sister bought."

"Top."

"What?"

"It wasn't a dress. You didn't even see it."

"You didn't stay long enough."

"No reason to."

"I wanted it to be *special*," he said.

"You wanted a friendly face in the audience, that's all."

"I've played there lots of times, why would I need that?"

"Because those stiffs aren't your kind of people."

"It was a date. I wanted you there," he said.

"A *date* is where the man actually sits at the same table as you."

"I was going to. As soon as I finished playing. I'd ordered a bottle of champagne to take out on The Terrace. It was going to be dead romantic, oysters and champagne. Looking at the moonlight. Thought you'd like it."

"I might have done. If I'd known."

"Sorry, Stevie. Have I blown it?"

"Maybe."

"Can I make it up to you?"

I didn't mean to be manipulative. Honestly. But the thought just zipped straight into my head and came out my mouth before I could stop it.

"How'd you fancy being a rehearsal pianist for The Sound of Music?"

"What!"

"It's either that or knocking up some scenery."

"Pass."

"Take it or leave it," I said.

"That's putting the boot in, Stevie. A bloody musical." But he laughed despite that.

"Well?"

"Hell, why not? But I won't have that awful Endersley woman bossing me around. She knows as much about music as my hamster does."

It was news to me that he had a hamster. But then people can surprise you. "Okay then. Done. But if you don't want Gloria on your back, you might as well take on the job of musical director as well."

He walked me back to the table with the others, all cosy; his arm round my waist. Across the faded red and gold carpet. Past the pocket size dance floor where Eli was just finishing his cabaret set, to thunderous applause from the Hotel Royalites. Then he went and bought me a bottle of champagne from the bar. I didn't tell him I'd given up drinking. It wouldn't be right, would it?

Everybody helped me drink it. That's what mates were for. The whole thing turned into a proper party with cheese nibbles that Eli had lifted from the bar and those strange white cocktail onions that tasted of plastic. Don't know how they got there. And I thought about Harry, stuck behind, holding the fort. Harry who must be in some kind of pain right now, but who hadn't even flinched when his cast came off.

"Hear what she's dragged me into?" said Matt. His words were starting to slur. He was like me, not much of a drinker. One smell of cork and he went into orbit.

"Should we be hearing this?" asked Joe.

"It's not *that* kind of stuff," said Matt. And he blushed which was sweet. Well Matt can be really sweet.

"What kind of stuff, then?" said Wilbur.

Joe put a warning hand over his partner's.

"Only that I'm the new M.D. for the local Am Drams. *And* the rehearsal pianist."

"She stitched you up, eh?" Wilbur grinned.

"Nah. Did it for love," said Matt. He put an arm around my shoulder and squeezed. "It was either that or design the sets. No contest."

"Hey, Joe's a fantastic designer. Took a course in it," gushed Wilbur.

Joe looked appalled. "That was interior design. Not the same thing."

"Still, in for a penny and all that," said Matt and winked at me. And I guessed we'd just found ourselves another *volunteer*.

Matt walked me home. He'd come in his van, but he'd had a few drinks so he left it at the club, "pick it up in the morning," he said. His morning was everyone else's afternoon.

We walked arm in arm, looking out to sea, waves lapping gently, their crests painted silver in the moonlight. Real Mills and Boon; couldn't have been more romantic if we'd planned it. And we stopped along the way for some gentle groping that turned into a long hot French snog.

By the time we got to the Royal, the passion had soared, so I was sure we'd end up in my tiny bedroom. I did a mental check. Had I even made the bed this morning?

"I'm waiting to lock up." The words were clipped and Harry looked teed off. He stared angrily at Matt, said "Pull the door behind you on your way out."

"What are you – the morality police?" I said.

"Just the bloke who's been working all night while you lot been off getting pissed."

"It's okay, Stevie. I'll give you a buzz." Matt closed the door behind him.

And that was it. The image of Matt and me locked in hot steamy sex, faded - and in its place came a picture of Harry with his double chins and sweaty armpits and one of those vests he insisted on wearing under his shirt. He reckoned they sop up the sweat.

My stomach churned slightly and the cheese and the cocktail onions and champagne tried to fight their way back up my throat.

"Harry."

"What?" he snapped. And I noticed he was massaging his bad hand.

"You're a bastard."

The idea seemed to cheer him up. "Better the bastard you know, though." He let out a piercing whistle and Benjy, Harry's black Labrador came bounding out of nowhere. "C'mon, mutt," he said. "Let's head for bed. Stevie can lock up. And don't forget to put the alarm on when you close up out back." He chuckled.

"I should have shares in this place."

"You're always good for a laugh, Stevie."

"It's why you keep me around. That and my superior intellect and good looks."

Harry tickled Benjy under the chin and the two of them went waddling off down the corridor towards the lift. Man and dog. An aura of contentment surrounding both; a statement of belief in doggy treats and Betty Stogs.

*

I locked up, punched in the code for the burglar alarm and went up to bed. Alone. Still, things were looking up. Matt was back in the fold, and we now had a rehearsal pianist and a set designer, and with any luck the golfers Harry was expecting in two weeks' time would start to turn the tide of bad luck for the faithful old Royal. She'd give her best. She always did. And so would we, that strange collection of souls who relied on her for our daily bread.

The bread! Shit! I'd forgotten all about the phone call from Alfie. I'd promised to take the bread for tomorrow morning out of the freezer for him. I yawned, put on the tatty old navy dressing gown that I kept promising myself I'd replace with one of those sexy negligees in some decadent flimsy material. But my old ratty towelling one was warm and I was glad of it as I made my way downstairs. Harry had the heating on a timer.

It was dim in the front corridor, the only light came from the meagre glimmer of the night lights and if Harry had his way even those would be switched off. But some health and safety measures you just had to go along with, or they'd shut you down. The green glow gave the whole place a ghostly, eerie feel and a slight shiver ran up my neck.

Imagination told me there was someone walking behind, ready to put a knife between my shoulder blades. But of course when I turned round there was no one there. Even so, I couldn't shake off the spooky feeling and walked on tip-toe past the bar, towards Reception. I didn't fancy going down the back stairs to the kitchen, there was no light down there. I should have brought a torch.

Something clicked in my head. Something wasn't quite right in the bar. I'd only glanced in there for a split second, but my brain gave me a poke in the guts. I froze, stood in the middle of the hall in front of Reception and listened. The only sound was my own strained breathing. I turned round slowly and for an instant saw a dark figure with the face from my nightmares pasted on it. That's the last thing I remember before the pain exploded in my head, and all the lights went out.

Chapter 34

"Six stitches *and* I had to have a patch of hair shaved," I said. "You call that nothing?"

"'Course not. Just that it could've been worse."

"Thanks for the sympathy, Harry. Nice to know I'm appreciated. I nearly gave my life for the soddin' cause."

"I got you to the hospital, didn't I? *And* gave you first aid."

That was a surprise, the fact that Harry put a towel on my head to stop the bleeding and kept up the pressure till the paramedics arrived. It wasn't one of the skills I'd have put him down for. And there was a *lot* of bleeding, but the ambulance guys said that head wounds were like that. Often they looked more dramatic than they were. I took their word for it. It wasn't something that had happened to me before. Someone whacking me on the back of the head.

"I'm grateful, Harry. My head thanks you." I tried to smile, but it didn't work. Maybe it would get easier.

"Your head and my bloody cash."

"That's where we differ. I think my head's much more important than your cash. Anyway, thought you didn't have any."

"It's a contingency fund, that's all. In case of emergencies. Right, nearly there."

Harry had ordered a taxi to take us home from the hospital. He'd been given a pamphlet about the follow-up to a head injury, in case of concussion. I didn't have concussion. No dizziness, confusion, double vision or nausea. But I had one hell of a headache. They'd given me pain killers. I hadn't mentioned the champagne, but I figured it would be okay, that had been hours ago.

"So, you keep a stash behind the bar?"

"Hardly a stash," he said. "Just something to help out with the cash flow, something the taxman can't get his hands on. It's well hidden."

"Not well enough."

"If *one* of us hadn't forgotten to switch the alarm on, I'd still have it," he said.

"Don't go there again. I told you. I switched the bloody thing on. Whoever nicked your cash knew the sequence, or knew how to override it. You think burglars don't go on Utube, Harry?"

"Shit, Stevie. It was a mistake. I ain't saying you did it on purpose. You'd had a few."

"I did *not* forget to put the bleedin' alarm on Harry. I made a point of it. And I'd only had one glass of champagne."

"Yeah, well. Let's see what the cops come up with, eh?"

"Good luck with that," I said. They hadn't been much help to me. That's when the steamroller ran over me. "Holy shit!"

"You're not gonna throw up are you?"

"I know who it was. And he probably knew all about your little stash and the alarm."

"They said if you started talking gibberish I should take you back. You gettin' dizzy and stuff?"

"No, but *you* might. I knew there was something familiar about that bastard. It was our friend the barman, Christopher Newly. He's back." I started to shiver. And that's when I threw up, all over the back of the cab.

*

"Thought you and I were mates, Stevie." Joe sat on the end of my bed in the attic. His critical eye had already taken in the random decoration of my room. The mismatch of furniture and soft furnishings. It probably upset his sense of design.

"You know we are," I said. I didn't feel well and Joe was giving me the third degree. Probably didn't fancy covering my morning shift again. He'd been drinking last night as well, but Harry didn't want to face another stint on the front desk. He was still waiting in his office for the police to arrive. They both figured I wouldn't be safe let loose on the few remaining guests, and nobody wanted me throwing up in Reception. But I hadn't puked in ages.

"And that's what mates do, is it? Set you up." Joe had his famous pout on.

"Might be fun. All of us together. Anyway, I think you'll find it was Wilbur and Matt parcelled you up between them."

"Noted. But you stood on the sidelines cheerleading. What in God's name do I know about set design?"

"More than I know about being a nun." I laughed. It hurt my head.

"Or singing," said Joe.

Everyone's a critic. It's enough to give you a complex. My phone rang.

"Want me to get that?" said Joe. "Probably Harry asking why I've abandoned Reception."

"Thanks."

Joe spent a long time listening and his face became tight. "She's right here. I'll pass you over. Sorry Stevie," he said and handed me the phone like it was a bomb.

Funny how quickly your own problems fade when the pain of others much worse off takes over. I couldn't even feel my stitches and the sickness receded straight off when I thought about Sophie's chemo. She sounded terrible.

"How good are you at holding hands and mopping fevered brows, Stevie?"

"The best."

"Come up for a few days?"

"'Course. I'll look after you, Soph. You won't have to do a thing."

"Hey, little sister, I don't need a babysitter, just a friend."

"That's me."

"You sound weird," she said.

"Had a night on the town. You know me, your sister the alcoholic. I'll be all dried out by the time the train gets in. Don't worry."

"How'd the dinner-dance go?"

"Terrific."

"And the top? Bet you looked great. Did he like it?"

"The man was practically drooling," I said. It wasn't really a lie. Just a question of the time frame. "Now what about these side effects of yours?"

"Nothing other people haven't had. You know: bleeding gums, nose bleeds, food tastes like shit. Like you've been eating metal. Not that I'm eating much. Can't stand the thought of food."

"You need to eat, Soph – keep your strength up. You'll be losing weight."

"You'd think so, right? Think of Miss Piggy and double it. The bloody chemo makes you put weight on."

"I'll cook you something special."

"We'll go out," said Sophie. "You can't cook."

"How'd you know?"

"You told me, remember? Just get yourself up here; I need to see your gorgeous face. Can you get a week off?"

"I'm on my way." I put the phone down and cried. All that pent up emotion and the strain of trying to be cheerful. Joe looked uncomfortable.

"You're going?"

"Booking my ticket now," I told him. I wasn't of course. I was still in bed. But he got the idea and left quickly. I guess he was relieved, and he'd already earned his brownie badge for the day.

Harry tried to stop me, but I was a human bulldozer. My sister needed me and Harry and the Royal could wait in line.

We were in his office and Benjy was under the desk, playing with something that looked suspiciously like a mouse. I didn't have the heart to tell Harry. He had enough problems.

"I don't think you're up to it," he said. "You might have a head like concrete but it took a right wallop. You need to stay in bed for a week, Stevie, never mind gallivanting round Bristol."

"You telling me I can't go?"

"I'm *advising* you not to. But who could tell you anything? You're like a soddin' tsunami."

"So, you'll be okay, then?"

"Reckon we'll struggle through. It's not like you do any work round here anyway."

*

The signboard swinging outside the Old Duke pub was a painting of Duke Ellington. I hadn't expected that. When Sophie suggested we go there I hadn't been keen, but that was before I realized who the 'old Duke' was.

The place was a famous Bristol jazz venue, right in the heart of the city on one of those ancient cobbled streets that gave it an atmosphere before you even stepped through the door. There'd been some kind of watering hole there for centuries.

Inside, you could feel the history coming out of the walls at you. Years of jazz coated the place, framed pictures of bands covered every available wall space; posters were plastered to the ceiling - most of them faded and clinging on by a sheer act of will. A massive blackboard announced the week's bands, and some enthusiastic artist with a moderate gift for drawing had chalked a treble cleft sign on there and a large baritone saxophone.

An electric ceiling fan was battling away full blast, its propellers straining with the effort to overcome the heat and the sweat of customers and the build up of beer fumes. It was moving the air around and looked dangerously close to coming off its mountings.

Sophie grabbed my hand, led us to a table beside the trio. The three young musicians crammed into a corner were practically in our laps. The audience was a mixture of ages and characters; there'd be a few hardened jazzers there; trad, mainstream, fusion, smooth. Jazz could be many things. And maybe not everyone here was listening to the music, for it seemed to be a hangout for the town's students as well. Every so often you'd catch a snippet of intellectual and pretentious conversation. All bollocks. Kids trying to impress.

That sort of thing didn't impress me, except the trio did. They played their own version of *So What*. The tune had become a jazz classic, came from the Miles Davis iconic album Kind of Blue. It was one that took jazz off in another direction and brought together so many talents: Miles, Cannonball, Coltrane, Cobb, Chambers; and my favourite melodic pianist of all time – Bill Evans. The album was ancient now, made in the late '50s, but every so often new musicians rediscovered it, brought their own slant. Like this young guy on piano now. Sounded like he'd listened to a lot of Bill Evans. This guy would be good if he stayed the course. If he didn't kill himself with booze and drugs, like Evans had.

Yeah, okay. So I'm not against a drink or two myself, but I've always figured drugs were a slippery slope. Not that I'm sanctimonious. People have the odd spliff, fair enough; but I've seen the damage the heavy stuff can do and steer clear.

"You know that guy?" said Sophie. She was looking at a long haired student at the bar.

"Never saw him before." I squinted over at him. The bar was a distance away, so his features were fuzzy, or maybe I really did need to think about laser surgery. "You can see his face?" I asked Sophie.

"'Course. Why, can't you?"

"Bits of him," I said.

Sophie laughed. It was the first time she'd laughed since we'd met up. "Some bits of him are quite tasty," she pursed her lips. "Think he fancies you."

"I've already got a man."

"You sound like an old married woman."

"What? You think I'm boring?"

She chuckled. "You're good for me, little sister. It was a joke! So, it's going all right with the romantic boy pianist?"

"He's not a boy. He's twenty-nine, though sometimes he acts like he's ten."

"They all do," said Sophie. "Comes with the package. But he's cute, right? Look out the guy's coming over."

"Shit! Oh my God he's still got zits. Help me out here, Soph."

I fled from the table, headed for the loo. I hurried past the gents; it had a large sign up outside saying *Dukes*. I figured that after a heavy night at the bar, there wouldn't be too many Dukes going in there.

I heard footsteps hurrying behind me, trying to catch up, and someone put a hand roughly on my shoulder, spun me around. My instincts took over. The part of my brain, the reptilian bit that had made its way out of the prehistoric sludge, when we had to choose between fight or flight, took over. *Fight* won.

I didn't analyse, I didn't speculate, I just balled my hand into a fist and smacked the guy as hard as I could. He went over like a stalk in the wind. I'd caught him under the chin. I'd been aiming for his face, but I'm small and the guy was tall and skinny. I sunk to the floor beside him, hugged my knees tightly and rocked backwards and forwards.

Chapter 35

"No need to drag the cops in. Let's just call it a misunderstanding." The guy, named Jimmy, was massaging his jaw which didn't seem to have suffered any permanent damage. He had a wry look on his face as he spoke to Sophie, not me. Like she was my keeper or something.

"Not keen to meet the police then?" said Sophie. She wasn't stupid.

"Doin' your sister a favour, that's all. They'd press charges. But I'd keep her away from normal people if I were you, she's a whacko." The guy left the room, but not before he'd given me a look that confirmed my whacko status.

We'd all been crammed into the manager's office. Sophie, me, the pub manager Sam, and Jimmy, the tall skinny idiot with zits who still looked like a stalker to me. He hadn't been keen to give us his last name.

"I've got his face in here," said Sam and he tapped his forehead with an index finger. "Reckon he must be on something. He was a bit too quick to rule out the police. Don't need trouble like that in this place. And as for you . . ." He gave me a strange look. "I'd think about therapy if I were you. Or some kind of anger management. And I don't want to see you in my pub again."

"You don't understand," I said and burst out sobbing. I'd promised myself I wouldn't. I didn't want Sophie upset, didn't want her to know about Christopher Newly. She had enough on her mind. But sometimes things don't come out the way you've planned. "When that creep put his hand on my shoulder like that, it brought it all back. A guy indecently assaulted me."

Sophie's skin went grey and she sank into one of the scruffy office chairs. "We're not supposed to have any secrets, Stevie. You should have told me. Do the police know?"

"They know. They're looking for him. It's complicated."

"You should get her home," said Sam. "She doesn't look too good."

But you ask me, neither of us looked that good.

"Could you call us a cab?" said Sophie. *My big sister, taking care of stuff - w*hen it should have been me looking out for her.

Sophie looked drained when we got back to her place. Just climbing the stairs seemed to take all the energy she had, and when I led her to the sofa and made a cup of tea, she didn't protest. And it was good for me, focusing on her, putting the stupid stuff in the pub behind me. I guessed that was one place Sophie wouldn't visit again. Not that she was a jazz fan. I reckon she'd done that for me.

"I'm cooking pasta," I said.

"I can't eat it." She gave me a weak smile. "And you should have told me, you know. What's the point, if *we* can't trust each other?"

"You had enough to worry about."

My mobile went off. It was Harry. "They got him," he said. "Turned up drunk in *The Sailors*. Spending my bloody money, Stevie. Bragging about it; hell of a nerve."

"Sorry, Harry."

"Part of life's spilt milk." He gave a resigned sigh. It didn't sound like the Harry I knew. "Least the bastard can't do another bunk. They're remanding him in custody till the trial."

"And when's that?" Not that I wanted to know, or even think about it now. One thing at a time.

"Your guess is as good as mine. Justice moves at its own pace."

"Won't hold our breath then, eh?"

"How's the head?" he asked.

"Fine. Can't stop, I'm cooking for Sophie."

"You can cook?"

"I can boil pasta. How's the hand?"

"Good as your head!"

"Great."

"So, you'll be back in a week? Only we got a bus from Leeds coming in . . . and the golfers."

"Good news."

"You'll be back then?" he said.

"You miss me. That's sweet."

"You're a pain in the ass, but you've grown on me."

"Cute. See you in a week," I said. And as I put the phone down I found myself smiling.

*

"My twin, the boxer," said Sophie. "What are you – lightweight?"

"The guy had it coming. He was a creep."

"Sure. But you can't go round smacking every creep you find. There'd be no guys left," she said.

"What? You think there aren't any good blokes out there?"

"'Course there are. You just have to look in the right places, Stevie. And pubs probably aren't ideal. Not that it matters. We've been banned." My sister laughed.

"It's not that funny, Soph."

"Yes it is. Give it a day or two little sister, and you'll see the funny side. I've never been banned from a pub before. Have you?"

"Rarely go into one. Bottle of rotgut from the Offy in a brown paper bag usually suits me," I said.

If Sophie could see the funny side, then I guess I could as well. Last night had been something to put in the autobiography, if I ever got around to it. There were other things as well, but some of them made me come out like an airhead – and I don't think I am.

My sister was looking better this morning. Maybe because she'd had a proper night's sleep or it was one more day away from her last chemo. These things went in three week cycles and she was due her next treatment at the end of the week. I wanted to take her there, help her get through the day after. That was her worst day, she'd said, the day she usually threw up.

"Sure you'll be okay to stay? The hospital's a bit grim, but it'd be great to have you there for my 'C' day."

"I'll be here," I said. "You reading my mind again?"

"Yep. This twin thing really works."

"So 'C' day is Chemo Day."

"That and my crap day. But this time it'll be better. You're here."

Her hair was coming out now, but there were still wisps of it left. It looked so bizarre that she'd taken to wearing a turban. It was lime green. Sophie had this thing about vibrant colours. I think if I'd been feeling sick after chemo, lime green wouldn't be a colour I'd go for. But I guess it was my sister's way of sticking two fingers up to cancer. Don't know if I'd have been that brave, but it was good that one of us was.

"Breakfast here or in the park?" I asked.

"You remember that?"

"'Course I do. Best breakfast I ever had. Cake and ice cream."

Chapter 36

"I like the ones with Minnie Mouse on. How about you, Soph. Think they're cute?"

"Sure they're cute. You got a friend with a toddler?" Sophie picked up the plastic cutlery set. Examined it closely. "Nice. Good sturdy handles for chubby little fists."

I put it in my basket and we moved on to the smellies section in Boots. We were in the Mall at Cribbs Causeway. Sophie said we should come: shop-a-bit, eat-a-bit, talk-a-lot. We were still on the shopping bit and I was about to dive into all the aromatherapy stuff. I thought it might be good for her.

"How about I give you a massage, Soph? Here listen to this. Bergamot, Rosewood, Clary Sage and Ylang Ylang. Herbaceous Aroma, it says." I laughed.

"Let's see that. Hell. What's Ylang Ylang?"

"Search me," I said. "Some sort of flower, I guess."

Sophie turned the bottle over in her hands. "Says here it calms, relaxes and might help release feelings of anger, tension and 'nervous *iratibility*' – figure they mean irritability?"

"I guess."

"Maybe you should have tried some last night, Stevie. Before you punched the creep out."

"Maybe. C'mon." I linked arms with my sister and steered her towards the long line of people at the checkout. "I'm taking you to lunch. Anything you fancy, long as it's under a tenner and has nothing to do with raw fish."

"You don't like Sushi?" she asked.

"Not everybody likes Sushi."

"Is that *all* fish, then?"

"No. I like fish," I said. "Just not the kind that's still alive. Oh and Crustaceans."

"What crabs, crayfish?"

"Yeah, that sort of thing. And lobsters."

"Is it the shell? Or those funny little antenna things they wave about. Or the big bulging eyes. Some of them have eyes that come out on stalks," said Sophie and stuck her two index fingers either side of her head and wiggled them.

"Carry on like that and I'll be sick."

"Wow. My sister the Crustacean hater."

"I don't hate them. Matter of fact I sort of like them."

"What then?"

"Bad experience with some lobsters. I'll tell you about it one day."

The line had moved on and the woman behind the till glared at me like I was eating into her day. Customer service. The Americans had the whole thing down pat. It was like they really *wanted* to serve you and you weren't just an inconvenience interfering with their plans. We were crap at it. The British. We were good at other stuff. Donkey sanctuaries. Winning wars. We invented the computer. And the Cornish were good at making pasties and cream, and had Richard Trevithick. He built the first full-scale working railway steam locomotive. Some people say that was Stephenson with his Rocket. But they'd be wrong. Richard Trevithick got there over twenty years before him, and he was Cornish. Ask the folks from Camborne all about that, and they'll tell you.

Richard Trevithick was one of their own, and he definitely invented the steam train.

"You buying those?" The assistant looked from me down to her nails. They were like talons and had a French manicure with white tips. She seemed more interested in inspecting them than in taking my money. She'd probably missed the induction day where staff got reminded that customers paid their wages.

"It's why I'm here," I said, smiling. Trying to be pleasant. Not a sarcastic bone in my body. The sun was shining; I was out with my sister, buying aromatherapy oil that would get rid of nervous *iratibility*. All was right with the world.

We took a taxi to a place Sophie said served good food. Not that she was interested in food, it tasted weird, she said; so I guess she did that for me.

The place was Lebanese and there was a massive buffet set out with every kind of food you would ever want to make its way onto your plate. I had Hummus with pitta and a dollop of Tabouleh, Baba ghanoush (some kind of Aubergine concoction with olive oil) and baked Kibbee. I'd never heard of it before, but the smell coming from the Kibbee was enough to make me want to dive into it like a caveman. The smell of herbs and spices and meat kicked off messages of lust in my brain. But I held myself back. At least until Sophie had brought her own small selection back to our table and the drinks had arrived. Strictly non-alcoholic. Sophie didn't drink before she had her chemo, and I was teetotal from here on. Until the next time I had a drink.

"What's in that?" My sister wrinkled her nose as she pointed at the precious baked Kibbee.

"Pure angel dust."

"Smells like industrial cleaner," she said. "And it looks worse."

"You can't wind me up. I'm unwindable. And I'm looking forward to this." I waved a fork at my plate.

"You sure it's safe to eat angel dust?"

"Sure. Try some. It's ground steak and bulgar-wheat and onions and mint and cumin and cinnamon and basil and . . ."

"How'd you know all that?"

"I asked the waiter," I said."

"Looks like plain meatloaf to me."

"Ah yes, but then all food looks and tastes like crap to you right now. You said so."

"It's the chemo."

"And it's metallic. Am I right?"

"Same taste for everything. No matter what it is."

"That's the metal cutlery you're tasting," I said.

"What?"

"But we're about to change all that."

"We are?" Sophie looked cynical.

"Sure. Here." I dug down into my shopping bag and unwrapped the package. "Your very own plastic cutlery. And don't give me that look. You can't refuse to use it. You said you liked it and it's got Minnie on the handles."

She laughed so much it attracted the stares of other diners. People wearing suits. Upwardly mobiles who came to this fancy restaurant to be seen as much as to eat. They could all go to hell on a skateboard for my money. For the first time in ages my sister Sophie was laughing like a drain, coarsely, loudly; hardly an elegant noise. A cross between a snort and an elephant giving birth. But it was the sound of pure joy. And it was real.

She unearthed the plastic spoon from its bubbled container. "Give me that thing and let's see what all the fuss is about this bloody Kibbee stuff."

A rogue tear fought its way down my face. I couldn't help it.

*

"I hate those words, Stevie. I don't see myself like that."

My sister's face was flushed and her eyes had tiny stress lines under them.

"'Course you don't. I understand. You're far more positive than that."

We were sitting in a plush anti-room, going through a glossy catalogue of wigs. But the thing that had got Sophie out of kilter was the introduction page. The wigs were for all kinds of people, it said. Alopecia sufferers. Victims of Cancer.

"I'm not a *victim*. Or a *sufferer*." She denounced the words with a kind of venom, as if that would rid her body of the thing that had taken hold of it. I said I understood. And I really did, for it was as if I was inside Sophie's head. We were one person.

"No, you're not," I said.

"If you can understand that, why can't these bloody people?" She smacked the glossy brochure with an angry fist. "I'm not staying here."

"Look, Soph. They're just insensitive. Doesn't mean they can't make beautiful wigs though, does it? Look at that one. It's got YOU written all over it."

"You like it?"

"I love it."

"Right. We'll go see that assistant. I'll get measured up."

"Great!"

It wasn't that easy, of course. Is anything? I'd imagined we'd walk out the front door with Sophie wearing her new copper red wig, looking like a model straight off the catwalk, like the girl in the brochure. As if! That was just me, being naive.

The elderly woman who measured Sophie's head was more sensitive than the wording in the brochure. She'd done this many times before; you could tell. But every wig was tailor-made to the head it would end up on and that took time, she explained to us. She almost took my eye out with her elbow. The three of us were squashed into a tiny private cubicle. Cosy.

"Couple of weeks should do it," said the woman.

"That long? But I wanted to see you strut your stuff in it, Soph."

"*Stay then*," said my sister. Her voice wavered and she looked away.

"Right. I'll go fill out the invoice." The woman pulled back the curtain of the cubicle and hurried away. She seemed to sense the tension and wanted to leave us to it.

"You really want me to stay?"

Sophie didn't speak. It was as if she didn't want to force that choice on me. But she gave a small nod. It was just as good. She needed me, but she wouldn't push it; didn't want to back me into a corner. *Her. Or my job.*

Neither of us mentioned it again when we left the wig makers with its waiting room and cubicles and soft piped musak. It was a tacit, unspoken agreement that just hung there in the air; we would both think about Sophie's words. And I would have to come to a decision. I would do anything for my sister, the woman I'd waited thirty four years to find, but it would mean my rejection of the Royal and Matt and Joe and Harry and Doris and . . . even Gloria Endersley. What the hell. There was no choice. And I reckon I wouldn't have made a very convincing nun anyway.

*

Sophie had said the hospital was grim and I'd expected something very different. But then I guess if you had cancer and were going there for chemotherapy, then everything would seem grim.

It was the opposite. The waiting area was bright and cheerful, a bit like Disneyland. One wall had a rainbow painted across it and there were photographs of smiling people underneath; happy people with their families, shaking hands with nurses and staff. They would be the survivors, the lucky ones. The grateful ones. I couldn't imagine people who'd lost mothers, fathers, grandparents, kids, smiling like that.

The receptionist nodded at my sister, pointed towards the coloured plastic chairs, said: "You know the form, Sophie. They'll be out to get you when they're ready."

I took the cue from my sister. She didn't want to talk, just held my hand and stared off vacantly into some place where I couldn't go. Even the twin thing didn't help me read her mind. She didn't look angry, which is what I would have been; just wistful, like she was carrying a deep sadness. I thought back to the restaurant a few days ago, when she'd laughed till she cried. That person was gone. But hopefully she'd be back, and I'd do all I could to help her return.

There were others in the room – waiting, thinking, going through their own private hell, perhaps. Sophie nodded to several people and they nodded back. It felt like some sort of club; staff, patients, they probably got to know each other.

A few seats away, an elderly man and woman sat together. I tried to use my people-reading skills to figure out which one was sick. It was hard to tell; they both looked sad and ill and they never spoke a word to each other. A teenage girl sat with her mother; well I figured it was her mother. The woman kept on asking how the young girl felt, kept fussing over her, like I guess you do with your children. It's your job to protect them. Take their problems on your own shoulders, make things right for them. It was easy to see who had cancer there. The girl was wearing a hat and her skin was like thin parchment.

The teenager shrugged her mother's arm off from around her shoulder, said: "Stop fussing. You're always fussing. Go for a walk." Teenagers were teenagers I guess, whether they had cancer or not. Her mother looked deflated. But she stayed where she was, even if she wasn't wanted, she was still a mother. I wouldn't know much about the job description, but I guess in general there were expectations of the brand. The teenager got up and walked away.

A middle aged man opposite me shuffled about in his plastic chair. He reminded me of Harry, although he wasn't quite as rotund. The man looked at his watch and up at the clock on the wall, got up and took one of the magazines.

"His chemo takes five hours." Sophie nodded at the guy. "I saw you looking at him," she said. "You're a people watcher too. Like me."

"Five hours, Jesus!"

"You think that's bad, Stevie? Some of them are hooked up to IVs all day."

"What about you?"

"I'm one of the lucky ones. Three hours and I'm done."

A nurse came out of a doorway and headed in our direction. "This is obviously the twin I've been hearing about," she said and looked at me. She smiled. All the staff seemed to have caught the happy bug. I figured the cheerfulness was a mask and helped them deal with the sad shit that came their way. I couldn't have worked here.

"This is Michele, my nurse. If it wasn't for her, I'd have reduced this place to rubble by now," said my sister.

"Now you know that's not true. You're a model patient. Perfectly well behaved. Not like that guy last week, tried to slug me."

"Stevie's the boxer in our family. I leave all that stuff up to her."

"Right, let's get on," said the nurse.

I struggled out of my plastic seat and wondered how easy that job would be for the man opposite me. The moulded plastic chairs were made using a template suitable for anorexic midgets. I guess there's only so far the NHS budget will stretch, even for cancer patients.

"No. You stay, Stevie. I don't want you in there."

"But I thought . . ."

The nurse, Michele took my sister by the hand. "It's okay," she said. "You can wait here or go shopping. We'll be finished by 3. That's when you'll *really* be needed."

They went off together into some secret hinterland where I couldn't follow. A scary place, where, if I'm honest, I didn't want to go.

I went shopping instead. Bought Harry a tie. He liked ties. I'd post it to him, although it wasn't much compensation for leaving him flat when he had a coach coming in from Leeds. But life's like that; full of surprises.

Chapter 37

Harry had bombarded my voice mail with messages, more desperate as time went on and heavily punctuated with swearing. I'd ignored them and dumped his texts without even opening them. *Call me cold and hard-bitten, if you like. But I've had to prioritise.*

I didn't think I could be this brave. I don't mean about Harry. Losing your job doesn't take bravery. And I'd lost it once before, so I'm guessing I'll live through it. No, about my sister.

I've looked after her and cleaned up her puke. Put damp towels on her head to bring her temperature down. And today, I sang to her. She laughed at that; the first time she's laughed since her chemotherapy session. So either my singing has improved or I could earn money from stand-up. I may need to.

I don't know how she does it. How other people who go through this bitch of a chemo manage it. I'd gripe like hell and make everybody around me miserable. Or maybe I wouldn't; who knows until it happens to you. At any rate, all these people are heroes in my book, including my sister Sophie.

I've been brave about something else too. Last night my sister asked if I'd like to see the *battle ground*. She meant her breasts, of course. I took a mental gulp and tried to be all upbeat about it, for the awful picture I'd painted in my head was nothing short of gruesome. The sort of thing that might have come out of the Spanish Inquisition. But if Sophie was prepared to let me see this humongous crater, this butchery where her breast used to be, I knew I had to be brave too.

"Wow!"

"What?"

"You've got breasts," I said.

"What did you expect?"

"I don't know. A huge hole, I guess, where your left one used to be."

"This is the twenty-first century, Stevie. Not the Dark Ages. They can work all sorts of miracles."

"Wow!"

"You said that already."

But my reaction had pleased her. It couldn't be easy. Letting somebody look. Not when the mental and physical scars were still so raw.

"But how . . . ? I mean – it looks real. Is it one of those plastic implant thingys?"

"No. It's all me. That's the best bit. They bring muscle tissue round from your back. It's natural. It even grows with you. You get fat – it gets fat. You loose weight, it does too."

"Cool."

"It's incredible," said Sophie. "They harvest muscle, skin and fat from your back and pass it inside this skin tunnel thing into your armpit and through to your breast. Then bingo. It gets folded into shape to make your boob."

"Yeah, but doesn't that mean you'll be lopsided? Won't they both be different?"

"Do they look different to you?"

I have to be honest; I was trying not to stare at her boobs. "No," I said. "They're the same."

"And you're right," she said. "The new one. The *manmade* one . . ." Sophie laughed, "was higher up, like a teenager's. So they just pulled the other one up to match it. My tits have never been so great, Stevie. It's like gravity never took hold."

"They did all that when you had your op?"

"Sure. Immediate reconstruction. That's why it took so long. Eight hours."

"God, Soph. I didn't know."

"I didn't want you to. Not till it was all done."

So you see. We're both brave. My sister and I.

I went over to the park café to get us a couple of lattes. Sophie suggested it; I needed to get out of the flat, she said. She didn't come, too many people out there with bugs to be passed on to that struggling immune system of hers. Chemo does that to you.

I bought cake, luscious death-by-chocolate for me, and a plainer carrot cake for her. She might not eat it anyway, for most things seemed to make her queasy. But even so, I kept encouraging her to eat and drink.

"I've had enough water to fill a bleedin' reservoir," she'd complained. But I'd kept on bringing her glasses of it and sometimes lemon barley. Water was good for you. Your cells needed it. I'd remembered that from somewhere and my sister had grudgingly gone along with my badgering, taking small sips, her face screwing up in disgust.

Time I got back, Sophie was on the phone. "I'll get her to call you right back," she said and put down the landline.

"Your friend Doris wants you to phone."

"Doris?"

"She sounded real sad."

"Doris *sad*? I said. "She doesn't get sad. She gets *mad*."

"Phone her Stevie."

"She say anything else?"

"Only that Harry's been a royal pain in the rear."

"And that's new?"

Sophie handed me the phone. "Phone her and I promise to eat my cake and drink my coffee. Deal?"

"Deal," I said, reluctantly. I didn't want to talk to Doris. Or Joe. I hadn't spoken to either of them for the last two weeks. Matt, yes. He'd phoned me twice. He missed me, he'd said. I missed him too.

Doris was on one of her famous long coffee breaks.

"Like one of them bloody great bulls, he is," she said. "Smoke coming from his nostrils. Snarling at staff. Alfie threatened to deck him if he didn't get his arse out of the kitchen."

"Nothing changes," I said.

"You know how to handle him, Stevie. You got the knack. He won't listen to nobody else."

"I can't come back."

"What, never?" she said.

"Who knows?"

"We miss you, Stevie."

"Yeah? Well, I miss you too, Auntie D. But I can't leave. Don't ask me to. How's Morris?"

"You know my Morris. He don't change. He's building the Swiss mountains out of hardboard in the back garden."

"What?"

"For the Am Drams. Joe's dragged him in – for the sets, like."

"Sorry, Doris."

"Oh he don't mind. Keeps him busy and outta my hair."

"They got a new Maria yet?"

"Gawd knows. I don't 'ave nuthin' to do with that Endersley woman. Her and my Morris nearly come to blows – till he offered her his saw to build her own bloody sets."

The line went quiet. Doris was waiting for me to say something, I guess. I couldn't think of a thing.

"The golfers are here. They come, like His Lordship promised."

"That's good."

"Lotta toffee-nosed gits. Wives glad to get rid of them, shouldn't wonder. Treat the rooms like crap."

"Gotta go, Doris. Sophie needs me." Sophie was waving a hand, like she wanted me to carry on, but I ignored it.

"Sure, babe. You take care and remember - you need anything, I'm right here."

"Thanks."

"Joe sends his love, wants to speak to you."

"I can't." It was hard not to blub. They were my family. I loved the lot of them, even Harry.

"Okay. Look after yourself, girl."

"Sure." I put the phone down. My hand was shaking and Sophie was looking sad, but she didn't say anything. And I didn't have to explain. She knew. Her pain was my pain; my pain was hers; we were twins. Mostly that was good, but sometimes it wasn't and you wanted to cut the invisible cord that joined you. But only sometimes. I'd waited a long time to find my sister, and I wasn't going to let anyone or anything come between us; not the Hotel Royal and certainly not bastardin' cancer.

Chapter 38

It was the middle of the night and my mobile was having a fit. At first I'd tried to ignore the constant beeping as texts flooded in one after another. I should have put the thing on silent, for it would wake Sophie from her fitful sleep. I'd been sleeping in a duvet on her bedroom floor. My sister didn't ask me for many things, but last night she'd been upset, had an attack of the gloomies and asked me not to leave her alone.

The mobile beeped again. I stumbled through the darkened bedroom and bashed my knee on the old fashioned chest of drawers. It would be Harry. I found the phone, the glow of its screen puncturing a small hole in the blackness, and I grabbed it.

It had been hard enough getting Sophie off to sleep last night without her being disturbed by Harry and his incessant texts. I took the duvet from the floor and went out to Sophie's small lounge. It was freezing in there and I wasn't happy. You'd think Harry would have the idea by now. I wasn't playing. I wasn't coming back. My sister needed me, and as much as I *wanted* to help him out, there wasn't a choice. She was going through a bad patch and seemed to be sliding downhill.

I shivered and looked up at Sophie's Mickey Mouse wall clock. God, it was three thirty in the morning. What was Harry thinking? Unless he was drunk and feeling sorry for himself.

It wasn't Harry. This last text was from Matt.

"hi", he wrote. "its me" ♪ "luv u. heres my heart" <3 and heres wot u did to it </3. C, Stevie? Its brokn. ☹ n im drunk. lol matty. Wen u comin home???

He *loved* me? Wow. He'd never said that before. Then again, he was drunk. How could he do it to me? Did he think this was easy? Did they all think it was easy? Well it bloody well wasn't. I sat in Sophie's armchair, shaking. There was a creak of floorboards in the hall outside. That would be my sister getting up to go to the loo. I should go out there and help her, but I didn't have the energy. I fell into a weary sleep.

Next morning I woke up to Sophie acting as a waitress, bringing me coffee and biscuits. She had this massive grin, but my insides curdled when I saw the colour of her face. It was like day old ashes, and she walked with a stiffness that said she was suffering. But her whole manner was . . . I searched for the word, chirpy. Yeah, I guess chirpy would cover it. And it didn't make any kind of sense.

"Drink your coffee, sleepy head. We're going out."

"We are?"

"Wig's ready."

"Great. We taking the bus over there?" I said.

"Nope, celebration. I'll swing for a taxi."

It was what I figured. All this cheerful stuff was a front. Sophie didn't have the energy to make the long walk to the bus stop. But she was still smiling about stuff. So I did too.

Later, we passed the landlady in the hall. She knew all about Sophie's treatment, but I could see it in her face; the old woman was shocked at the toll it had taken. But we all did the smiley thing and pretended stuff was great.

And my sister really did seem happy about the prospect of having hair again, even if it was somebody else's hair.

*

Sophie was over the moon with her wig, so I tried to be just as happy as she was. The stylish bob suited her, but the splash of deep red made her face look even paler. Still, it was better than having no hair at all.

When we got back to the house, Sophie had to ring the bell. In all the excitement she'd forgotten her keys.

"Like a proper movie star, me dear," was the landlady's verdict. "You'll have gentlemen queuing up. Now, do you need me to open up upstairs for you, as well?"

"Lovely, thanks Rosie. That would be kind. Sorry to put you out, but this chemo thing takes your brains out and puts them back upside down."

"I understand, dear. No need for apologies."

The elderly woman led the way upstairs. It was a hard climb, but she made it look easy. She was nimble, her body bobbing easily from one tread to the next, as if she were on springs.

"Talk about *you* being forgetful, Sophie," she said. "They'll not be using my brain for medical science. It's mush right now. I forgot all about your visitor. I told her you'd gone out and she said she'd come back later."

"Visitor?"

"Yes, a lady of advancing years; though I can hardly speak." Rosie smiled and put her hand up to her mouth to stifle a laugh.

"What sort of build was she, this lady?" I asked.

"Build? Well, I suppose not particularly tall. A little on the portly side, perhaps. Though one shouldn't judge."

"Doris," I said. "Now why on earth would she come? I thought I'd explained it all to her the other night."

My sister giggled. "Might not be Doris. Why not Gloria Endersley? From what you've said, it's the sort of thing she'd do."

"Holy God! She's the last person I want to see."

Rosie took a step back and a shadow passed across her face. She was a little genteel, so perhaps she was shocked by a blasphemer. Or maybe she was religious. I don't rule out the possibility of a deity overseeing things, myself. But in my mind, He'd forgive the odd lapse on my part, and blaspheming wouldn't be one of the things He'd be hot on. Not when there were people out there doing far worse things to each other.

I couldn't settle after that. If I'd known for certain it was Doris, I'd have phoned her mobile, asked her what the hell she was playing at. But what if it really was Gloria Endersley, come to extract her pound of flesh? Well I was out of the flesh donation business. She could clear off back home to Cornwall and leave me in peace.

That was the sort of stroppy mood I was in when somebody knocked Sophie's door. She didn't have a doorbell. I hadn't had one either. We had lots of things in common, but then we were twins.

The knock came again, only louder and more insistent this time. I signalled to Sophie to stay where she was on the sofa and let me deal with Gloria Endersley and then I stomped to the front door, ready to do battle. The woman could damn well find herself another nun. It couldn't be that difficult; there must be star-struck people in their droves out there just waiting for the chance to play Maria.

But it wasn't Gloria Endersley. I drew in a shallow breath and leaned against the door jamb for support. It was my mother.

Chapter 39

Her shoulders were heaving with great heavy sobs. I'd never seen my mother cry like that before, always thought there was nothing she cared about enough to make her weepy. Shows me, right? And now I'm confused, for she seemed genuinely upset. The tea I'd made her was still untouched, and she stared hard at Sophie, waiting for an answer.

"It seemed the right thing to do," said Sophie.

"You should have told me you were ill."

"I didn't want you feeling sorry for me. I guess I wanted to protect you, as well as me."

"But that's *my* job Sophie. That's what mothers are for. To protect their children, keep them safe. That's why I let your grandmother take you away. Why I didn't try to get back into your life. You think I wanted you to go?"

That was one question too far for me. And a discussion I figured Sophie and my mother should have alone. I left the room. Maybe I just wasn't brave enough for any more confrontations; I'd used up a lot of courage in the last few weeks, watching my sister spitting in the eye of cancer, and me powerless to change a thing.

Sophie came to get me.

"Pleeese, Stevie. Come back in. Don't make me do this on my own."

"She still there?"

"Just listen to what she has to say."

"I've heard what she has to say, and I've been listening for years."

"Give her another chance. Everybody deserves one of those."

I followed my sister into the lion's den and I was scared, for something told me that things were about to change. Stuff I had no control over.

My mother's eyes were puffy and she looked beat up. Life hadn't always been kind to her, and in a flash of uncomfortable insight, I realized that neither had I. So . . . she hadn't been perfect; but had I?

"Can we call a truce, Stevie?" she asked.

"Maybe."

"Only, this cancer thing has knocked me for six," she said.

"Welcome to the club. But then you're a late comer." *God, why did I have to do that? It's NOT me. I'm NOT a bitch. But she brings out the worst in me.*

"Take as many cheap shots as you like. Maybe I deserve some of them, but I want to make up for lost time. I want to help Sophie."

"I'm helping her," I said. "She doesn't need you."

"Oh? Maybe we should ask your sister about that?"

"Soph?" I said.

My sister looked miserable. "I want us all to be friends. I want us to be a proper family. What's wrong with that? It's what Grandmother wanted too. You said so, Stevie. She asked you to reunite us, didn't she?"

"There you are." My mother sounded triumphal.

"Look, Mother wants to stay for a while," said Sophie. "She was going to get a B and B, but I'm not having that. We can fit her in here somehow. Maybe you could take the couch, Stevie. We can't ask her to do that. She'll help."

"I will," she said eagerly.

"But I'm looking after you. We don't need her."

"Then I'm to keep paying for something *you* think I did. Is that fair Stevie?"

My mother got ready to leave. "I'll not stay where I'm not welcome," she said.

"Stevie! Tell her to stay," my sister said angrily.

"Oh, she can stay all right. For I'm going. I'll miss you, Soph. But you don't understand. You didn't have to get your own dinners. Or have a mother who didn't come to your school play."

"Look, you guys. You can't put me in the middle like this. I won't take sides. And I'm the one who's sick, if you'd both forgotten," said Sophie. "I'm disappointed in the pair of you. I thought I had a family, but now I'm not so sure. I wish I'd never left Canada."

*

I'm home again. My real home. And everybody made it easy for me. The prodigal daughter who walked out when they needed her, and then walked straight back in to hugs from Joe and a cup of tea from Doris. What is it about the British that we think the world's ills can be cured by flinging a small bag into a mug and drowning it in boiling water?

It wasn't all plain sailing, though. Harry had me back okay, but he couldn't let it go without the odd jibe about people letting you down when you really needed them. I'd been crying a lot. I'd tried not to, as my face isn't at its best with humungous red splotches covering it, but I reckon my head was coming to terms with lots of complicated stuff and tears were the safety valve.

Matt arrived. You could tell he'd made a special effort, for it was only ten thirty in the morning and he was already out of bed.

He lunged at me. Practically ate my face off with his sloppy kiss. And it hit me with the force of an explosion, how much I'd missed him. How good it was to have someone on the planet who cared you were alive.

When we came up for air he looked serious.

"What?"

"We need to talk about this."

"I'm all talked out," I said.

"And cried out too, according to Joe."

"He's a blab."

"He's a friend, and he's worried. You can't just pretend this didn't happen. What about your sis? How's she feeling? You even know?"

"I know how she's feeling, Matt. We're twins. She's in my dreams with me."

"Then call her back. Put things straight. You think it's fair she's had to choose between you and her mother? Not that you gave her any choice, not running away like that."

"Not you too? Thought I could rely on you."

"You can. But I call things as I see them, Stevie. You know that. She's not happy."

"How'd you know?"

"She's been calling. Give her a bell. Can't hurt, and it might make you less miserable."

"Who says I'm miserable?"

"Everybody whose head you've chewed off. C'mon, Stevie. Take a chance. What can you lose and we can't have an unhappy nun, can we?"

"I'm not playing Maria."

"I think you'll find you are. The battleaxe has started rehearsals and wants to slot you in 'at your convenience'."

"Bet she didn't say that."

"Exactly what she said. Think you've scared her."

"As if."

"What's she gonna do with a whole load of posters with your name on them?"

I could have told him. But I don't always say the first thing that pops into my head.

"Your mother's a gem," said Matt.

"Think so?"

"Well obviously not, I was going for irony there. She told Joe he was rude and called him a fruit."

"Sounds like her. Joe tell her about Sophie's cancer?"

"Even Joe's not a saint. I guess being called a fruit does something to you. He wanted to make her hurt."

"How'd she get Sophie's address? Joe tell her that too?"

"Who knows? Maybe your sister did, when you two went up to Plymouth to see her."

Harry passed by Reception, he was wearing a ridiculous pair of knee-length plaid shorts, like baggies gone wrong, and a fancy jumper that was too tight for him. He was hefting a golf bag over his shoulder and walked side by side with an equally stout individual whose clothes were almost as bizarre as Harry's. My boss threw me his most charming smile and I looked behind to check it was meant for me.

"Back later, Miss Anderson," he said, in his business voice. "Anyone wants me, I'll be on the course up at St Mellion."

"Very well, Sir." I played along.

Doris came rushing up just in time to see the back of the Mercedes as it pulled away from the front drive.

"Who the hell was that?" she asked.

"God knows, but Harry's going all the way to Saltash to play golf instead of Newquay. Must want to impress with a championship course."

"Think the bloke'll be impressed with them shorts?" laughed Doris.

Agata came out of the restaurant, a massive grin on her face. "Mr Evans just give me pay raise. He say he was pleased with *exemplary breakfast service.*"

"He didn't happen to be taking breakfast with anyone in there?"

"Sure, man with the Scottish trousers."

"Golfing trews, Agata. Big tartan patterns," I said. "Means people can spot you easily on the golf course."

"Ah. Well, both of them smile at me. And Mr Evans tell me to take pay raise."

"Right." I smiled at Agata too. Didn't want to spoil her day. But sometime I'd need to go into the finer points of Harry's sense of humour with her. I'd do it soon. Before she went ahead and ordered that new Smart T.V. she had on her wish list.

Chapter 40

"It ain't natural," said Doris.

She was right. Harry had been whistling cheerfully everywhere he went, and there was a general feeling of optimism in the air.

"Money," she said, plugging away at it.

"What money?" I asked.

"Sure to be about money. Harry ain't interested in nuthin' else."

"He likes golf," I said, for some reason leaping to Harry's defence. He had a heart in there somewhere and could be sentimental about his dog, Benjy.

Speak of the devil. Harry stepped out of the lift like he'd just got his cue from a stage manager. "They need you up on the 2nd floor. Work your magic, Doris."

"Magic?"

"Sure. Maureen don't know what to do with red wine stains."

"Simple. Just throw white over them."

"White?" said Harry.

"White wine. Should work. Mind, depends how long ago it happened."

Harry grinned. "Always said you were a magician, Doris."

"You did?"

"'Course."

"Fair enough." Doris walked towards the lift, muttering under her breath "Abra-ca-bleedin'-dabra."

"You sound happy,"

"Why not? Looks like I've sold the house," he said.

"That's great, Harry."

"Yeah, bloke came down from the smoke to see it yesterday."

"The golfer?"

"Well, he ain't much of a golfer, but he wants to set up down here."

"Brilliant."

"Yeah. He's got a few bob. Hedge fund manager."

"A *banker*? Thought you hated them?"

"His money's good as anybody's." Harry rubbed his hands, doing his impersonation of Scrooge. "And he runs his business online, so it don't matter where he lives."

"Result all round then." I was pleased for him. Pleased that he was happy, for he'd worked hard to try and pull the Royal out of the mire.

"Not signed, sealed and delivered yet. But lookin' good. What about you?"

"What about me what?"

"You still sellin' tickets for the Am Drams?"

"You're not thinking of coming? Don't think it's your sort of thing, Harry." I imagined him sitting on the hard, wooden benches we'd be setting up in the school assembly hall. Not an ideal environment for his piles.

"'Course it is. Put me down for two."

"Two?"

"Sure." Harry winked.

Maybe he'd found love.

*

"Looks like we got ourselves a court date. You okay with that?" Harry asked.

We'd both had the letter. The *call to arms*, he called it. No idea what he meant by that; sometimes I think Harry lives in another world, in a different century. There'd been a pamphlet as well, about Witness Support and stuff. I binned it. Maybe I should have read it, but I guess I was in denial about how grim this would be.

"Stevie!"

"What?"

"You don't have to do this, you know. We'd still have him for the robbery."

"Yeah? And he'd get what for that? A tap on the wrist and community service?"

"You're bloody cynical."

"I read the papers," I said.

"So, you're okay to stand up in court?"

"I'd rather be in the Bahamas, but that's not the point."

"So, see you in court, eh?" he laughed.

I knew why Harry laughed. It wasn't my boss's first court appearance, but at least this time he'd be standing on the right side of the dock.

I'd had *another* letter. And its contents had both shocked and thrilled me in equal amounts. I'd have to do something about it soon. I'd been tempted to show it to Matt, but maybe Joe would be better. He had a more keen business head on his shoulders than Matt had. Matt was a musician, had an artistic temperament and as far as everyday problems were concerned, he floated about a foot above the surface of the earth, slightly removed from the rest of us folk.

The Ottawa solicitors, who'd been the executors for my grandmother's will, needed some further input on my part (and my sister's). Mr Clarence Adams from Harding and Willis had signed the letter himself. Both Sophie and I needed to sign some documents in the presence of a Notary Public, and Clarence - I have always thought of him irreverently as simply 'Clarence' - had suggested that as my sister and I were in the same area (what map did he have?) we could get ourselves the same local solicitor.

It looked like we would both end up with some money. And part of me thought that was great; I might even be able to get myself a cheap car. But another part, where I keep my negative emotions and fears locked up, could have done without having to face Sophie. Tell her I was wrong. That I'd abandoned her. There! I'd finally said it. Everybody else who cared about me had already hinted at it.

I'd screw up my courage and phone my sister. Swallow my pride. I could do that.

"Hey, do I pay you to stand and daydream?"

Harry's face looked like he'd eaten a lemon whole, pips and all. *What now?* Ten minutes ago the man had been positively chummy. You hear about this bi-polar stuff, radical mood swings and what not. But I'd never put my boss down as having the sensitivity or the temperament needed to be bi-polar.

Skelly came out of nowhere. Crepe soles on his shoes, I reckon. So people couldn't hear him coming. Harry put on a brave front. "My office, NOW!" he growled.

I remembered the broken hand. Who could forget? Especially not when you've had to wriggle your fingers between Harry's sweaty arm and the Plaster of Paris. I phoned cook.

"Alfie, reckon you could make a guest appearance in our illustrious leader's office? At your convenience, but sooner might be better than later. Skelly's just gone in there and he looked like he meant business."

"Bastard!"

I didn't know if he meant Harry or Skelly, but the word seemed heart-felt.

"Little toe-rag Skelly's all mouth and steroids," he said. "He ain't up to no real action. Count me in."

I only heard about it later. I kept well away from Harry's office, for I figured I would just complicate stuff. Harry, Skelly, Benjy and now Alfie. Too much testosterone in a relatively small space. It could only spell trouble. But for who, or was that whom?

Doris came running up to Reception. "You see what I see?"

Obviously not, for I was trying to keep busy, after all Harry had said it himself. He didn't pay me to daydream.

"I'm like the three wise monkeys rolled into one," I told her. "See nothing, hear nothing, say nothing."

"Sometimes, Stevie, you worry me. Ain't you even curious? It's WW3 in there and you ain't interested?"

"Nope."

"And if I was to tell you Alfie went in Harry's office with a meat cleaver in his hand?"

"I'd say you're hallucinating. I've got bills to make out and you got floors to clean Auntie D. Let's just stick to what we're good at. And keep our noses out of things that don't concern us."

Doris went off muttering and I went out back to my office to sort out some admin. My stomach was doing complicated double-flips, so I reached for the antacid tablets and thought about what I'd say to my sister when I phoned her to eat an oversized portion of humble pie.

I didn't have to. Phone, that was. For twenty minutes later she was standing in front of me. Looking unsure of herself. Of the kind of reception she'd get. But looking better. Looking *far* better than the last time I'd seen her.

I threw my arms around my big sister, squeezed her till it hurt. And she looked relieved.

"I was going to call you today," I said. "Just got up the courage to say what a prat I've been. I was wrong. I should've stayed and tried to work things out with mother. You shouldn't have to pay, Sophie. Not for stuff that we've got going on."

"It'll be okay now," she said quietly.

I wasn't sure how. But I trusted her. She was my blood.

*

We made an appointment to see a solicitor in Newquay, Sophie and me. The woman didn't have an available date until the middle of next week. I suppose we could have shopped around, tried to get one somewhere else quicker. But I liked the woman's name. Vivienne Hardcastle. I'd never met anyone called Vivienne before, but it seemed like a serious name and anyone who was booked up solidly with clients, I figured must be good at their job. Sophie decided to stay until then. She only had one more chemo to go and it wasn't for a while. Besides, she wanted to come to rehearsals, see how her little sister cracked it as a singing nun. And I could hardly refuse, could I?

Chapter 41

My sister knows *everything* now. All about the assault and how it traumatized me, and the way our ex-barman had come back again to steal from Harry and smack me around the head. *I* hadn't told her; I wasn't looking for sympathy. Somebody else had snitched.

Harry had given her one of his best en-suite rooms, where the heating worked and you could take a reasonable shower without having to thump the pipes with a wrench. I'd offered to pay for it out of my salary, but Sophie insisted she should pay herself. Harry had given her a good rate. It wouldn't have hurt him to give her a freebie for a few days, but I guess there's only so far the man will go. His wallet was welded to his body.

We'd been shopping in town for a serious looking suit. A suit to wear for an appearance in court as a witness. I could hardly wear my staff uniform, which was the only formal bit of kit I possessed. It had H.R. embroidered on the pocket, Sophie reminded me. They might think I was taking the piss. Matt and Harry were also on the witness list, but they already had dark suits. Funeral clothes. Hopefully the only funeral would be Christopher-Scumbag-Newly's.

Sophie sipped her latte and beamed. "That was a real find." She patted the bag affectionately, said: "designer cut, good colour on you too. And dead reasonable."

"Reasonable?" I said, astounded. It had cost me a whole week's pay.

"Sure. Try shopping in Canada. Crazy expensive."

We lapsed into one of those silences where both people feel happy to just kick back and think. I don't know what Sophie was thinking about, but I was glad she was here. Especially now, though I didn't want her sitting in court tomorrow.

"You miss it?" I said.

"What?"

"Canada and your life there."

"A bit. But I won't go back if that's what you're asking."

"But it's where you grew up," I said.

Sophie laughed. "*You've* moved on from where you grew up."

"Yeah, but that's different. My life wasn't that good before. I like this one better."

"Me too," she said. "Now that I've found you, I won't go back home. I'll make a new one."

"You will?"

"Sure."

I didn't dare ask her where. I was too scared of the answer. Maybe she'd move closer to our mother.

We walked back to the hotel. It was a fair distance through the town and along past Tolcarne beach, but Sophie managed to keep up and didn't look nearly as ill as the last time we'd walked together in Bristol. It felt like a holiday. Harry had hauled Joe in and given me the day off. The man can be sensitive when he wants to be, it seems, and I guess he was thinking about the ordeal I'd have to face in court tomorrow. Not even a serious looking suit with a designer cut would make that any easier.

But tomorrow was still to come and I reckoned we could both enjoy our day, my sister Sophie and I; have dinner in the restaurant for a change instead of the staff room, go into the bar, have a few drinks (only a couple) and listen to Harry's lame stand-up, and maybe even join in the Karaoke.

As it turns out, somebody else sat at our table as well. An older woman, with a friendly smile and hair whose sleek, blonde sheen had been helped along by some high class hairdressing product. It was Harry's idea we should sit with her to watch the Karaoke. Keep her company, he'd said. And as he'd asked, his eyes held a pleading look. Very un-Harry like.

The woman's face crinkled into deep laughter lines when Harry told his corny jokes. It struck me as loyalty, her laughter. For Harry's anecdotes had little backbone to them and only the faintest trace of humour.

Her name was Grace. And she bought a bottle of wine for Sophie and me, although she didn't drink any of it herself. Her manner was like her name, gracious. She possessed a quiet dignity, and brush strokes of humanity were clearly visible on her, but she could also throw back her head and laugh without feeling embarrassed. I felt I'd known Grace Harper my whole life.

None of the customers seemed too upset when Harry knocked it on the head early and exchanged his duff Karaoke tracks for the bar's usual piped muzak. He came to join us, a glass of scotch that Eli had poured for him earlier grasped tightly in his hand. He looked nervous.

Eli came over to the table and made a large production number out of opening a bottle of champagne. He was an old ham at heart. Note to self; get him to join the Am Drams.

"Here you go," said Harry, smiling at Grace and handing her a glass of bubbly.

"Oh Harry. You know I shouldn't." But she sipped it delicately all the same.

"We celebrating something?" I said.

"Grace's birthday - and tomorrow's happy conclusion." Harry winked, first at Grace and then at me. He poured out the champagne for the rest of us. And we all raised a glass to Grace Harper.

"One of those is a shoe-in," I said. "Not sure about the other one though."

"Don't be so negative, Stevie. Maybe tomorrow will be an easier ride than you think." Harry tapped the side of his nose, like someone with insider information.

"You know something I don't?" God, let's hope he wasn't going to try something dodgy. That's all we needed at Truro Crown Court in front of a judge and a jury, and the court reporter from the local paper all wired up for something sensational.

Harry's look of innocence was pure gold. "What me? What could I possibly know? The man's going down, though. I feel it in my bones," he said and massaged his bad hand.

"Touch of arthritis, dear," said Grace. "That's what happens when you break bones. You should take better care of yourself, my lovely. Let the barman put out the empties in future." She put her hand on top of Harry's large one, and smiled. It was a look that said from now on someone else would be happy to take care of him.

Everyone has their own cross to bear, I'll grant you that. But anyone who would take Harry on, and cheerfully call him 'my lovely', must have a fairly robust psyche. Or be totally naive. And although Grace might seem like a fine woman with a generous heart, she didn't strike me as anyone's fool. Maybe at last Harry Evans' luck had changed. I found myself hoping it was true.

Chapter 42

"Be upstanding in court." *They still say that.* The old fashioned words jarred; seemed out of place in a world of technology's super highway. But we all stood up just the same. It was more than a bit scary, and I've done scary things. That's when I had second thoughts. Not about testifying, but turning down the help offered by the Witness Care Unit. They would have taken me on a visit to the courtroom before the trial. Explained the court process. But it was too late for all that now.

I knew the truth. But somehow THE TRUTH won't stand up automatically on its own two fragile feet. I'd never thought about that before. But now it was important.

I did my best. You need to believe that. I told the whole truth. But the defence barrister was a bastard in his cross-examination, or maybe he was just doing his job. And that job was to make me look like some kind of slut who would jump the bones of any guy on my radar. At any rate, he made me out to be a cross between Mata Hari and the local bike; a liar, who had all men under her spell. *I wish.* I thought about the guy who had stolen my furniture, the one who still owed me a hundred quid, and the fish-man. Men were bastards, I was right. Okay, not all men. Matt had slipped a tiny silver horseshoe into my hand for good luck before I'd gone into the inner sanctum of the courtroom.

"Remember, Miss Anderson, that you are under oath," said Newly's barrister. "Now, have you ever had a relationship with a married man?" His look said *home-wrecker*.

My brain hit a glitch, just for a second, but I guess that was enough to plant some kind of negative seed in the minds of the jurors. How had he managed to dig that up? I looked over at Christopher Newly sitting there looking smug. Of course he knew. All the staff knew about me and the fish-man and the fact that he was married.

"It wasn't like that," I said. And I think I mumbled, for it had taken me off balance.

"Oh? And how exactly was it? Perhaps you'd care to explain to us all." The slime-ball smirked at the jury.

"It was a perfectly normal – *innocent* – mistake to make," I said. "I had no idea the man was married."

"Okay, leaving aside your other liaisons . . ." the emphasis he put on liaisons made it sound like a grimy, dirty word – "isn't it true that you always smiled at my client when you passed him in the hotel? That you'd encouraged him to think you had feelings towards him of a sexual nature?"

"What?" I spluttered. "I did no such thing."

"You're telling us you *didn't* smile at him?"

"The truth is," I said quietly and tried to be calm. "That I smiled at him to annoy him, to rile him, because he always scowled at me." *Sometimes the truth can hang you - especially when you're innocent.*

I don't believe that old cliché anymore. You know, the one about truth setting you free. It's total bollocks. It doesn't work.

I could tell by the looks on the jurors' faces, they believed I was the guilty one. That the scumbag who'd done this to me was as pure as the driven snow. That I'd encouraged him. It was *consensual*. A horrible word that had been bounced around the courtroom and was totally, totally untrue. I had not invited him to slobber all over me, stick his filthy tongue in my mouth, shove his hand between my thighs, slam my head into the wall and smack me in the mouth.

The picture taken by the police photographer straight after the assault, with my bruised face and swollen lips, had already been entered into evidence by the prosecution, but I guess jurors can rationalise stuff like that, especially when the defence barrister was far more compelling than the prosecutor. Maybe the jury figured I'd led the guy on, so he'd be justified in smacking me around a bit. *You think?*

We recessed for lunch. The lunch was free, I had a voucher for it, but if you thought I could eat, then you don't know me. Next up was the man of the moment, and what kind of lies would he tell about me? He was good at lying.

I could lose the case. I imagined the report in the papers already. My reputation tarnished; the home-breaker, the other woman. The frustrated bitch who'd brought an unjust prosecution against this poor guy; a maligned, misunderstood, and victimised man only doing his job, when I'd continually picked on him and finally tried to get him into bed. Shit!

I'd be the one accused of perjury. I wanted to be sick, but I thought about my sister then. She'd had far worse to face. I could do this. And maybe a miracle would arrive. Such things happen, of course. But not often.

I didn't hold out much hope. But that was my mistake. For when we all processed back into the courtroom to hear from Christopher Newly, a small miracle did take place. As the accused walked from the dock into the witness box, he went through an odd transformation. His eyes popped. His face became a whiter shade. And the cockiness drained from him like someone had pulled a plug. I followed his eyes and they were linked by an invisible thread to someone in the public gallery. I looked back. *Alfie!*

Alfie hadn't been there in the morning, but for some reason had come this afternoon. I inanely wondered who was prepping tonight's food. He winked at Christopher Newly and put a stubby finger in the air, like he was testing the wind direction or velocity or some such thing.

Our ex-barman looked as if he might throw up any minute. His voice cracked as he asked the judge if he could have a private consultation with his counsel. After that everything was confusing. At least I was confused. The judge temporarily dismissed the jury, said they'd be recalled when appropriate, and both sleezeballs (the defendant and his barrister) went into a huddle.

The barrister looked rattled; he wrote a note on court stationery and the usher handed it to the judge. The judge didn't look rattled when he read it; either he was made of sterner stuff than the barrister, or he was a good actor. The jury was herded back in and the judge thanked them, dismissed them finally from the trial, like musical-bloody-chairs it was. You couldn't blame them if they were totally pissed off.

The jury could go home. We could *all* go home, for the defendant, Christopher Newly, had changed his plea to guilty. The usher told us to 'be upstanding' again. The judge left the courtroom through his own private door. Newly was taken away, remanded in custody for sentencing. And that was it.

That's when I started to shake, and Alfie came to get me. Steered me out of the wood panelled room with its witness box and its jury box and its raised bench where judges sat. I felt like Alice must have done when she fell through the rabbit hole. Light headed and my feet were walking through a treacle-like sludge. Alfie deposited me in the small lunch bar and went off to get Matt and Harry who'd been waiting in the witness room in case they were called.

"You okay, Stevie?" Matt put his arm around me and still I couldn't control the shaking in my body.

"Here, drink this," Harry ordered. He shoved a mug of disgustingly stewed coffee in front of me and piled in four packets of sugar.

"I don't take sugar."

"You do now."

"What the hell happened in there?" asked Matt.

"Search me," I said. "Ask them."

But both Alfie and Harry gave innocent shrugs. Neither of them looked like fairy godmothers. One slightly chubby, past his prime; the other a hard, mean face, a shaved head, earring in one ear, and a tattoo across the top of his arse that said *just try it mate*. No, they weren't fairy godmother material. But they were nothing short of angels, with great big shiny wings.

Chapter 43

"I love Christmas, don't you?"

"I do," I said, and smiled at the elderly woman who'd planted her feet firmly in front of Reception. She looked solid as a rock, though top heavy. But the woman had a smiley face on, so I figured she wasn't here to complain.

"It's a brilliant idea," she said.

"Oh?"

"I've been on turkey-and-tinsel breaks before, but most hotels start theirs in October, when Christmas is just a wee bit away. I've never heard of one in *May* before. It's wonderful. I'm looking forward to the carols in the Cabaret Lounge tonight," she said. "Can't believe it's Christmas Eve."

Neither could I. Or anybody sane. But that's Harry for you. He was down on bookings; no golfers this week and still too early in the season for family holidaymakers to pull him out of trouble. So he'd got onto the good folk at Pearson Travel and offered a turkey-and-tinsel mid-week pensioners' special.

We already had the decorations and the lights and the two artificial Christmas trees, so as far as Harry was concerned it was a no-brainer. Tonight was Christmas Eve and tomorrow the guests would all be stuffing themselves with turkey. Not real turkey, though. Turkey roll with stuffing that Harry had got cheap as it was about to go over its sell-by date and Alfie was busy knocking out mince pies that bore a fair enough resemblance to the real thing.

The woman idly picked up one of the leaflets from the stand at the end of my reception counter.

"Cyder Farm? That's a funny way to spell it."

"It's traditional," I said.

"What? The farm or the spelling?" she asked – although she didn't seem too bothered about an answer. "I find most people can't spell well now," she said. "We used to get a thump round the ear with a blackboard duster if we got things wrong."

"Right."

"I was wondering about the sherry," she said.

"The sherry?"

"Yes, the coach driver says we'll have a glass of sherry when we go in to sing the carols. Would that be free, or would we be expected to pay for it?"

It was the first I'd heard about it, and Harry wasn't one for throwing complimentary drinks around.

"I'll check and let you know. Which room are you in?"

"The one where the floor slopes," she said, "and the heating doesn't come on. Number thirty."

Ah. She was *here to complain after all. Complaints by stealth. Ones that creep up on you, take you unawares.*

"We don't usually put the heating on in May," I explained.

"Well, maybe you should," she said, "you might get more customers." The woman plastered a superior look on her face and walked away like she'd won a victory.

Doris sidled up to the desk. "Not her again. She's right high and mighty for somebody paid 60 quid for a two-day-all-inclusive. She gave me a proper going over 'cause she only had one toilet roll in her loo. Said that weren't enough for a two day stint for normal folks. You ever hear the like, Stevie? Me and Morris between us don't get through a roll in two days." Doris took up her fighting stance.

"Maybe she eats a lot of fibre," I said.

"You been dragged into this carol singing lark?" Doris asked.

"Nope. Joe's got something special on tonight. I'm doing his shift for him."

"Lucky you. Thought his nibs would've had you in there round the piano leading this lot. You bein' a singer an all."

"Matt's been roped in."

"Make sure he gets paid cash," said Doris, a knowing look on her face.

"You've not been listening at key holes Auntie D?"

"Just saying. Tell your Matt to get the money upfront."

"Matt can look after himself," I said. "He's a big boy."

"Is he now? Well ain't you lucky?"

Doris winked, making sure I got her innuendo about my sex life. Then she roared with laughter and headed off in the direction of the staff room. She was gone before I could retaliate and ask about her own sex life. Her and Morris. Skinny little Morris, and Doris who looked like a battleship. It was an image that made me smile.

Smiling came easier now. Now that I didn't have to worry about court appearances and could try and wipe Christopher Newly's face from my memory. Last night Sophie and I sat up late drinking wine and talking it through. I felt better about the bizarre outcome after that. For what did it matter how the guy got nailed, just as long as he *did*.

I hadn't been happy at first. I'd wanted proper justice. Where he got convicted because everyone in that courtroom believed *me*. Believed the truth. Not because of some strange threat that Alfie held over the guy's head. That didn't feel right. It was like cheating. But it was done and like Sophie said, I'd need to move on and not let the bastard ruin my life.

"Hey beautiful."

"Hey yourself," I said. "What got you out of bed before three?"

"Unfair," said Matt. "I went for a jog at ten this morning."

"My hero."

"*And* I'm thinking of joining a gym."

"Impressive."

"I thought so. Joe says he'll introduce me to his trainer. Get me a good rate."

"Joe works out?"

"Not *your* Joe. My drummer."

"Ah."

"I'm setting up for tonight. *God Rest Ye Merry Gentlemen* and all that."

"Won't that feel weird? Carols round the tree in May."

"You know me," said Matt. "Weird and kinky's my middle name." He stretched across the reception counter and held my head in his hands. Hands that could span a tenth on the piano, he'd boasted. I didn't know if that was good or average. I'm not much of a musician. Some would say I'm not much of a singer either, but I've been working on it. And I reckon I'll pull off the role of Maria – on a good day.

Harry arrived, adjusting his tie; looking flustered. "Get a room, you pair. And not one of mine, eh."

"Sorry, Harry," I said.

"All set for tonight?" he asked Matt.

"Definitely. Looking forward to it, Mr Evans," said Matt without flinching.

Liar.

"Half an hour should do it. Don't want to spoil them," said Harry. "Or have them going through too much of my sherry."

"Sure. But an hour, half hour, it's still the fee we agreed."

"What, no reduction for only playing thirty minutes?"

"I charge by the *session*, Mr Evans."

Harry went off grumbling and I tried to stop myself sniggering – and wondered what Doris would make out of that.

*

Sophie's going home today. I'll miss her, but the final chemo's not something she can put on hold. Quicker that's done; the closer she'll be to the end. After that she's got some radiotherapy to get through, and then there's the hormone therapy with Tamoxifen. To me it seems never ending. But Sophie takes it all in her stride, ready to give cancer a bloody nose.

She sat through one of our Am Dram rehearsals and smiled all the way back to the hotel. Don't know if that was because it was incredibly good or incredibly bad. And coming face to face with Gloria Endersley in full flow didn't phase Sophie one bit. But then she was brought up in Canada; I expect that gives you a broader outlook on life.

Matt drove us all to the station in his gig van. It was great of him. Some guys wouldn't bother giving your sister a lift to her train. Some only take from a relationship without putting much back in.

I'm in A RELATIONSHIP. I hadn't wanted to admit it. I'd wanted to be cool, you know. Not put too much pressure on my expectations. But Matt was one of the good guys. Now I know I don't have a great track record when it comes to judging men, but he had a lot going for him. More plusses than minuses. And we've all got flaws, it's what makes us human, I guess.

Matt gave Sophie a friendly hug as she boarded the train. *Me?* I hung on to her for dear life. Like I would never see her again. She was off to fight her demons. She'd agreed that our mother could go to the hospital with her, but in my book that was the same as fighting your demons alone.

Chapter 44

Life isn't your average fairy tale. It has rough edges, and loose ends that can't always be neatly fastened to make a perfect ending, but we all have to work with what we've got. And that includes Harry, my boss.

His house sale fell through. Not only was the banker not much of a golfer, but he hadn't cut it as a hedge fund manager either. He was under investigation for 'misdirecting funds'. His clients' investment funds had been siphoned off into the banker's own account. Can Harry pick them or what?

So the Royal is like a man about to be hanged, the noose is around his neck, but no one has actually kicked the stool out from under his feet yet. But there's always hope we might get a reprieve. We've got a few families staying right now, although Harry won't make a fortune out of them. They're on a tight budget (that's why they came here) and don't spend money in the bar. Harry hasn't even bothered putting on the Karaoke. He's languishing and it's hard to watch. The only faint light on his horizon is the new love in his life, Grace Harper.

"Brought you a coffee." Doris put the mug down on my office desk.

"Cheers."

"Hear from your sister yet?"

"Just had her chemo," I said.

"She'll be feeling poorly then," said Doris, her tone hushed, almost reverential. Her mother had died of cancer.

"Says she's fine."

"No point complaining, eh? What about your mother?"

"What about her?"

"She still there?" asked Doris.

"Guess so. Sophie didn't say."

"Gone running back home, I 'spect," said Doris. "That's her style, ain't it?"

Had she though? And what exactly *was* her style? I couldn't tell anymore. And Doris was being loyal of course, for she'd heard me whinge on about my mother at great length. About the woman's lack of support when I'd been a teenager. But looking back on it now, I don't suppose I'd been an easy teenager. And she'd been on her own, trying to earn money to pay the bills. She'd had a job on a factory production line, making Wellington boots and hot water bottles. Heady stuff. She must have been bored witless, but then I'd never thought of mother as having much imagination anyway. She'd done a shift in a bar at night, collecting glasses and washing dishes. It can't have been easy, having to work at night when you'd been on the go all day. It was the first time I'd thought about that.

Harry shuffled into my office, gave Doris a scathing look that would have sent any normal human scuttling off, but Doris stayed rooted to the spot.

"Bit of privacy if you don't mind, Doris." He scowled. "And shut the door behind you."

Even Doris couldn't argue with that, for Harry paid her wages. *But for how much longer?* The man looked fraught and if I didn't miss my guess, he'd lost some weight from his puffy cheeks. Could be that Grace had put him on a diet. She'd have a job to wean him off his Betty Stogs though.

"Policeman to see you, Stevie. I've put him in my office. Thought that might be a bit more private for you."

"Dear God! Not Sophie?"

"Shouldn't think so," he said. "Same bloke as last time. From Truro. You know, when that bastard . . ." He couldn't say it. Harry still had a way to go before he'd be in touch with his sensitive, feminine side. And in a way I was glad. For he wouldn't be Harry otherwise.

"Think it's about Newly then?" I surprised myself. I could say his name without feeling sick anymore.

"Could be."

The man waiting in Harry's office, puffing away on a cigarette, was Detective Constable Alan Winter. So, the guy smoked. He also liked Kit Kats as I remember. He was pacing when I went in, like he was anxious to get to the business in hand and on to the next thing on his list. Police were short handed, stretched thin in these harsh economic times. Made them like the rest of us. Pick a number, join the queue mate.

"Good to see you again, Miss Anderson." He stuck out a hand and I shook it. It seemed a strange thing to do. But he didn't look self-conscious, he looked happy. So I figured he wasn't the bringer of bad news for a change. He must get pissed off with that, with people treating him like a leper. But I guess coppers had to grow a thick skin.

"Can I get you a coffee?" I said.

"No thanks. Just popped by to give you the good news. Judge has handed down a sentence."

"Already?"

"Courts don't hang about once there's a guilty verdict."

"So, he's going to jail?"

"He sure is. A year. Eight months with time off, I reckon. Bit less than we figured, 'cause he saved the courts some time and pleaded guilty."

"But that's ridiculous. He didn't plead guilty straight off," I said.

The policeman just shrugged. I guess the police were used to this kind of stuff. They did their best to catch villains and the scumbags got let off easy by the justice system.

"A *year*! Is that all?" I said, trying to drag a reaction from the guy.

"Don't knock it; some of them get off with a slap on the wrist and community service."

"For God's sake. What's the point?"

"The point is," said Alan Winter, "that the guilty are punished."

"Not much punishment, is it?"

"Don't forget he's still on the court docket for the burglary. Could add some more jail time for him. And from what I hear, there's some in Exeter Prison looking forward to meeting up with our Mr Newly again. He owes them big time. He'll hardly do easy stir."

D.C. Winter made his way to the door. He looked disappointed. He'd been pleased with the outcome and I'd poured cold water over him.

"Thanks for coming over," I said. "I'm sure you're busy."

"Thought you'd like to know right away. It's really a *good* result, you know. The system's not ideal. Jail's are crowded. We were lucky to get prison time for him."

"Sure. I get it. The world isn't perfect," I said. And I tried to keep the bitterness out of my voice, for the policeman had looked pleased with the outcome.

"Walk a mile in my shoes, Miss Anderson, and you'd see just how far from perfect it is. But it is what it is." He sighed. And I felt like I'd somehow let the bloke down.

*

"Place is a feckin' joke," screamed Alfie into the phone. Then he'd slammed it down, so I had no more information to go on.

I'd been the patsy elected to go and pacify our unhappy cook. *Not through choice, obviously*. Harry had been missing all morning, and Agata had totally freaked out when I'd asked her to go and find out why Alfie had thrown a pot at the kitchen door. She told me she was pregnant and that having one of Alfie's cast-iron catering pans flying at her was not a good way for any baby to start life.

I threw my arms round Agata, congratulated her. It was a wonderful surprise. A small oasis of joy and hope when the poor old Royal had seen precious little of either lately. Our small family was about to expand, along with Agata's waistline, although I couldn't see any sign of that at the moment. She looked just as slim (and tall) as she always had.

"Is okay?" she asked. "You don't mind?"

"What? About the baby?"

"No - that I don't see Chef."

"'Course not. We'll keep you as far away from Alfie as we can. Though his bark is worse than his bite. He's a big old pussycat really." I couldn't believe I'd said that. But, in a way it was right.

"Chef bites?"

I'd forgotten Agata's fondness for taking things literally. "No, you're fine. He won't bite *us*. Not sure about Harry though."

"Boss has thick skin," said Agata. "Maybe Chef not bite through so easy, eh?"

Agata laughed, and so did I. She'd made her first joke.

I wasn't laughing five minutes later. Neither was Smithy, the young Kitchen Porter. He was cowering in a corner of the still-room, too frightened to come out. And Alfie was busy arranging baking trays around the kitchen floor. It had been raining non stop and most of it was coming in through the roof.

A part of the flat roof of the kitchen extension had fallen in and water was flooding through. One of Harry's mates had put the thing up two years ago. Cheap materials. Cowboy builders.

"Does he think I can cook dinner in the middle of Niagara Falls?"

"Be a good one for the C.V.," I said.

"Don't be a pillock, Stevie. Where is he?"

"Not a clue. Harry's been missing since this morning. Didn't say where he was off to."

"I warned him. Said this would happen. Didn't I, Smithy?"

The K.P. nodded. Seemed too scared to speak.

"I'll phone Morris," I said. "Maybe he can get a tarpaulin over the roof."

"Better get a priest as well," he told me.

"A priest?"

"Sure. When I get hold of his nibs, he'll need the last rites."

Chapter 45

I'm terrified. It came out of the blue and the man wasn't even drunk. Matt has asked me to move in with him. He used all sorts of arguments to back his case: it would be more fun; there was far more room; Harry wouldn't be able to drag me in when it was my day off (I liked that one); it would be easier for rehearsals for The Sound of Music, us being in the same place. And the sneakiest of all – he would cook for me. Unlike me, Matt was a great cook and could make the most luscious banoffee pies. And the things he could do with cream should be X-rated. (We'd been experimenting.)

But there was one thing he hadn't said. He hadn't mentioned the *love* word. The only time he had said that was in his drunken text to me at Sophie's. In a way it was a relief. You bring too many expectations to a relationship and you usually end up disappointed. At least I have. So, I'm trying to play it cool. Terrified on the inside, cool on the outside.

"I've got a delivery for a Stevie Anderson. Know where I can find him?"

I scowled at the man. "The *him* you're looking for is a *her*," I said in my haughty voice. "And you've found her." I pointed at my name badge. Why did people do that?

The guy from Interflora went back to his van and brought in a massive floral arrangement in a purple vase with an incredible lavender ribbon tied around it. I love purple, but I was surprised that Matt remembered. Men don't always, do they? I don't know what the flowers were, apart from the pink roses, as I'm not much of a horticulturalist, but the colour scheme was purple, pink and white.

The bouquet was stunning and I felt tears well up. Joe arrived carrying a bottle of champagne that he plonked down on the reception counter.

"Here," he said. "That's to go with the flowers. I tried to get the guy from the florist to deliver it as well, but he wittered on about some health and safety thing because it's glass. Brave new world, eh?"

I must have had my mouth open, for Joe gave me an odd look.

"They're okay, aren't they, the flowers? I told them to give you a mix of purple and lilac. Those are your favourite colours, right?"

"*You* sent the flowers?"

"Well, don't look so shocked. I've been known to walk into a florist before now."

"They're gorgeous, Joe. But why?"

"Thought you looked a bit down yesterday. We can all do with a cheer-up at times. And to celebrate, of course." Joe gave me a small peck on the cheek. My blood pressure spiked and I could feel my face redden.

"Celebrate?" I said.

"Sure. He's asked you, hasn't he? Don't tell me I've made a boob. Matt's asked you to move in, hasn't he? He said he was going to. He asked me what I thought."

"He asked me," I said. "I thought the flowers were from him."

"Ah. Well – 'spect he's busy. Practising and stuff and whatever else these musician types do."

"Sleep till noon. That's what they do."

"Stevie!"

"What?"

"You *are* going to move in with him, aren't you? You two are great together."

"And that's what you told Matt, is it?"

"'Course it is."

"So, you've both been sitting chewing the fat. Sorting out my future. Discussing me like I was some sort of merchandise. Women have the vote now, Joe. Or hadn't you noticed?"

I left the champagne and bouquet on the counter and rushed out back to have a cigarette. Joe's confused face was imprinted in my head. He wasn't the only one confused. Why would he give me a huge bouquet and a bottle of champagne? It seemed over-the-top, even for a friend. Was Joe trying to tell me something? And why had my heart rate sped up when he'd kissed me? And why had I been so cruel to him? It was too late to take both feet out of my mouth. Normally I only put one in there at a time. But that's me. Mouth open. Brain disengaged. *Why do I do it?* Maybe my mother is right. Perhaps I should go and see a shrink.

*

"What's *wrong* with you? Matt's just phoned me, says you're avoiding him."

My sister sounded angry.

"He's asked me to move in."

"Well? That's okay, isn't it? He's a great guy," she said.

"Yeah, I know. But . . ."

"But what?" she asked.

"I'm scared, Soph."

"Something else you're not telling me?"

There was. And I didn't know if I should tell her. But then, she was my twin. She'd understand.

"It's Joe, isn't it?" she prompted.

"How'd you know?"

"I've seen the way you look at him sometimes, Stevie."

"Forbidden fruit," I said miserably.

"VERY forbidden fruit."

"I know. I'm confused – and I feel like a heel."

"So you should. Matt's a straight up guy and he wants to be with you."

"I know."

"Okay. And Joe. . ."

"What?" I asked.

"Well, Joe's a lovely man, but he's already *taken*, and he doesn't have any of those feelings for you."

"Maybe. Maybe not."

"*Definitely* not. You just find him exotic 'cause he's off limits."

Put like that, it sounded bad. It made me come out like a spoilt kid. I really don't think I am.

"Phone Matt, Sis. He's miserable," she said.

"I just panicked. Got cold feet."

"Tell him that, but for God's sake don't tell him why. He'll think it's a commitment thing."

"It is – in a way. I've been let down loads of times."

"Okay, so go with that. Men are wonderful, but they don't need to know *everything*. Especially not if it hurts them. Or attacks their ego."

"Thanks, Soph. You've been a big help. You're wise beyond your years," I said.

"Nothing less than a sage. Now, go and phone Matt."

"I will," I said. "You okay?"

"Feel great. And the consultant is pleased with me."

I felt better when I put the phone down. Sophie sounded real upbeat and of course she was right. Matt was a good guy.

I phoned him and apologised. Told him that his sudden offer had thrown me off balance and the commitment bit had frightened me. Or rather, I told his voicemail. He wasn't answering my calls. But maybe I deserved that. I hadn't been answering his.

Joe wasn't speaking to me either. He'd just taken over on Reception and gave me a pained look. I'd tried to apologize about flouncing off and leaving his flowers to languish, but he wouldn't listen. He passed me a postit-note with a message scribbled on. It wasn't in his normal handwriting; it was an ungainly scrawl that I could hardly read.

"Brain gone," he said, "along with your manners."

"Sorry, Joe."

"You should be."

I shrugged my shoulders. It's not like I could explain stuff to him. That would only make things worse.

"It's from the chief," he said.

"What's Harry want?"

"Not Harry. Harry's still missing," said Joe. "It's from Gloria Endersley. She wants you to go for a costume fitting."

"What – for a nun's habit? I thought one size fits all."

"Maybe for the robe, but what about that starched wimple thing you wear round your head and chin," he said. "You wouldn't want it to strangle you." The emphasis Joe put on 'strangle' made it sound like that wouldn't be a bad idea.

I wondered when he would forgive me and things could get back to normal again. I'd said sorry. Did he want me to open up a vein, like Harry's bank manager?

"I expect there's more to this Nun business than meets the eye," I said, as he threw me a withering look. I took the postit-note from him and sighed. The tension in the air could have been sliced and diced, but I suppose that was my fault as much as Joe's.

This was the point where Gloria Endersley came charging through the front door of the hotel. You couldn't fault her timing. She noted the coat I was halfway through putting on.

"Good," she said, "you're ready. Jump in the car." She threw me the keys like some enthusiastic rugby player handling a 20 metre pass. "I'll be out directly. Just need to clear up a few points with our master set designer." Her beady eye settled on Joe.

Chapter 46

Harry had been missing for two days when he finally phoned in. He sounded cheerful, happy, even. Or that could have been the line. The connection was fuzzy.

"Everything okay?" he asked.

I thought about Alfie, a cook still trying to produce food under a tarpaulin. And his threat to buy Harry a coffin.

"Just peachy," I said.

"Sour grapes is it, Stevie – 'cause I've managed to nip off for a bit? Or is the place falling down round your ears?"

"Only bits of it," I said. "You want a list?"

"Save it. We'll be back tomorrow."

"We?"

"Fill you in when we get home. I'm in Scotland right now. Pissing down; beginning of June, you don't expect it."

Great! He'd been missing without a trace, leaving me to carry the baton, face the flak. No messages. No apology. And now he calls me up with a weather report. Not that I told him that. He was my boss after all, and I hadn't had my wages yet.

"Want to know what I'm doing in Scotland?" He sounded excited, like a kid showing off. Could be that he'd finally sold the house.

"Okay Harry. What are you doing in Scotland?"

"I'm in Gretna Green."

"Gretna Green? Are you drunk?"

"No, but we put away two bottles of champagne last night. Me and Gracie. Stevie - I just got married."

"To Grace?"

"Well of course to Grace. Who else would I take up to Gretna for a quickie marriage?"

"Wow!"

"Yep. Still getting used to the idea myself."

"Grace is a wonderful woman, Harry. I'm pleased for you."

"Be back tomorrow night. How's occupancy?"

"Same as when you left. Oh, except we've got two walk-ins, only here for the night, though. Couple of reps, passing through."

"So, can you have Doris make up the suite for us? Nobody in there, is there?"

"Will do. Honeymoon, is it?"

"No point wasting a good hotel room, when it's free."

I wondered what Grace would think about that. If she wouldn't rather spend her honeymoon in the Caribbean, somewhere warm. Especially if she'd already been freezing in the heavy Scottish rain.

"So, tomorrow night then," I said.

"We might be too late for dinner. Can you ask Chef to lay on something special for us? A late supper?"

"See what I can do." *Chef might be keen to lay something special on all right, but somehow I doubted it would be supper.*

I didn't have to go and find Doris. She'd heard Harry's name when I'd been on the phone and had been hovering till I finished the call.

"Well?" she said.

"What?"

"Did I get that right? He's run off and got hisself married."

"Sounds romantic, eh?"

"Not much like his nibs. Reckon that was Grace's idea. She's a lady on a mission."

"You're an old cynic Auntie D. Grace is a lovely woman."

"I'm not saying she ain't. Just that after the right do he had with his last missus, Harry was a confirmed old bachelor. She'll have been steering him in the right direction."

"Not our business, though. Oh, and he wants the suite ready for tomorrow night."

"All right for some. He didn't happen to mention no satin sheets while he was at it? And some of them cute little mints on the pillow?" Doris folded her arms over her chest in a challenge.

"It's his hotel, Doris. He can have what he wants."

"No skin off my nose. You moving in with Matt?"

The sudden switch in topic jolted me. "How'd you know?"

"Jungle drums. There ain't nuthin' goes on in this place I don't know."

She was right, of course. Doris made it her business to know. "Finger on the pulse of the good old Royal, eh?"

"Sure. And right now that pulse don't feel too strong to me," she said. "The place's in Intensive Care; 'less, of course, Grace has money. Figure that's why he married her, Stevie?"

"No idea. But it's not something we need to be broadcasting, is it?" I said. "Marriage is hard enough to make work, without them having to fight rumours as well."

Doris shrugged her shoulders. "I'll get on with the lovebirds' honeymoon nest then." She walked away, but not in the direction of the rooms. She headed straight for the back stairs and the kitchen. She'd be putting Alfie in the picture. And somehow I doubted that cook would be thumbing through wedding brochures looking for suitable gifts. But at least Doris had done the groundwork for me; I hadn't been looking forward to asking Alfie to prepare a special wedding supper.

I thought about the pair of them, up there in Gretna Green. Like a couple of eloping teenagers. I hoped they both knew what they were getting themselves into. Grace obviously had deep feelings for Harry, but was that love? And what about Harry? He never wore his heart on his sleeve, so it was hard to tell. Maybe Doris was right and it was a marriage of convenience. *Especially* convenient if Grace had money. Money to pour into a hotel that – according to at least one of its staff – was gasping out its last breath in Intensive Care.

No. I couldn't go along with that. Grace was a fine woman, but she was also a strong woman and she didn't come across as someone would let herself be manipulated. True, Harry wasn't ethical in all that he did, but he had a good heart. I couldn't see him taking on a wife and giving up his independence just for money.

*

Things have been hectic lately. It's a time of change, what with Harry and Grace newly married and settling into a house – *her* house. It's just a small place but close to the beach, so I suppose it has a healthy price tag on it.

I was pleased to see there are no moves to sell it. So Harry didn't marry the lovely Grace for her money after all. If that was the case they would have lived in the hotel and put Grace's house up for sale along with Harry's – but there's been no mention of anything like that. Not that they'd have confided in us (the staff) but then Doris has a way of getting information that can only be equalled by the CIA.

Alfie's got his roof fixed at last. It took three weeks of living under a tarpaulin to get it sorted. But when he finally handed in his notice and packed his cooking knives – and Morris threatened to take his tarp back, it did the trick. We hired a proper builder this time. One with certificates.

And me? Things were strained between Matt and me for a couple of weeks. He told me he was reappraising his life, and in particular the two of us, where we might be going. I just wonder why any of us need to be going anywhere. I'd told him that, and he said I wasn't ready for a grown-up relationship. Can you believe it? I mean, he's practically a child compared to me.

But it's all sorted now. The wheels are no longer coming off the relationship that was *Stevie and Matt*. We are back where we were before, and I'm happy. I just wasn't up for the next stage, so I'm still living in the 'penthouse'. It's small, but manageable, and it feels secure. And Matt and I have recaptured the excitement of first love. *Or first lust*.

It happened after a harrowing rehearsal with the Am Drams. Gloria was on my case for not hitting the high notes and the more she shouted, the worse I got. Then I bumped into the Swiss mountains behind me and knocked them over. Not my fault. They hadn't been anchored down yet, just propped against a wall.

Matt rescued me. He stopped playing, said he couldn't work in an atmosphere of tension. Walked out, just like that, and left Gloria with her jaws flapping. I was proud of him then, especially when he grabbed me by the hand and waltzed me off the stage with him. Knight in armour, or what?

It wasn't that he felt sorry for me, he said. He reckoned I just looked cute with my nose wrinkling up and the feisty look on my face – even though he knew I was fighting back tears. That's when it happened. When we got our relationship right back on track. And I know it's a bit personal, but I ended up having the best sex of my life. Right there, in an improvised and draughty dressing room and me in a nun's habit. That probably added spice to it. For both of us. And Matt said afterwards that it was the first time he'd ever ravished a nun. I would hope so.

"C'mon then. You'll be late." Joe had snuck up behind me in Reception. "Miles away again. Off on one."

"Just thinking," I said. "You know, about how funny life is at times."

"Hilarious. Tell me about it," said Joe. "I'm stuck here with a convention of crazy bird-watchers while you're about to swan off and be a nun."

"Swap you," I said. "I'm scared stiff. Throat's closing already and I can't sing a note."

"It'll be cool, you'll see," he said. "All right on the night, and all that."

"Really? You think so! This is real life. And it *is* the night."

"You'll be great. It's first night nerves, that's all. You got two weeks of it. Might as well enjoy it."

"Enjoy? I've thrown up twice already. Thank God Sophie isn't coming yet. I've put her off till the last night.

We should have it right by then. I feel like running for the hills, Joe."

Joe put his arm round my shoulder and squeezed. "Good! For I've heard they're alive with the *Sound of Music.*

I punched him in the arm, but he didn't flinch.

"Think that lot really are proper *twitchers*?" I asked.

"They've got the gear and the fancy binoculars, but I reckon they're as bad as those golfers," said Joe. "Any excuse to get away from their wives and have a good old piss-up. They kept the bar open till early this morning; Harry's rubbing his hands in glee."

"And is there a rare Swift do you reckon? This White-throated Needletail they're all on about?" I said. "Figure they made that one up, don't you?"

"Could be. Anyway not your concern, is it? said Joe. "And I know what you're doing. It's called procrastination. That means . . ."

"Thanks Joe, but I'm not retarded. I know what procrastination is. Stalling. Putting off the evil hour. And I'm not procrastinating. Believe me; I haven't even *begun* to procrastinate yet."

"That's what I figured. That's why *he's* here." Joe nodded towards the figure coming in through the front door.

"Ready for the big night, Stevie? Thought I'd give you a lift." Matt winked.

They'd stitched me up between them, in case I got cold feet. But I guess that was good. Good friends are hard to find and I'd got two of them right here on my doorstep.

Chapter 47

Time had no meaning. Act I came and went. We had an interval, or so people tell me; when the audience could stretch their legs and have a rest from those awful wooden benches. Wine was on sale. If I'd known that, I would have had some. But I remembered little of it, just glided through the whole three hours in a dream. It might have been tremendous. It might have been woeful. People clapped at the end, but then most of the audience were family or friends of cast members. Your granny would hardly be a critic.

I was a fine Maria - according to the Stage Manager, at least. But he would say that, wouldn't he, for we had another thirteen days of this to get through and we hadn't managed to find an understudy for my part. The after show party was low key and Gloria said she had 'notes' for us, but she'd hand them out tomorrow. *Not that brilliant then.*

"Hope she has notes for herself, as well," said Gregory Witchal in a stage whisper. He was our Captain von Trapp, and apparently he'd tripped over one of the children, gone headlong into a sideboard (you could still see the mark on his forehead) and forgotten the words of Edelweiss. Nobody's perfect.

Still, that's the good thing about amateur dramatics. You're doing it for love. *Well, aren't you?* No one pays you to go through all this anxiety and rehearsals and self-doubt. But it can only get better. First nights are when you stick your toes in the water and test the temperature. I guess the temperature was tepid right now. But we had two weeks to warm it up, and luckily my sister wasn't coming until the final show, along with the drama critic from the local paper. Most came opening night, but he knew the score.

There was one good thing about it. The relief of actually having stumbled through opening night meant that for the first time in months, when I finally made it home, I fell quickly into an exhausted, dreamless sleep. The hotel didn't sink into quicksand. My mother didn't hover over me in the shape of a giant black crow as she had in several nightmares. And Sophie didn't fade into the distance, me running to catch her up, waving a red wig in the air. The subconscious can sometimes be a hard taskmaster. But I think I've cracked it now. I'm trying to make my mind a blank and throwing it off the scent.

The next morning the 'notes' arrived from Gloria. Joe brought them into my office along with a cup of strong black glutinous coffee. I guess he thought I'd need it. I drank the coffee, it was a Smithy special, one of those stand back and light the fuse brews. Glorious. But I filed the notes in the bin. If you knew Gloria Endersley, you'd understand.

Joe grinned. "That's what I love about you, Stevie. You're a rebel."

"Sure," I said. It was an exciting thought, but hardly true. If it was, would I still be wearing a blazer that said H.R. and working as a receptionist?

"Hear about the tragedy?" he asked.

"I was in it," I said.

"Not that! Anyway, I heard it wasn't too bad. Doris reckons your singing's improved, and she's not one for sugar-coating it."

"Doris was there? I didn't see her."

"Sure. Her and Morris. What planet were you on? She said she spoke to you."

"When I wasn't on stage, I was busy throwing up."

"Worst is over," said Joe. "More than you can say for our twitchers."

"Oh?"

"Like a bloody farce in here last night. All walking round with long faces; drowning their sorrows at the bar."

"Good bar takings then."

"Harry was pleased. But looks like they'll be leaving. No more reason to stay," he said.

"So, no White-crested Needletail. I thought that was a wind-up."

"No. No wind-up. It really exists and it's the White-*throated* Needletail, Stevie. Keep up. And all those crazy bird people were holding a wake for it last night. They got quite maudlin."

"It's gone then."

"You might say that. Apparently it took to the skies majestically. *Soared* was the word used, I believe. And flew straight into the bloody wind farm. Turbine blades made minced meat of it."

Joe made it sound comic, but it wasn't of course. It was sad. A poor little Swift that had come to grief; and in my mind it joined the gloomy inventory of the badger and cat that I'd managed to maim when I'd been driving – and the two innocent lobsters that had been murdered in Alfie's kitchen. Sometimes life isn't all that kind to small animals.

I've come to a decision. When these two weeks of the show are over, I'm moving in with Matt. I haven't told him yet. I haven't told anyone, not even my sister, but I know she'll be happy. It's time I started *acting like a grown-up*. Those were Matt's cutting words when we'd had our row. They'd stung, but he was right. In a way I'd been putting life on hold, God knows why. Fear of the unknown, I suppose. And it doesn't work, for life marches on without you whether or not you try and hold onto the present.

We have good times together. Far more good ones than bad, and like all people, Matt and I have our quirks but mostly we try to see each other's point of view. I'm not saying we're perfect. We'll both have to make adjustments. But he's one hell of a cook and he gives great cuddles. And he seems to care for me. It's not something I could say hand-on-heart about any other man I've been involved with. He's teaching me to cook, and I've bought him an alarm clock.

We're learning to get along with each other's differences. Vive la différence! Matt says. But then he sometimes has an exotic turn-of-phrase. It's not the only thing about him that's exotic and exciting. Our sex life is thrilling and unpredictable. He wants me to keep the nun's habit. Maybe I will.

Apart from Matt being a decent bloke, one more thing prompted me to think about moving out of my safe attic bolthole. It was watching Harry and Grace. Sounds crazy, I know, for they're a very odd couple; a total mismatch, but it works for them. She's older than him, but well preserved and more sophisticated than Harry, though that wouldn't be hard of course. The more I see them together I realize that Harry is sincere. Even our Doris has given them her royal seal of approval. He *dotes* on the woman, Doris had confided in me.

I've become friends with Grace. She treats me as an equal even though she's old enough to be my mother and she tells me things; I guess everyone needs someone to confide in, especially if you live with Harry.

Grace has re-mortgaged her house to put cash into the hotel. Harry didn't want her to, he tried to get an extension on his overdraft and wanted to sell his car, but Grace wouldn't let him. The good news is that the bank has agreed to let Harry and the hotel struggle on until Christmas now, as he's made efforts to refinance. Grace has insisted that they move into a room in the hotel and I wouldn't be surprised if she ends up putting her house on the market too - whether Harry likes it or not.

The poor old Royal is in a tight spot. A Catch 22 pickle. It desperately needs an upgrade to entice in more customers, and without enough customers Harry won't have the cash to do that. The plumbing needs sorting and the restaurant could do with a complete overhaul. It's very old fashioned. Harry calls it quaint and homey. Don't get me wrong, we all love the place and it has a character all of its own, but that won't stop it crumbling around us. Or the bank taking it. So, Christmas is crunch time. When the miracles need to be wheeled out.

*

The last time I moved my belongings they had the smell of fish on them. It was something to think about, and made me even more convinced that moving in with Matt is the right thing to do. Nigel Jameson had been a totally different kettle of fish (puns notwithstanding). Do people still say that, notwithstanding?

At any rate, I've got this funny sort of jellified feeling in my stomach. I guess it must be excitement, because now that I've taken the plunge and am about to share a house with someone else, I find myself looking forward to it. As you know, the last person I did that with took all my furniture. But I don't have anything really valuable anymore and besides, Matt's not particularly into furniture, it was hard enough to get him to go shopping for a double bed. He reckons it's cosy to cuddle up together in the miniscule one he has in his place. But I've put him right. Buying a bed together is a good solid way to start a serious relationship. Like putting down proper roots. And I've explained to him that the only notches I want to find on the headboard are mine.

Sophie arrived last night and she and Grace went shopping today. I couldn't go, for Harry's been acting like one of those slave masters on a galley ship. Don't know if Soph is clothes shopping or what, but it's Matt's thirtieth birthday bash tonight, so that could be it.

It's also the final night of that rip roaring musical *The Sound of Music* and I'm feeling a little sad, but most of the gang from the show are coming along to help Matt celebrate. Soon as the curtain comes down we'll all be hitting the high spots, minus Gloria Endersley, who's going home to henpeck her husband. She's been invited, but Gloria doesn't socialise with the rest of us, for at heart she's a diva who likes to encourage an air of mystery.

Soph's hair has started to grow back. Right now it's just a fine down and her eyebrows still haven't grown, so she's pencilling them in, but my sister's thrilled and so am I. It's like a signal. There is light at the end of this scary black tunnel.

"They not back yet?"

It was Harry, and he was getting on like an expectant father again. It was the second time he'd made a pass by Reception, looking at his watch.

"You okay?" I asked. Although he'd lost weight recently, his red face still looked like he should be on blood pressure tablets.

"Why wouldn't I be?" He checked the clock behind me.

"We expecting more guests?" I said.

"Like who?"

"I don't know, Harry. But you seem a bit on edge. Bank manager not on his way, is he?"

"None of your business. Just get on with what I pay you to do, Stevie, and don't be a smartarse. You can type up next week's menus. Get them from Chef."

He took off before I could reply.

Alfie looked at me strangely when I went for his menus. They were written on scraps of paper and he thrust them into my hand, closed my fingers over them like they were precious jewels I'd been entrusted with.

"You're still here then?" he said.

"Where else would I be?"

"Thought you'd be off getting ready for your show. Big night, ain't it?"

"Joe's not here yet."

"When's he due?"

"Twenty minutes," I said.

Alfie looked at the kitchen clock. What was it with everybody and clocks?

"You'll need to get a move on then, if you want to get them typed up." He nodded to the notes I was clutching.

They were all busy telling me how to do my job. I wanted to bite back, but Alfie had already gone back to inspect something in his hot-cupboard and an argument with cook was rarely worth the hassle.

I was behind the front desk when Harry came by again and I tried to look busy, for he seemed to be on the warpath. I'd been excited before, thinking about the show, about my sister, how well she looked, and Matt's birthday party, but I was as jumpy as Harry now. Still, nothing that a leisurely soak in a bubble bath with a good book wouldn't put right. Matt wasn't much of a reader himself, couldn't understand why people got so caught up in fictional worlds, but even so, he'd bought me my favourite author's latest title. In expensive hardback too. If that wasn't sweet, I don't know what was.

Chapter 48

There was a parcel outside my bedroom door, with a note from Sophie.

"Hey little sister, see you after the show. And I hope you'll wear this. Remember you promised we'd both go out and celebrate and wear purple. Now you wouldn't go back on your word, would you? And I'll be wearing exactly the same to Matt's party, so we'll be like two proper little twinnies. Break a leg, girl. You're loving and excited sister, Sophie."

Black satin flowing Palazzo pants, totally glam; a deep purple silk shirt and black evening pumps seeded with tiny diamantes. I tried to picture the outfit times two, both of us side by side against the slightly faded backdrop of the Con Club. It seemed out of place and I didn't know if I'd be brave enough to wear it. Sophie was right; I always felt better in clothes that didn't stand out, *camouflage*. But if she could do it, then I suppose I could, and I'd made her a promise.

I couldn't find her in the hotel. She wasn't in her room and when I asked Harry if he'd seen her, he gave me an odd look. Told me to get going or I'd be late.

I ended up walking down to the school alone. It was a bit of an anti-climax as Matt didn't come for me as usual and I couldn't get him on his mobile. But then maybe he was still off sorting stuff out for his party. *I'd* wanted to do that, but he'd insisted that he get the venue and sort the food and do the invitations. He knows I'm a good organiser, and usually he's happy to let me get on with things. So I have to own up that I felt a bit hurt. Couldn't understand what he was playing at. Weren't we supposed to be sharing a life together now?

He was late, came breezing in ten minutes before the performance was due to start. *Whistling. Looking pleased with himself.* Gloria was practically swooning with nervous exhaustion, her wimple threatening to choke her. But Matt just smiled that big innocent grin of his. And during the performance, while he was playing in the improvised orchestra pit, he winked up at me several times. Like he knew a joke that I didn't.

It was the final night and I might never get to do this again. The thought made me throw caution to the wind. I held my head high, stuck my chest out, pinched my bum cheeks in as far as they would go, and found a voice that seemed to come from outside of me. I knew it was good. And it had been there all along. The look on Matt's face as I soared towards the high notes, didn't bump into a single mountain, and got the choreography right, was a joy to see. I reckon it was pride. But then, I was pretty proud of myself.

It doesn't happen often when you're performing, that you totally lose yourself in the role. You fit it on like an invisible skin; it's who you are. I wasn't even aware of the audience, didn't know if my sister was there, but the amazing burst of applause that came at the end suddenly jolted me out of my dream-like state.

That's when I finally looked out at all those people, clapping, *standing up*, cheering. And I saw her. She was crying. Crying and smiling at the same time, her arms raised high above her head and clapping furiously. My mother.

We didn't fall into each other's arms like we'd walked out of an episode of some cheesy soap. But she smiled, and I smiled. It was a start. We stood in the middle of the makeshift theatre, people milling around us, and she took both of my hands in hers. No words. Not right then, but her face said everything. She was happy I was her daughter.

"You were incredible," she said, "but then you always have been."

"I *have*?"

"Maybe you didn't always know it, and that was my fault."

"Hey you! Where did all that come from?" Matt bounded up and planted a messy kiss on me. "Sorry, Isobel, didn't mean to butt in, but this woman was fantastic."

"Isobel? I said. "You guys know each other?"

"Not really. Your sister roped Matt into picking me up from the station."

"Where is Sophie? Wasn't she here?"

"Oh she was here all right," said my mother. "Whistling and stamping, and calling for you to take another bow."

"So, where is she?" I was disappointed.

Matt grinned again. "You'll see. Now get yourself dressed up in that new outfit and we'll get on over there. Got a mini bus waiting for us outside. We've got a party to go to."

"Happy birthday," I said. "If you're good, you can have a special pressy later."

"Oh, and what might that be?" said Matt, all innocent.

"Don't tell Gloria, but I'm keeping the costume. And we can play the naughty nun game. You know you like that."

My mother coughed. I'll wait for you pair in the bus then. That okay?"

"Sure, Isobel," Matt said. "We won't be long."

He helped me get changed. Out of one costume and into another.

"This really isn't me, you know."

"What? You look bloody gorgeous, good enough to eat. Bit of cream on top, like the other night." He planted a kiss on the back of my neck and a ripple ran along my spine.

"Behave," I said. "And you know exactly what I mean. Sophie means well, but can you imagine the two of us turning up like this, all glammed-up. It'll be embarrassing. It's the sort of thing you'd wear on the red carpet, not the Con Club."

"We're not going to the Con Club," he said.

*

It was just like the Oscars. Mind blowing. Except instead of stepping out onto a red carpet, it was a midnight blue one. Matt and I walked along the carpet, me in my purple, him in his white tux, our arms linked. It was like one of those posh receiving lines, and on both sides there were hoards of cheering people. People taking photographs on their phones, shouting happy birthday at Matt, yelling "well done, Maria."

I felt drunk, and I hadn't had a drop. No, really.

My sister was there, grinning. Most of the cast from the show. Matt's band, The Syncopated City Slickers. Joe and Wilbur. Doris with her husband Morris, his worn overalls exchanged for a black 'weddings and funerals' suit that didn't quite fit. Harry and Grace. Even Alfie.

Bless him, he'd put a shirt and tie on, but I doubted the tie would last long, for he was already tugging at the shirt collar trying to release his large neck from its unnatural confinement.

I flung my arms round Joe. "You rat. You knew and you never let on."

"I can keep a secret. Worst bit was sneaking your mother into the hotel without you knowing."

I looked round at my mother. "You're staying at the hotel?"

"Of course. Where else? It's where my daughter is."

I didn't know if she meant me or Sophie. But she was smiling at me. So maybe it was me.

Harry came up with Grace and I gave them both a hug. "So?" said Harry.

"You were all in on it, even Alfie?" I got it now. It's why everybody seemed so interested in the clock.

"Sure," said Harry. "Worked out okay. Mind, I could've given you a real good rate for the party. This'll be costing a bomb." Harry looked around at the grand entrance hall, the opulent furnishings. Grace dug him in the ribs.

"So, who's holding the fort? Looks like everybody from The Royal's right here," I said.

"Not everybody. Eli offered to be night porter and keep an eye on Reception."

"Eli?" I said. "*On Reception?*"

"Yeah," said Harry and he gave me a wink. "*You* do it. How hard can it be?"

Chapter 49

"Thirty eh? You feel old?" I asked Matt. We were snuggling up in the new king size bed. Our bed. We'd been busy christening it. And not with sleep. Now we were wallowing in that drowsy after glow that comes with satisfying sex.

"No, do you?"

"In my prime," I said. "And at least now we're both in the same decade."

"Thirty's good," he said and wriggled in closer to me. "Shouldn't have let you talk me into this massive bed, though. We'll lose each other in the night."

"No way. I'll be sticking to you like a limpet," I said.

"*Romantic*. That's some kind of sea slug, right? What is it with you and crustaceans?"

"Molluscs," I said.

"And molluscs to you too!" said Matt, and he stroked my hair slowly and sensuously. The movement was seductive. The man was downright sexy and his hands were very long and thin, elegant. Like you'd imagine a pianist's should be. And I moved them to somewhere more interesting on my body.

"Molluscs are different from crustaceans, is all I'm saying. I've been looking them up – since my depressing experience with lobsters." I moaned softly, and it was nothing to do with the memory of the lobsters. I moved his hand farther down.

"Tonight was good, eh?" he said sleepily.

"Brilliant," I said. "You're a master of deception. And that was the loveliest surprise I've had in my life. The hotel was beautiful, the food was great and the music wasn't bad."

"And who'd have thought your mother could sing like that? Did you know?"

"Lots of things I didn't know about my mother," I said.

She'd got a bit tipsy and asked if she could sing with Matt and his band. I'd wanted to disappear. Couldn't bear to sit through something that would humiliate her, not to mention me and Sophie. But I ended up with my mouth open when she'd sung Moonlight in Vermont. It's got one hell of a range in it, and yet she nailed it and the sadness that came through her voice was gut-wrenching. At least for me. The audience cheered her, and there seemed to be general agreement that this was where I got my singing skills from.

People clapped her, all except Doris, I noticed. But then she was my surrogate mother, and I guess she was being loyal to me. Plus of course Doris remembered the wailing noises I'd made when I'd been going through my vocal training exercises. My mother had been nowhere around then. But maybe it was right. Some things are inherited.

*

She's gone home now, my mother. Back to Plymouth. But it looks like she'll be coming down to the hotel for Christmas; she seemed to like the place. And we're taking it in easy stages, this new relationship of mother and daughter, where we both learn things about each other. I can't see it ever being perfect between us, but at least my sister is pleased that we're trying to find common ground.

Sophie went back up to Bristol and has almost finished her treatment now. She's having her nipple areola tattooed next weekend, to make it look like a normal boob again. Apparently there's someone attached to the hospital does that sort of thing. It's something I'd never thought about, but it's amazing the stuff you learn when you're forced to look cancer in the eye. My sister refuses to call it the big 'C', but has demoted it to cancer with a very small nasty little 'c'. And she reckons she's managed to boot it into touch.

I hope she's right, for she seems real sparky about the whole thing. She goes back to the hospital to help out and talk to women who are setting off on the same journey that she did. It's her way of saying thank-you to those people who helped her. All those hard working dogged professionals who fight this crappy thing every day, and even when they're weary still manage to smile at their patients. I'm going to say thank-you too (though I haven't told Sophie yet). I'm registering for next year's Race for Life. It's only 5K and I'm going to run it in a pink fluffy bunny suit. No, don't laugh; I reckon I can make it. I've been practising. And I'm getting fitter now, for I've been doing a lot of walking lately.

It felt strange at first, walking into work every day from a house on the other side of Newquay. But I soon got used to it. And Matt was right, there are lots of perks. One of them is that after only a month I've lost eight pounds without even trying. The main perk is pretty obvious, for I've found a man who cares for me (he even used the 'love' word the other night) and who thinks I'm *pretty hot*. He said that when we were in the middle of taking a steamy bath together and getting heavily into bath oils and stuff. So maybe that's one of those pinch-of-salt things.

But even so, the man has changed my life. The way I look at things, the way I laugh out loud now, even when people are around, and the confidence I have in my own body. I am *attractive*, even though I'm not a leggy six footer wearing size eight. He's told me I'm gorgeous so many times now, that I truly believe it. All that stuff about beautiful things coming in small packages, he reckons is true. I'm short and he's tall. Maybe I shouldn't have said that, because I've suddenly thought about Doris and her lanky husband Morris. But it seems to work for them. So why not?

"Stevie, There's a missed collection card for you there. Bloke came yesterday, with a special delivery," said Joe. "You'll need to go into the office at Newham."

"Big, small?"

"What?"

"The parcel, Joe."

"One of those document bags. He wouldn't let me sign for it. Made a song and dance about it being confidential material."

I didn't feel like going into Truro on the bus. True, I was off now that Joe was here for his shift, but I'd been looking forward to going home, having a glass of wine and one of Matt's special lasagnes. I was still thinking it over when my mobile rang.

"Hey gorgeous. You get yours yet?"

It was Sophie. "Hi Sis. My what?"

"*No* to that then. Thought your special delivery would've arrived. Mine came this morning."

"Ah." I picked up the missed delivery postcard that Joe had left on the counter. Looked at the office times.

"Ah *good*, or ah *bad* is that?" asked Sophie.

"Office in Truro might be closed by the time the bus gets me in. Maybe I'll wait till my day off."

"*Stephanie Gloria Anderson*," she said, "take a tip from your big sister and get a taxi right this minute. Get a bloody fleet of them. You can afford it."

Joe called me a taxi. It felt weird, but Sophie had been adamant. So I sat in the back of the cab with my heart pounding, wondering what it was about and hoping that when I took the taxi back home again, Matt would be there. I didn't have enough cash on me for the fare.

I went into the pokey office with the glass partition keeping people away from the two post office workers. Why was it there? Did they think people were going to attack them? I slipped the missed delivery postcard through the slit at the bottom of the glass.

"I'll need some form of I.D." the man said, "and there'll be a small charge."

I pushed my passport under the glass.

The guy checked it, looked at the photograph for a long time.

"I've had my hair cut," I said.

"And you are Stephanie Gloria Anderson?"

"That's me," I confirmed.

"Okay, sign here."

I signed. And the '*Gloria*' thing? Not many people know about that. I only use it for official documents, like my passport, because it's right there on my birth certificate. But that's hardly my fault. I don't think it's a name I'd have chosen for myself, but it means things like praise, honour, distinction. So, maybe in her way, my mother *was* giving me something special. Even so, it's not a name I toss around.

The same taxi took me home and on the way back I undid the fastenings on the document bag and stuck my nail under the fancy seal of the large white envelope inside. I read the impressive document twice. I'm not an idiot, but it took a minute to come to terms with words like 'testator' and the other legal jargon that's meant to separate lawyers from the rest of us.

"You all right, love?" The driver seemed to think there was a problem.

I might have squealed. I can't be sure. But I think anybody in my position would have done the same. It was the figure that did it. The numbers swam before my eyes and I found myself laughing hysterically. For the cashier's cheque that was attached to the document had my name on it and it was written in Sterling. Five hundred and fifty thousand pounds. Over one million Canadian dollars. It was official. I was a millionaire.

Chapter 50

The man had rung the bell on Reception, so I'd come rushing out from my tiny office. It didn't do to let people ring twice. Harry had ears that could hear around corners. And even though there'd been a change in the dynamic of the hotel, he was still the same; his management style more bolshie than benevolent. It wouldn't be Harry otherwise.

"You do take guests?" the man said in a haughty voice. And he looked down his long, pointed nose at me - real superior - like I was the scullery maid in some Victorian household. You couldn't get much lower in rank than the scullery maid.

"We do, Sir. It's our raison d'etre."

"It's your reason what?" he said.

Not so clever then, was he?

"It's why we're here, Sir," I explained, forming the words slowly. But not enough for him to complain I had a smart mouth. You take your fun where you can get it, and Reception had been quiet this morning. We were undergoing a general refurbishment: restaurant, some of the older bedrooms, the lift, the heating. Harry reckoned you wouldn't recognise the old place soon.

I hoped that wasn't true. For we all loved the Royal and apart from the obvious things that needed an upgrade, wouldn't want to see it change too much.

"The scaffolding outside might give customers the wrong impression. I thought you were closed," said the man.

"The sign out front explains all that," I said patiently. "Though we're only operating a limited service in the restaurant. Just breakfast, I'm afraid. But Chef makes a splendid full-English."

"No doubt. No doubt. But the Continental I find is more the ticket nowadays." He patted his stomach, like it was a weight thing. "Your Chef's heard of that, I suppose?"

"Chef's been in France, Sir." *Yeah, on a day trip.*

"Glad to hear it. So, who do I have to see about registering?" he asked.

"That would be me, Sir." I felt like pointing out my name badge. It did say Assistant Manager, after all. But that would be a step too far. Plus I'm a professional. It's not that I need the job, but I like the job. And all guests meant business for the brave old Royal, who'd taken a battering through tough times.

The man wrote his name with a flourish. "Refurb eh? Gearing up for Christmas, I suppose."

"Exactly," I said.

I handed the man his key. "Unfortunately, the lift is currently undergoing some routine maintenance, but your room is only on the first floor."

He looked at me cynically from under his heavy bushy eyebrows. *I'd have had those trimmed if I were him.* "No doubt there will be a small recompense for such inconvenience," he said.

Sophie snuck up behind me. She handed him one of the complimentary drinks slips that were sitting in a large pile. We'd used a lot of them lately.

"That entitles you to a free drink at the bar, Sir," she said.

The guy struggled up the stairs with his suitcase, but he'd seemed pleased that he got one over on us. *You think?* Maybe he wouldn't feel that way when he'd drunk Harry's cheap brandy. He could end up spending the next day in bed and his internal plumbing might never be the same again. I'd tried to discourage Harry from buying the stuff in from his dodgy sources, but I guess old habits die hard.

Sophie laughed. "Think I'd make a good receptionist?"

"No way. You'd never stand the pace." I ruffled her hair. Bright orange it was now, with a streak of shocking pink running through. Sophie loved colour. And she loved having her hair back. It was still thin, but it was getting there. Her eyebrows hadn't grown back and she was resigned to them having gone forever, so had booked an appointment in Bristol next week when she went home. Can you believe that you can have eyebrows tattooed on?

"Right, when's Joe coming in?" Sophie looked at the clock above our heads. "Shouldn't he be here by now?"

We were going to look at yet another house. Sophie had been down in Cornwall for a couple of weeks now, house hunting, but I have to say that she was real picky. It had to be close to water. It had to have trees and a large garden. There should be a hobby room. The list went on. But we'd had fun looking at places.

I'm thrilled. Still can't believe that she wants to buy a place close to me. But my sister feels the same way I do; we're making up for lost time, thirty four years of it. We're alike in many ways. We're twins, so I guess that's why. But it doesn't mean we'll always wear matching outfits. I draw the line at that.

The in house phone rang. "Got a message from Joseph. He can't make it in; got an emergency on. He's out at that Aga woman's place. She's having a baby for God sake."

"I know Harry. Christmas baby. We're all thrilled."

"Christmas be damned. She's having the bloody thing now and her husband's gone up England," said Harry, like it was a foreign country (which it was).

"You sure?"

"'Course I'm sure. What am I, an idiot?" *No comment.* "Get your ass over there and do something. You're a woman."

"Thanks for noticing, Harry. But there'll be a qualified midwife in Treliske to take care of all that."

"She's not in bloody hospital. She's at home and Joseph's over there panicking. I'll come out to Reception, take over for a while, and you get your butt over there. Can't afford to lose our Maitre d'."

We didn't look at houses, Sophie and me, not that afternoon. Instead, we watched a baby being born; a tiny little person with a scream on him that could curdle milk. Luckily the paramedics got there at the same time as us, and we ended up only as spectators at this miracle - when the wrinkled little chap shot out of his mother like a slippery rugby ball.

Happily, one of the paramedics played rugby for a local team and managed to lunge for the baby before any damage was done to either him or his mother. The paramedic who saved the day was called Harry, and a crazily happy Agata, drunk on gas and air (it's not called laughing gas for nothing) immediately promised that this tiny new life would be christened Harry.

My God, there'd be no living with Harry Evans now. Of course no one would be able to convince him that the baby wasn't named after him.

Epilogue

My big sister Sophie has bought the most wonderful house. It's opposite the River Truro and Boscowan Park, two very special ticks on her wish list. The river turns into mud flats when the tide goes out and it's a haven for all sorts of wild life. She's about to buy herself a dog too, a Labrador. I guess it's a substitute for a man, for Sophie's not into men, not yet anyway. The sorrow of her past is still a shadow that won't let go. And I understand, for I saw the look of sadness on her face when Agata's baby was christened this week.

I had to hold it. The baby I mean. And you know *me* and babies. I'd never been tempted to get within a mile of one. But all things change, don't they. And Agata's Harry (I can't say the name without smiling) doesn't seem a bad little chap. Apart from the screeching of course and the humming nappies and the projectile vomiting and the early morning feeds. But I watched him smile and he came out with a gurgle like he was really happy about something. Well, it was an eye opener, I have to tell you. It made me go all hot and woozy. (Probably some sort of bug going around.)

Matt was at the christening as well. I watched his face as Harry was passed from hand to hand. (Not *our* Harry, obviously.) It was a mixture of awe and fear. I recognise the feelings. I used to be that way myself when invited to pick up something two feet long dressed in a baby-grow. It's a scary business. So, shouldn't think the pair of us will be up to anything like that any day soon.

It's Christmas next week, and I don't think I've ever looked forward to one so much. Matt's going to be playing a lot over the holiday, but then that's his job. And I'm going to be busy as well. Harry's made me Assistant Manager; he baulked at the idea of me having Deputy Manager on my name badge. I guess he figured assistant was a better description, meant I wouldn't rise too far above my station. But they're both only a name, for I'm doing the same job I always did – out on Reception and fire fighting; trouble shooting stuff that Harry can't be bothered with.

There's always something that needs sorting, that's the hotel business for you. Guests have expectations and some people can be real pains, even at Christmas. The Royal is a pretty decent hotel after its refurb, but then it always had a great heart. It's the staff mostly who give it that; even ones like Doris and Alfie.

The place is safe now from greedy bankers' hands who want to repossess it. People interested in profit and loss accounts who don't understand the concept of loyalty, and maintaining some kind of value in an age where that's an outdated idea.

And my sister Sophie and I have become sleeping partners. Not that either of us do much sleeping nowadays. We both had this money from our grandmother's will and what use is money if you don't do something positive with it. So we decided to invest it in a hotel with sloping floors and dodgy plumbing. It seems to be working out okay.

And me? I've found my lovely sister and she's working her way back to health. She took me out for ice cream and we sat on a bench in the park opposite her new house and watched the tide go out. Ice cream for breakfast, you can't beat it. And I've got a man who's honest and caring, even if he sometimes sleeps in till noon. Right now life is perfect. But who knows what the future holds? Sometimes, it's better we don't know. Don't you think?

THE END

Author's note:

Many thanks for reading *Ice Cream for Breakfast*. The Royal has been loosely based on a Cornish hotel where my husband and I played music for several years. However, it has been fictionalised. The 'real' hotel may have had a few minor ailments, but these do not include sloping floors or less than ideal plumbing. The staff are all hard working professionals and pretty cool people who are very welcoming to visitors. My characters are purely fictional and none of the 'real staff' actually have tattoos that say *just try it mate*. I have taken the liberty of using our son Matt's name as he too is a jazz pianist and have repositioned our younger son Sam – an engineer – as the bar manager in the Bristol pub!

A friend of mine was kind enough to explain to me all of her treatment for breast cancer and generous enough to allow me to write about it. I am interested in issues like that which affect many women and also feel strongly about women (and men) being abused either physically, sexually or mentally. Everyone is entitled to a life free from abuse and to be valued as a person.

However, the book wasn't meant to be a social commentary, but first and foremost to entertain, which I hope it did to some extent. Thanks once again for reading it.

I'm an avid reader myself with wide ranging tastes, including chick lit, historical fiction and crime/thrillers. My favourite authors include Lee Child, Lisa Gardner, David Baldacci, Vince Flynn, Nora Roberts, Marian Keyes and Carole Matthews (to name just a few).

Other Books:
Look on the Bright Side
The Last Climbing boy

Short Stories:
Living with Benjy
The Good Life

Following pages:
Sample chapter of *"Look on the Bright Side"*

Look on the Bright Side

Chapter 1

Okay, so I'm not perfect. But is life this complicated for everyone? I stepped over a mountain of toys and junk, stuck my head in a cushion and screamed. It was better than sticking a fork in your eye.

The cat did a runner. But then I've never been fond of the cat. She was a hangover from the days when Bill (my ex) thought the house needed an animal in it. She was his cat, but he'd left her behind. He'd left me and the kids as well.

"When will there be some me-time?" I yelled. But the cushion didn't answer, had never heard of one parent families.

It sounded like a great idea, time for yourself, where you were number one. And yes, it really did exist, claimed Alice, who'd been my best friend since college. *Sure, Alice. If you say so.*

"Get yourself off to a spa, girl", she'd said. "Do you the world of good."

Alice is a gem, but she doesn't get it. She lives in her own bubble. Has a publishing job up in London, gets to take clients out to dinner in real restaurants, not McDonald's. And doesn't have to think about what to feed the kids for tea, try to get the boiler working again, write a lesson plan for tomorrow, or figure out how to scrape up this month's child minding fees. They'd gone up again. Nothing seems to go down. Only your bank balance and your energy.

But things would improve. I knew it. And hey, I can still smile, which makes me an optimist - except not tonight. Not with Millie whingeing on about new trainers, and Tom refusing to eat the macaroni cheese I'd whipped up after collecting these two ungrateful brutes from the after-school childminder.

A glass of wine waited. The saviour. But only after the kids were asleep and I'd written that lesson plan for tomorrow's class. It's being observed.

I'm not that fond of lesson-observations. They're like auditions, as if you have to prove yourself all over again. Prove you can do the teaching job they hired you for in the first place, and that you're still giving value for money. And they don't really work, because you'll always give your best performance for this one-off stellar moment. But how can you keep up that sort of thing all year? Demonstrating *best practice*. How I hate those words. Seems like I hate everything tonight, but it's not true. It's just been a bad day. Tomorrow will be better.

*

"Thought you looked tired yesterday, Jillian."

"I'm fine," I said, giving the words an extra little spring in their step, "autumn term's always a long haul."

"Sure," agreed Emily. "For all of us. Soon be half-term though. You'll be looking forward to spending time with the kids, I expect."

She could expect all she wanted. She didn't have kids. Had a husband who paid the mortgage. And she and the old man were off to the Med on a cruise for *their* half-term.

*It's not that I'm bitter. And don't get me wrong, I really **do** love my kids. But I wouldn't say no to a Mediterranean cruise myself.*

My boss, Emily Thomson, is a decent woman who tries hard to be helpful while doing the impossible job she's been lumbered with. She insists on calling me Jillian, though. And I'm not a Jillian, more of a Jill.

Jill Webster: Mother, English teacher, cook, cleaner (only in extreme circumstances, when the carpets change colour and the washing up reaches 3-days' worth) payer of bills (not always on time) and sole householder.

I looked at Emily. Her face was expectant, so I nodded. She'd been waiting for some kind of reaction before I'd wandered off inside my head. I sometimes do that and it can be confusing to spectators.

"I could've put my observation feedback in your pigeon-hole," she said.

"Right . . ." I waited for the other shoe to fall, the one that gives you the kick in the rear.

"But I wanted to see you face-to-face. Credit where it's due, Jillian. That was a great lesson today."

"Thanks." *Wow! Still, I was waiting for the 'but'. There's nearly always a but.*

"I wish I saw more like that," she said. "You had them in the palm of your hand. And all outcomes fulfilled. Excellent."

"Great." Fulfilling 'outcomes' isn't easy. They're slippery little devils.

"If you were being OFSTEDed it would be a one."

Good God! Things were looking up. A 'one' was the highest you could get, like reaching the summit of Everest.

"Just one small detail and I've written that in my comments…"

Ah, here it was. The one 'point for future development'. Something to show that you were never perfect; could always do better. Still, not too dusty – considering the time I'd taken writing the lesson plan last night. And the two glasses of wine that had helped it along.

"Right." Her eyes flicked over to the clock, and she seemed to be making some sort of weighty decision. "Get yourself off to the staffroom for a coffee break."

"Okay."

"Have a chill and while you're there I'd like you to think about something," she said.

"What?" *God, not more new initiatives. I was still working on the last lot.*

"There's a new vacancy about to come on line."

"Oh?"

"Mandy's moving up to Bristol and I'm looking for a new Deputy. I'd rather keep it internal if I can."

"What, me? Management?"

"Don't fancy it?"

"Never even thought about it. But all that paperwork."

"Not much more than you do now, and I'd be right here next door to give you advice. You'd be my second-in-command. More money . . ."

She left the final two words dangling in mid air to work their magic. Emily knew I needed all the money I could get my hands on right now. There was the dodgy boiler for a start. I wish I'd never told her about it now.

*

"But that's crap. Of course you're up to it."

I'd told Alice about the job offer, and my own doubts about it. She'd brought over two bottles of 'good red wine' and her upbeat, life-is-what-you-make-it attitude.

"That's not what I meant," I said. *She knew what I meant.* Of course I could do the job, but it would mean even more time away from home. The child care bill would be humongous, and somebody else would get to know my kids better than me.

Alice sloshed more wine into the massive glasses she'd brought with her. She didn't like my economy wine glasses that, unlike hers, were not hand-blown by some arty bloke in Italy. Mine came from a supermarket, but were perfectly adequate. 'Adequate' was a quality I specialized in.

The kids were both on sleepovers with friends, a small miracle that had been thrown my way. Even so, I felt guilty about enjoying this girly night with a takeaway and Alice's fine Merlot. Guilt was something that dogged me, though I tried to ignore it. But they stamp the word across your forehead when your babies are born.

"What then?" Alice wouldn't give up.

"I feel . . . *conflicted.*"

"Bollocks," she said. "That's a fancy, copout word. You know you want to take it. So take it."

Everything was so much simpler for my friend. Like now. She'd taken a week away from her desk to stay at a retreat near Land's End. This was to arm her for the upcoming rigours of the Frankfurt Book Fair.

She'd been driving over to visit me when the spirit moved her. Or when she got bored with life in the tiny village of Saint Buryan where the nearby Merry Maidens Stone Circle was meant to power up her batteries.

I couldn't imagine Alice at a retreat. She was more of a city girl, like me. Or at least I had been, B.C. - before children.

The arrival of the kids kicked in all sorts of life style changes, most of them driven by me in that headless-chicken-time following birth. Like a migrating bird, I'd dragged the family down to the West Country.

I had this pattern in my head for how children should be bought up. It didn't come from any parenting book, but had spookily arrived the moment Millie thrust her tiny, quivering body into daylight and set up a wail strong enough to wake the dead.

It seemed a no-brainer that our pokey London flat was no nesting place for kids. But Bill didn't see it that way, for he was nostalgic about the London borough of Hackney. Don't ask me why. Years ago it had been one of the most crime affected places in London. And I instinctively knew that no amount of change would turn it into a place I wanted my kids to remember. Note the "my kids". I think that even back then, I realised any offspring would always be *my kids* and not "our kids".

I was a driven woman, and put my size fours down with all the force of a Jackboot. I marvel now when I think about it, where the strength to oppose him came from. I suppose your children do that for you. Turn you into this fierce tigress protecting her cubs.

Bill finally gave in when Judith - my fire breathing mother-in-law - pointed out that moving to Cornwall would bring us closer to her in Exeter. Nothing's ever perfect in life. *If it was, I'd be in the Caribbean sipping a rum punch.* She put the thumb screws on him and I pushed from my end. It's the only time the woman and I have been on the same team.

The insistent buzz at the front door brought two immediate results. One - I yanked myself from inside my head, and two - the wine glass went spinning off into space. Sticky red wine cascaded down my coffee table and onto the beige carpet.

Beige is never a good colour when you have kids, but Bill had insisted on it. It was the one his mother had, so if it was good enough for her etc. . . . The woollen carpet was one hell of an investment at a time when we couldn't afford it. But as Bill had pointed out, it was there for life. Pity he hadn't felt the same way about our marriage.

"You can chuck some white wine over it," Alice said helpfully.

Well maybe she could afford to use Chardonnay as a stain remover, but I couldn't.

"Hey! Is there anybody in there?" a disembodied voice yelled urgently through my letter box.

"Shit no!" I shot Alice a frantic look. Put a finger to my lips in a for-God's-sake-be-quiet mime. Things were complicated enough without him pestering me again.

"Who's he?" she asked, in a voice loud enough for the nearest deaf man to hear. She'd never been good at picking up on signals. "Didn't know you had a man on the go."

"Shussh," I hissed. "And I haven't got a man."

"Sounds like one to me."

Alice moved to the window, peering round the side of the lace curtains. They'd been a present from Bill's mother who had them in every room in her house. I'd been meaning to dump them for ages.

"Get away from there, he'll see you."

The ringing in my ears finally stopped, and I figured James had taken the hint and his hand off the doorbell. It was a surprise. The man was usually more persistent.

"Nice car."

Alice was impressed by cars. Not my old banger, which ran on low-grade petrol and luck. But I lavished love on Jemima, and gave the old girl a friendly pat every day to show her she was just as valuable as Alice's Beamer.

My friend had offered to buy me a 'decent' car. She had a generous heart and her family had mega-bucks, which always helps. They'd given her an expensive flat for her twenty-first and told her to go out into the world and make her own way. She had. But she'd never had to scrimp and save, like the rest of us poor stiffs. Even so, Alice never flaunted her money, or her looks, or her good luck. That's what I liked about her.

"Looks like he's gone," she said. "Go on, give."

"What?"

"Well, have you? And if not, why not?"

Her eyebrows shot up dramatically into her fringe. Alice had a flair for interrogation, something she'd cultivated earlier in life working as a journalist on one of the lesser known scandal sheets. She also had a downright nosy streak. A gift she'd inherited from her mother.

"Jill-i-an . . . You have – haven't you?"

"No I haven't!" I said indignantly. "We had one date, that's all. And now he's practically stalking me. It creeps me out."

"Not bad looking, maybe not eye-candy, but he's got style. And a nice ass." My friend grinned. She considered herself an authority on asses.

"You got all that from one curtain-twitch?"

"Body language - reading it's crucial in my job," she said.

We went back to the wine. Correction, Alice did. Mine was still decorating the beige Wilton. The poor old carpet had taken a hammering lately, but a new one was a distant dream. It would need to line up behind the boiler repair, the gas bill; the phone bill . . . The list got longer every day. And now, Millie's trainers.

The synapses in my brain hurled across a new thought. Maybe I *should* take the job offer. Then I wouldn't have to penny-pinch the way I did now.

"Penny for them," said Alice, managing to look wise as well as sober, even though she'd drunk the lion's share of the two bottles. She was more practiced at it. All those late lunches. Me? It's normally a rushed tuna sandwich in the staffroom and a mug of stewed, tepid coffee, because no one's bothered to put on a fresh brew. And I'm certainly not in Alice's league when it comes to shifting alcohol.

"What?"

"Penny for your thoughts."

"Funny, that's what I was thinking about. Pennies."

"Jill," she said, her tone impatient. Like I was some sort of lost cause. "Get a man. Take the bloody job. And send the kids off to their grandparents for a week."

It sounded easy when she said it. A concise, three-bullet-point plan. Probably the sort of thing Alice had to come up with every day in the office. But life is far more messy. Still, if I'd known how much messier it was about to get, I might have given more than a passing thought to Alice's strategy for sorting out my life.

Made in the USA
Charleston, SC
13 May 2016